DREAMS OF SLEEP

DREAMS OF SLEEP

Josephine Humphreys

COLLINS HARVILL
8 Grafton Street, London W1
1985

William Collins Sons and Co. Ltd.
London · Glasgow · Sydney · Auckland
Toronto · Johannesburg

Grateful acknowledgement is made to
Front Line Management Company, Inc.,
for permission to reprint a selection from "Desperado",
words and music by Don Henley and Glenn Frey,
© 1973, 1979 by Cass County Music & Red Cloud Music.

BRITISH LIBRARY CATALOGUING IN PUBLICATION DATA

Humphreys, Josephine
Dreams of sleep
I. Title
813′.54F   PS3558.U4656

ISBN 0 00 222868 8

First published in Great Britain by Collins Harvill, 1985
© Josephine Humphreys 1984

Set in 12pt Baskerville
Printed at The Camelot Press, Southampton

FOR WILLIAM BLACKBURN

One

Before they wake, sunlight is on the house, moving on the high east wall and windows through old glass wavy as broken water, onto the hard bright floor of waxed pine. When Alice opens her eyes she sees its cool path stamped by the shadow of mullions, squares stretching to rhomboids of clear fall sun. Will sleeps behind her, his breath wisping her back. She loves the quiet of light and its mutable geometry, as those wizards did who chinked and slit their stones to let in messages from sun gods. The message to Alice is, Don't move. Not till that first stamp of light touches the wide crack in the floorboards. Till then she is frozen. The room is frozen. Only two things may move—the slow light, and his feathery perfect breath between her shoulder blades.

But he turns. Gets out of bed and crosses the room. Without looking she knows he is standing before the dresser, getting clothes. He shuts the drawer softly, goes into the bathroom, closes the door softly. All that stealth means he'll not want breakfast. He will be gone before she gets up. The sound of the shower is the same as every morning, a heave and sigh in the old pipes, the spitting showerhead. She hears the girls waking in their room; they'll scramble into their clothes in order to meet him downstairs, where he'll give them cereal. Once these house noises begin, her sunlight loses power. It is only ordinary.

She sees his shoes and trousered legs pass through the light without hesitating.

So she'll think of Claire now, the girl in his office who is lovely, whose teeth and eyelashes and hair shine. Claire must be awake, Claire is energetic. Has probably cleaned her little house and gone jogging. Alice saw her last week jogging along the seawall at the Battery, white wide-legged gym shorts flapping on her thighs, forearms against her chest.

When Alice was single, married women seemed extraordinary—their full sets of china, their nightly love. Married, she marvels at the single ones. White shorts, electric-blue running shoes; their bodies and clothing and cars are bright! They are all in one piece. Things that used to make sense to them still make sense. And they don't have husbands in love with single girls.

She can hear her family's voices, their footsteps downstairs. Sound is loose in this house and travels free, the ceilings are so high, the rooms so big. She seems to hear even the dry cereal falling into bowls, milk swirling and buoying the flakes, cold spoons touching cold china. She hears Will carry garbage cans to the sidewalk, start his car, fade toward Claire. The light touches the crack. She can get up, dress; have the children, the sun, the house to herself. With luck the day will be warm. There is no real autumn in Charleston, only summer jostling winter. One day cools, the next warms again, unpredictably.

When she steps into the hall, something catches her eye. A naked leg. On the floor just beyond the children's door a tiny pink doll's leg tapering to a pointed foot, a tiny high-heeled sparkly shoe. She stands in the hall looking at it, like a passerby happening upon evidence of a crime. The sun hits the shoe at the right slant to throw glints into the air. She can't see what else is behind the door, but she can guess. It will have to wait. She pulls the door shut without looking farther and tries to forget the leg.

Washing the cereal bowls she hopes she is not very different from other women. Don't they all stand this way, belly against the lip of the counter, hands going slowly in and out of the suds, eyes focused past the window? She is watching

her daughters, who are playing now in the sunny driveway
Another woman would have the same careless ease with
dishes, ceaseless care with children.

She doesn't see other women much, especially since her
husband took up with one. She doesn't have much to do
with them, or with men either, or with what is called the
world (the restaurants and schools and offices). She has
drawn back to a tighter world. The cause of the tightening-
down is no mystery: knowledge, a cankerous little node of
it concerning her husband and his receptionist, worse than
what Eve got from the apple. The mystery is what will
happen next. So far there has been no visible change.

But as in cancer and other metamorphoses, the change
from invisible to small is slow; the change from small to
enormous is wildfire.

Claire would never wear clothes like these, old jeans that
zip up the front and pucker at the small of her back; her
dear plaid shirt nearing the end of a fifteen-year life, its
limp collar frayed and soft, buttons chipped. The knack of
dressing up is something Alice missed in life. A dressy dress
on her has the look and feel of a Halloween costume. Her
mother used to hide her in the kitchen when clients came
for a fitting, since Alice's thin bony frame made any dress
hang wrong and was not a good advertisement for her
mother's dressmaking skills.

Last summer Alice bought some new clothes, "lady's
clothes," and took to dressing herself up. She would put on
a silk blouse and a tailored skirt and go down to Will's office
to see Claire. She even bought a pair of earrings, gold
clip-on fish, and she brushed rouge powder on her cheekbones. In fact Claire always looked the same, with the same
short black hair and white uniforms, but Alice was hungry
for new looks at her. She couldn't sit in the office and study
Claire as she wanted; but she could steal long glances at
her, at her nose, the back of her neck, the perfect turn of
ankle above white shoes.

These were snapshots in her mind: Claire cradling the
telephone between her chin and her shoulder; Claire standing before the gray metal files, a drawer pressing against
her breasts, arms reaching forward; and once, wonderfully,

Claire coming from the bathroom, the sound of the toilet still flushing, Claire smoothing her uniform. One time she went into that bathroom herself, locked the door, and studied the room. It looked clean as a bone. But then she noticed the mirror was a medicine cabinet. She opened it and saw toothpaste and a green toothbrush tipped with a nipple of pink rubber. It had to be Claire's. She touched it. She was at jealousy's highest pitch, when a woman's obsession with her rival tends to resemble love. Mornings she woke exhausted by dreams of Claire. She wondered what style of underwear Claire wore. She drove past Claire's address hoping to see if not Claire herself then her car or some sign of her—the mailman putting letters into Claire's box, for example.

But jealousy can't be long sustained at that intense, spiritual level. It wore her out. What she feels now is curiosity, not real jealousy. She doesn't drive. She never wears the new clothes she bought; just remembering them makes her edgy and tired. These old clothes are for her.

More mysteries: her two children. Why do they look so fragile? Milk-colored, their skin is like some paper-thin membrane holding together what's inside; their bones are like twigs, bird bones. But they've grown to be four and six without breaking anything, and for all their look of delicacy they can be dirty. Beth has ringworm in the soft crook of her elbow. She is six, pale, afraid to swim in the ocean. Marcy is less timid; the possibility of hidden danger has not yet occurred to her. Her eyes are small and close together, giving her a shrewd and unchildlike look, even at four. Her skin is pale, too, her hair light and fine; but under the hair her scalp is covered with a brown crust. Sometimes Alice rubs a lotion into it to soften the crust; then, holding Marcy's head still in her lap, she scratches at it, flaking the thin scabs off to leave naked patches of scalp. Mysteriously, Alice's mouth waters.

From the street she hears the noises of people going to offices and stores. Oh, the world appears to work smoothly enough, like a toy town where the only business is the constant shifting of goods and wastes. If that were all, how easy to live—buy your food, put out your garbage. But the toys and models and dolls and the world's looks are treacherous. They teach children it will be easy. The real problems of consumption and disposal are nothing like what children are led to suspect.

When her telephone rings she hopes it might be Will. But it is his mother.

"A woman was attacked in the newspaper," Marcella says. "Did you see that?"

"No," Alice says, bracing herself. Marcella follows the rapes in the paper faithfully, as if they were Dick Tracy.

"In my day there was no raping, that I recall. There wasn't even rudeness. Will's great-grandfather shot a Negro in the thigh when he failed to step off the sidewalk to let Will's great-grandmother pass by."

"I know. I've heard that tale."

"Nowadays they have to recover the sperm for evidence, like a bullet. You have to have counseling. I read where in one case the charge was dismissed because the girl didn't actually see penetration. So there was no witness to the crime. Can you imagine?"

"No."

"But that isn't why I called. I'm calling with a suggestion." Marcella often calls with suggestions. Get a job, get a housekeeper, get a new nightgown, something rehabilitative, something that will bring Will back. Since Marcella was the one who told Alice about Will and Claire, she has assumed a kind of responsibility for the marriage. She wants Alice to do something. She is getting more and more nervous as she sees Alice is doing nothing.

"You need a baby-sitter. I've been thinking about it, Alice. Your horizons are shrinking." An implosion, Alice thinks. The world collapsing into me; nothing on the outside, everything inside.

"And I've found a girl for you, a part-time college student. You could have your afternoons free."

"Free for what?"

"Jazzercise, the hairdresser. You could go back to work, or get involved in the arts, anything. The point is, cheer yourself up. Something. Don't say yes immediately, of course. You must interview and ask for references. And if I were you, I'd want to see where she comes from before I hired her."

Since one afternoon five months ago on Marcella's porch, when they sat in the sun and Marcella told, they have not talked specifically about Will and Claire again, not with names and the particular unpleasant words. Marcella did not say how she had found out, but it was no surprise that she had. She often found things out as a result of her job. In real estate it is part of the business to know of impending divorce and disease, the harbingers of real estate transactions. Marcella was direct with her news. "Will, I think, is having an affair with the woman who works in his office," she said, sitting in the high-backed chair, Alice in the glider, an afternoon in early June. Across the street Marcy and Beth sat on the Battery wall, dangling their feet out over the water. The summer heat made Fort Sumter a dancing dot in the blue-gray harbor, air and water shimmering together so that the line of separation between them swam. Only a few gulls broke the flat, ribbony gray. The children seemed to sit at the edge of the world; everything was precarious. Alice steadied a foot against the floor to stop the glider. If she could keep it still, maybe everything else would keep still, too: the come-and-go horizon, the speck of a fort about to vanish, the children about to drop into the sea. But the glider kept up its almost imperceptible swing, deep in its springs; and the world wavered.

She had to admit, later, the news was not a total shock. Three women worked in his office. She knew instantly which one was meant. There had been signs.

"Do me a favor," Marcella says. "Talk to this girl. Queen knows her from the project, but she's white. She's going to give you a call. Her name is Iris Moon."

"All right, Marcella."

"Keep your doors locked. You don't live in a safe neighborhood. I worry about the children."

Alice finishes lighting a cigarette, blows out the smoke. "No one is safe anywhere," she says.

If there were such a thing as a safe place, she knows it

would have to be here in Charleston. It was for safety these houses were built, crowded together on the peninsula behind a wall to keep out Indians, Spaniards, outlaws.

And now tourists come to see the place. Across the rivers on each side of town are regular American suburbs, Harborside and Creekmoss and Shadowwood, where the city is developing in the normal way; but hemmed between the rivers are what the tourists come for, the old high houses. Whites live in them at the southern tip of the peninsula, blacks farther north. Alice's house is in the middle, a transitional neighborhood where the Jews used to live before they moved out to Harborside in the fifties. Blacks moved in, now whites are moving in again; and the neighborhood has no real neighbors in it. In the suburbs as shown on television, women drink coffee together in their kitchens and men borrow tools from each other. But here people keep to themselves. The Reeses are the only people on the block who live in a family. The others live alone—students, homosexuals, Navy people—or in groups not identifiable as families. There are still some black people in the corner house, but Alice sees them only in the mornings when they leave for various jobs in different-colored uniforms.

Sometimes she wakes at night to the sounds of fighting in the street, or even weeping. It seems to her that people who cry in the streets at night must not be family people. Family people cry in private places.

She would not admit it to Marcella, but she carries in her pocketbook a slim metal canister siren. "The Shrieker" is its name. It isn't Mace or tear gas, just noise in a can. Beyond that she has no defenses.

Her husband does call. His voice over the phone is one thing she married him for. She remembers imagining and wanting exactly that: a man telephoning in the middle of a morning. Why did I want that? she wonders. I settle for so little. A voice, a bend in the air, nothing of substance. They have never talked about Claire.

"What are you going to do?" he asks.

"Clean up." That is not the truth, but it will comfort him. "I love you," she says.

He answers, "I love *you.*"

7

"Your mother called. To tell me somebody was raped."

"She wants to sell you a house in a safer part of town."

"Maybe that isn't such a bad idea. A house in a safer part of town. Why do we have to live here?" she says.

"Don't start on that."

"But even if you aren't worried for me, what about your children?"

"Alice, stop."

She takes a breath. She tries.

He says, "I love you."

"I love *you*," she says back. This marriage is like a place where the language is not her native tongue. She has managed to pick up the words and idioms and intonations gradually, so that now they sound almost right coming out of her mouth; but she knows they are his. Sometimes even the thoughts she has are his. Behind her the refrigerator hums, the self-cleaning oven silently bakes itself bright, and hidden under the stovetop the pinpoint blue pilot light burns with a tiny hiss. She does not feel at home, here at home's center.

She used to be a mathematician. Now she looks for omens and signs. At one time she thought math would clarify the world for her. She knew her link to real things was weak: she had never been able to catch a softball; couldn't remember the colors of eyes, or years in which given events occurred; lost valuable pieces of jewelry (heirlooms that other people had kept safe for years). She had hoped knowledge of mathematics, the world's rules, might strengthen her hold. But it did not. The world turned opaque and medieval, its every event mysterious. Now she uses a private mathematics, one made from omens and signs and dreams.

At thirty-three, she has gotten her first good look at the schedule of things, the timetable she could not quite see until now: how years move lives along; how, in spite of assassinations, earthquakes, wars, the sun comes up again. She counts its return a sign not of hope but of its opposite. Omen of omenlessness. When John Kennedy was killed, she telephoned her philosopher father at his office. "What will happen?" she cried. "Nothing," he said, and as the truth of his answer became evident, the world seemed to grow old, and more assassinations came, followed by more nothing.

A loud beep comes from the receiver. She hangs up and smokes another cigarette. She can't get things done. Marcella has a new husband, a big job, and the vigor to fill a day with hundreds of accomplished tasks; but Alice can't finish making up one bed. If she were left to herself she could spend whole days doing nothing, not even eating or bathing or cleaning or putting out trash. So she is never surprised by those newspaper accounts of old women found living in houses full of garbage (the neighbors complain of an odor, the health department sends men over to shovel the place out). There's no surprise in that. What's surprising is when solitary old people do put out garbage and cook meals for themselves and set a single place at the table, living as if everything were all right.

She is not left to herself. There are things she has to do, such as feed the children—a duty that weighs on her mind like a concrete block tied to sink something in a sea. Sometimes she dreams that she forgets to feed a baby. In this dream weeks go by, until one day she opens the dresser drawer and finds the baby still alive but stunted. Will wanted her to nurse Marcy and Beth, so she tried, but they never got enough milk. It was a bad start. They didn't eat much solid food either. She held the tiny spoon of pureed carrots toward the baby mouth, touching the silver rim against the tightened baby lips. Mysteriously, her own mouth opened; but the baby's did not.

"Look what we found in the dirt!" Marcy says. "Jewels!" She holds out five bright green gems. Beth has a handful, too.

"They were buried in the driveway," Beth says, out of breath. "Maybe somebody dropped them, or hid them in the Civil War."

"Let me see."

"They're worth millions. Wait till Daddy sees."

"Let's call him and tell him!" Marcy says.

"No, honey. You can show him when he comes home."

"But they're diamonds," Marcy cries. "We have to tell him."

"Emeralds," Beth says, staring into her hand. "Real emeralds."

"They're very pretty. But not emeralds. We don't know for sure what they are, do we?"

"I do," Beth says. "Emeralds are my birthstone. I know what they look like. I'm going to call him."

"Not now, baby, he's too busy," Alice says.

"This is important."

"No, it isn't, Beth."

"Mom, we found buried jewels. You say that's not important?"

"Listen to me. I said no and I mean it. They're not emeralds. There are no emeralds in our driveway. These are pieces of broken Coke bottles. Trash. And they have sharp edges, so please throw them away. Now."

They stand in the doorway looking down into their hands, considering her words, and not believing. What she says does not change the sparkle, the green that goes all the way through and is therefore true. They look back at her, unhurt. She can't reach them.

"And wash your hands. They're filthy."

Their obedience is frightening. They go straight to the sink.

"Did you clean up your room?" she asks. Little cold golden add-a-beads, these daily minor cruelties against her children. They gleam, she can't resist.

"Pretty much," Beth says, blowing soap bubbles through her cupped hands in the dishwater, still too young to tell a complete lie.

"Then I can inspect it now."

Beth shakes out her hands and glances at her sister. "Wait. We started on it. But we might not have cleaned it all good."

"Didn't I tell you both clearly not to go outside until your room was clean? And didn't I say that anything not picked up would go into the garbage?"

"Yes, but—"

"Well, then." Alice leaves the room too fast for them to

keep up with. The dolls, as usual, are lying in disarray on the floor, not soft baby dolls but leggy, bump-breasted dolls with platinum manes of hair, red pouts, their clothes scattered about them: ski pants, nurse uniforms, stewardess outfits, tiny sunglasses and bikinis. Her own dolls were either babies or storybook characters like Cinderella and Snow White who though past childhood were somehow not yet into the world, girls who kept themselves apart from the world without really knowing what for. Now girls know what for. They menstruate when they are ten, and their dolls are sluts. Cinderella's shy foot never resembled the naked raised leg on the doll behind the door. Alice picks it up, touches its unnippled breast. An invulnerable body, hard and mean, with unbreakable plastic bubbles of breast and rump. It is a pleasure to sweep them into a pile, a tangle of hair and limbs and clothes that she then stuffs into a garbage bag.

"What's in there?" Beth looks at the bag, then the floor. ' What are you going to do with the dolls? Are they in that *bag*?"

"Maybe you will learn to take care of things," Alice says, in a witchy voice. "I will not have this utter negligence and destruction."

"She won't do it," Beth whispers to Marcy. They follow her downstairs. Jubilation lifts her heart, carries her onto the porch and to the sidewalk, where she sets the bag on top of a can, and just in time; the orange garbage truck rounds the corner, black men hanging off the sides with the easy grace of cowboys. The truck passes all the other houses in the block because no one else has put out any garbage; some of these people don't even get up until afternoon. When the truck stops in front of Alice's house, the men are surprised and embarrassed to find this white woman and her children watching them. They don't look up. With long dark arms they toss the garbage into the truck; a panel swings down to mash everything together, and a yellow juice trickles onto the pavement.

It is a surprise the girls don't object, watching the dolls go in. Then she sees in their faces that they are too dismayed to fight her.

"Where does that truck go now?" Marcy asks, stunned.

"I don't know."

"To the incinerator," Beth says.

"Come inside, girls. Come in now." They follow her. Their silence is worse than tears.

"Let's have a snack," Alice says. "Let's all have a Coke."

"No, thank you," Beth says in the voice she uses with strangers and waitresses.

Her own daughters are afraid of her. How could she go so wrong? A woman who frightens her children, a woman who watches in fascination as her husband drifts out of reach, is not like other women.

She thinks of the baby-sitter . . . but they come out of nowhere, these adolescent girls, show up at your house with bangle bracelets, gum in their pink mouths, your children the last thing on their minds. They search the bathroom for rubbers and notice the supply undiminished week to week; they read the mail and let your children watch *Dallas*.

Still, this girl is in college. And she might be different, a white girl from the project. Alice didn't know there were any whites left over there. They have disappeared from public housing and public schools, one of the mysteries of the city: where did all the poor whites go? Maybe Iris Moon is the last of them.

"Here, Marce, want one of my emeralds?" Beth says quietly. "Want one, Marcy?" Beth puts her arms around Marcy's shoulders. "Don't cry," she whispers. "Hold it in."

That baby-sitter coming along just now is significant. When what you need appears just when you need it, it must mean something, Alice thinks. Iris Moon's telephone call, if it comes, will be a portent, a good one. Her name is a perfect emblem.

Two

The white girl makes her way slowly down the sidewalk carrying wet sheets in a basket against her stomach. With her back arched like a pregnant woman's, she watches the sky. It is too heavy and low in the west, weighed down with dark blue, the color it always takes before rain. Iris needs the sun so the sheets will dry in time for her to make beds for Fay and Randall, her mother and brother. Though she doesn't live at home now, she still has responsibilities there, certain final duties. She starts to pray, *Let it not rain.* But in the grassless square yards of the housing project the dirt is not even a solid anymore; it flies into the air, earth vaporizing. The black children in the yards have a dull, powdery look to their skin; their eyes collect tears and dirt in the corners. Let it rain, then. It won't kill Fay and Randall to sleep on bare mattresses. Let it rain and the earth settle back into itself, tight down and damp the way it's supposed to be.

From half a block away Iris sees the blurred outline of her mother behind the screen door. Fay doesn't come out much. She doesn't like to show herself among the blacks, as if by staying in she can keep herself white. Fay is the only white person living here now. She's friends with Queen next door but no others. Usually she does not even come as far as the door. Something out of the ordinary has brought her to the edge the way fear draws animals slinking toward danger.

Iris sets the basket down on the sidewalk. Dirt has drifted over the folds of the laundry like sieved gray flour. Suppose she were to leave the basket here now and walk north (there being water on all other sides of the city). Then? There is nothing north but the paper mill and the Navy Yard and places worse than Sub Heaven, where she works nights. She might walk to the bus station and buy a ticket out, but when you buy a ticket you have to name a town you're destined for. What town? She gives the laundry a kick, then drags it the rest of the way, bending down sideways, scraping the basket over the rough concrete. Maybe Fay found out Iris has been scheming for a job minding children. Fay would rather Iris stay on at Sub Heaven in spite of the sandwich maker's bug eyes and drooping mustache and fat turquoise ring than take what she'd call a colored person's job.

Fay is in tears. She follows Iris into the kitchen, sobbing.

"Now what?" Iris says. "Another tooth?"

"Randall," Fay wails.

"What has he done?" Iris's heart sinks. Randall was sent away last year for stealing a Honda. Iris had to go to family court to get him back, by guaranteeing a healthy home environment for him. Next time, she told him, she wouldn't go. They could keep him.

"He's gone. He's been stolen."

"What?" The idea of Randall stolen is backward.

Fay howls.

"Stop, stop," Iris says. "Tell me what happened."

"I heard a car. I said, Randall, see who it is. I didn't recognize the motor. Then I heard Randall come in and go back out, so I ran to the kitchen window. The car was waiting for him like a getaway car. He climbed in with his radio and his bird. He had come back for the radio and the bird! Then they drove away."

"Who was it?" But Iris already knows. Her skin prickles with the knowledge.

"Him! Owen! He's changed cars again; that's what tricked me."

"What does he want with Randall?" Iris asks.

That question doesn't interest Fay. She is astonished

instead by the efficiency of the operation. "He didn't even get out of the car," Fay cries. "Didn't even look this way. I wait sixteen months and all I get is a side look at his head?"

Iris can see that head, the chin dropped down, the hair oiled but still scruffy at his collar, the cigarette flattened wet in his mouth. "I have to hang the sheets," Iris says, bumping her way past Fay with the basket.

"But what do we do? Should we call the police?"

"The police are sick of Randall, Mama. They'll be glad he's gone. Besides, he's gone with his own father. What can they do about that?"

Iris pins the sheets to the clothesline. The deep blue cloud has vanished; the sheets will dry dirty and need washing again. Randall is fifteen years old. Well, Iris was fifteen two years ago and could have taken care of herself then. But Randall. Randall is a doomed combination of sharp-eyed suspicion and blind trust. She sees them driving toward Florida, the dirty parakeet bouncing in its cage on the back seat, Owen Moon grinning all the way, pleased with his marauding. Having deposited his family here in Charleston, South Carolina, and left it to hold together on its own, now he comes sneaking back to make raids on it, nabbing what he wants. Iris has no love for either of them, Randall or Owen, and maybe no love for Fay either; but since Fay is her mother she takes care of her, comes over to wash Fay's laundry at the Laundromat and fix lunch and listen to Fay talk. She holds back on anything like love, though, out of spite. Fay does not deserve love. Fay messed things up from the beginning.

Out of the same limited, dull spite, for years Iris kept her hair cut short. When she was small Fay liked to sit her down in front of the mirror and fix her hair, playing beautician. She rolled the girl's heavy straight hair up in pins, but the curls wouldn't last more than a morning, so Fay gave Iris Lilts. She would twist up the curlers so tight Iris felt as if her hair were pulling out at the roots. Then the setting lotion went on, stinging into her scalp, the acrid white liquid dripping like poisoned milk into her ears and down her neck. Once Fay left the lotion on too long and burned the hair. When she unrolled the pins, each curled strand came right off with its pin, leaving Iris with a short furry halo. Fay cried in horror.

"Don't cry, Mama. It's all right. Please don't cry, honey," Iris said.

After that, Fay lost interest. She pierced Iris's ears with a needle, and now and then she'd try something with Iris's hair; but it was all loveless attention, the kind a girl gives a doll she's growing away from. Eventually Fay grew out of it altogether and let Iris alone. Iris watched the holes in her earlobes fill in and kept her hair so short people thought she was a boy or a leukemia victim.

Fay had other children, two besides Iris and Randall. The first was taken from her, Fay said, because she was fifteen. It was adopted straight from the delivery room. Then Patrice was born but something went wrong; Fay couldn't handle both Owen and a crying baby. She kept Patrice awhile, then sent her to an aunt in Berkeley County. When Iris was born, the time was right. Fay kept her. Two years later Randall was born, kept, jailed at fourteen, home at fifteen, and gone now again, Iris hopes for good.

She's lasted longest of them all! Seventeen years, which is enough. Now she has her own place. She still takes care of Fay, but she has her own place and no longer trusts in a future with Fay; that life is a thing of the past, the struggle to make a family out of those scraps of people. Fay says Iris has abandoned her. She harps on it, as if her nagging might convince Iris to return.

But Iris is planning a new future. You have to if you want anything at all to happen to you. She doesn't desire more than life in a warm climate with some good children. Charleston is warm but might not do. It has drawbacks, like Fay, Queen, Emory—people looking over her shoulder. But there are children here with whom Iris is already smitten.

She used to eye every kid she saw, wondering if it were hers; for she imagined one was somehow meant for her and marked in some way so she'd know it when she laid eyes on it. And all the while two likely ones were under her nose, in photographs she'd seen for years at Queen's. One day they glowed suddenly in their frame, and Iris took a closer look. Queen is a maid in their grandmother's house; Queen keeps their picture on her dresser, an updated picture every year, so Iris has seen their looks from infancy and knows their names. They are little gold-haired girls but not namby-pambies. The older one has a serious straight-on look, she cares for people, her forehead is nobly high; and the small one is fierce, her mouth pulled into a pout and set tough—look at her fists, balled up secretly, not quite hidden in the folds of her dress, held ready. Iris knows that no one can love those children as much as she could. She could love them hard; she stares at the picture whenever she is at Queen's.

The loss of Randall is a one-day tragedy. Iris doesn't see much difference except that Fay's place is quieter now.

To fill in the silence Fay talks more. "Who is living over there in that house with you?"

"Nobody. In the other rooms there's the old men."

"Emory?" Fay says.

"No. Whatever gave you that idea?"

"Queen says he isn't home much these days. She doesn't know what he's up to."

"Neither do I," Iris says.

"You used to. You used to be with him every day."

"I moved, remember?"

"You never see him?"

"Sure I see him," Iris says. "When I come here." In fact she sees Emory every day; but she can hardly say it is from her window, glancing down into the street, or over her shoulder when she walks to Fay's, or backward down the sidewalk when she leaves Sub Heaven at midnight. There he'll be, sidling down the street, a skinny black boy suddenly taller and deeper-voiced than the one who has been her lifelong friend, but still his wiry, spidery self. Still looking out for her.

"There is no such thing as a part-white baby," Fay says, looking at the sandwich Iris has fixed for her.

"That's a vile statement. What are you getting at?"

"Well," Fay says, lighting a Kool. "I only want to warn

you. You needn't turn on me. Call your own mother vile."
She passes her hand over her eyes. Her shoulders quiver.

"Don't now," Iris says. "I'm sorry. You don't have to
worry about that, Mama, don't worry about me. I wouldn't
ever do it."

"Do what?" Fay looks closely at Iris's face.

"What you're talking about."

"How come?"

"What?"

"Well, why not? It's nigger babies I'm warning you
against, Iris. Not love."

Iris stares. Fay bites into her sandwich. "What's in this?"
she says. She leans her elbows on the kitchen table and
chews cautiously, then peers into the sandwich.

"Chicken salad."

"Something's crunchy in it."

"Celery."

"I hate celery." Her eyes narrow down.

"Give it back, then." Iris takes out all the pieces of celery
she can find and replaces the sandwich on Fay's plate.

"I don't think I can eat it. Celery gives me the creeps."

"But it's all out."

"I can still remember the crunching feeling of it. I'd be
dreading it the whole time, thinking you missed some.
What else do we have?"

"Chun King chop suey."

"Oh, no."

Iris shifts cans on the shelf.

"Bean and bacon soup."

"I'll have that."

Her appetite is not normal. If Iris did not fix her food
she'd starve. It doesn't look as if she eats breakfast or supper; she says she does, but so far Iris hasn't seen any dirty
dishes or garbage to prove it. A forty-year-old woman who
can't keep herself fed!

She is still beautiful. Her eyes are wide set, with low lids
that close down over a sliver of the blue-washed centers.
Honey hair, sort of a flattened face, and a long thin mouth.
Because of poor eating habits in early life her teeth are bad.
Iris once offered to take her to the Spartanburg clinic,

where in one day they will pull all your teeth and fit new ones in, cheap.

"Iris?" Fay put her hand to her mouth. "You want me to do that? You want me to be completely toothless?"

"You'd only be completely toothless for a minute. Then they would put in brand-new, pretty, perfect teeth."

"Right on top of the holes of the old ones! It's pure cruelty. They don't even let the wounds heal and the pain run itself out before they slam the dentures in. No beauty is worth that price. Just so you can see white teeth in my mouth! I won't do it." She shut her mouth tight.

"Mama, you're so pretty." Iris shaped Fay's wilted bouffant hairdo with both her hands. "With new teeth you'd look as good as a movie star. You'd look so good you'd feel more like going out. Shopping or to a show."

"Teeth wouldn't make me want to go out by myself."

"Well; Owen might like them."

"Ho ho! Your father never cared a thing about teeth!" But she looked in the mirror on the kitchen cabinet, one of many that she keeps in the apartment, at least one mirror in every room. She has never given up on Owen. Every minute of every day, with a crazy hope, she is waiting for him to come back through the door. This hope is not a long, slow dream aimed at some point in the distant future; it is immediate and intense, she believes at any given second his hand might be reaching for the screen door handle. And that is why she is always glancing into her mirrors. To be sure she is ready. You have to feel sorry for anyone in whom love grows so big it edges out the feelings of normal life, including hunger.

As a child Iris quickly learned that Fay had to be looked out for because of Owen. Even before she knew it for sure, she had a feeling that Owen put Fay in danger. When he was around, the world grew fragile.

"But we were different from other people," Fay told Iris. "We looked different, both being better-looking than anyone around. We were the finest thing ever seen in town, and neither one of us ever needed money to be happy, we just spent ourselves. And it was worth it."

(But evidently Owen needed something in addition to

Fay, since he now has a wife, as Patrice found out and kindly let Fay know, in St. Cloud, Florida, a wife he has had children with and has taken Randall home to. Last year he took Fay's stereo, and before that the steak knives and a driftwood table lamp.)

When Iris was eight Owen came back for the first time. In the kitchen Fay was yelling at Randall for calling her Fay instead of Mama. She let go the iron hot side down on the ironing board and went to swat him with her hand. They tumbled around the room, but he was too quick, and then the old sheet covering the ironing board began to scorch. Randall laughed, loving disaster; and Fay cried, frightened by the smoke and the smell of burning muslin, but Iris looked past them both to where her father appeared in the doorway, leaning up against the wall, wearing blue jeans, a dark green T-shirt, and boots of worn black leather studded with bits of green and silver in star designs. He was smiling. The lenses of his sunglasses were mirrors.
"Fay Moon, what is it causing you to cry now?" he said, tapping a pack of Lucky Strikes on the heel of his hand. At first Fay just stared. Owen pulled the cellophane off the pack and dropped it on the floor, and was neatly tearing off the silver paper when Fay flew onto him. She hugged him, caught his hanging-down arms in her hug, and if he had been off balance they might have landed on the floor together, but he was steady. He didn't get his arms out to hug her back, just let himself be hugged. Iris unplugged the iron. She knew it was Owen because whoever Fay hugged like that had to be him, but all she could think was *I thought my father was a grown-up man!* This man was no taller than Fay, even in boots.
He was not dressed in adult's clothes and not half as handsome as Fay had claimed. But then he pulled an arm out of Fay's hug to take off his glasses, and fixed his eyes on Iris and Randall, and Iris saw why he was called handsome—from his eyes. These eyes were green-blue. They had a laugh in them as well as a cold mean tint, and they showed him to be older than his style let on: no teenager, but a thirty-year-old man.

He moved away from Fay, who stepped aside to give him a look at his children. He reached out a hand and fluffed up Iris's chopped-off hair. "Which one's the boy?" he said.

"Oh, Iris, I told you. I told you to let it grow. She keeps on cutting her hair, Owen. Look, here's Randall." Randall was the one he might be expected to take most interest in then, not having seen him past babyhood. But Owen's eyes left Randall and went back to Iris.

"Her hair's fine," he said. "Quit whining, Fay. I didn't come to hear you whine, I came to hear you say some nice things to me. Now I'm going to take you out for a beer. Get yourself dressed up and get some money, and you can show me the new night spots in this town."

"But I haven't been any places, Owen."

"Then we'll just hunt them. You get dressed."

"All right," Fay said, shy. "Help me, Iris." Iris and Fay went back to the bedroom and looked in Fay's closet. They picked out a pink soft blouse with a ruffle and a white skirt with permanent pleats. When Fay got them on, Iris said, "That won't go with him. Not with what he has on." Fay looked in the mirror. "Maybe not," she said, and they picked out a knit top and blue slacks. Owen was smoking when they went back to the kitchen. He looked Fay over. Iris saw her mother's hand tremble as she picked up her pocketbook and put money in it.

Iris whispered, "You look real good, Mama."

They went out arm in arm. It wasn't even sunset yet.

That night Iris fixed Randall supper, and then they watched TV. Randall kept saying, "Don't I have to go to bed yet?" and Iris said, "No." Then the television signed off. "I guess I have to go to bed now," Randall said.

"I don't care," Iris said.

She could not call the police, of course, asking for her mother. She could not report Fay missing or hurt, since she was not.

In the morning Randall said, "How come we slept on the sofa? With clothes on? And who is going to fix breakfast, fix lunch, fix supper, iron the clothes?"

"Just be quiet, please, Randall."

"You. You got to do it."

"I said be quiet."

"Well, you got to."

She cooked grits and toast and gave Randall the last of the milk. Then she washed the dishes and took a soapy rag to the table and cupboard doors. It would be nice to have the kitchen extra clean for Fay. She fixed a lunch for Fay and put it in the refrigerator under waxed paper: Vienna sausages and sliced pears. Iris and Randall watched television all morning and into the afternoon. She let Randall get out all his toys. She let him dump Tinkertoys on the floor, build up shaky towers, and then bomb them to smithereens. When it got dark they ate the lunch Iris had fixed for Fay.

"Do you have any money?" she asked Randall.

"You can't have it."

"How much do you have?"

"I don't know." She got his bank out, a plastic pig, and cut it open with a hot knife. The blade moved softly and gently down the stomach of the pig, letting out eighty-seven cents. "You're not taking it," Randall yelled.

"I'm taking it," she said, knowing he would put up a fight. But he backed away quietly, and she could not understand why until she remembered the knife in her hand. She had not meant anything with it; but if it convinced him, fine. Then she got three dollars from Fay's secret money place in the closet. There had been at least fifteen dollars there; Fay had taken twelve to go out on. It was something that she had left the three. It might mean she was not willing to hand over to Owen every last bit of what she had. But more likely it meant she knew she would be gone long enough for Iris to need food money.

At the end of four days, Iris had hardly slept at all. Every night she lay stiff with fear in Fay's bed, wanting to be there if Fay came home during the night. She borrowed money from Queen next door, saying Fay was sick. Now the fear seemed to be creeping up her legs in the bed, paralyzing her and even getting as far as her brain, for she could not force her thoughts onto tomorrow. She never heard Fay come in, no sound of a key in the lock or a floorboard creaking. Fay must have been careful not to make noise.

But Iris heard something in the bathroom and got up. Fay was standing in the dark. She tried to hide her bruised face behind the shower curtain when Iris turned on the light.

It was Iris's first look at the work of love.

But she helped Fay wash, got her a nightgown, and led her to bed. Iris slept with her and dreamed about her, but that was not the same as loving her; and Fay slept two days straight. Now, nine years later, Fay lives alone, and Iris lives alone.

"And who abandoned who?" Iris wants to know, asking aloud as she pins up the last sheet. Down the clothesline, other people's laundry hangs still, legs and arms straight, like an audience that's attentive but has no answers.

She will always be taking care of somebody. She had planned to be alone when she found herself a rented room. But there turned out to be three old men living in the other rooms of the house, and no one taking care of them. How they survived before she came is a miracle. It is as if they had been counting on her arrival. Now she cooks for them at night and checks on them in the morning.

She will have no mirrors in the new room. It is not a permanent home anyway, just a station. The room is sunny and spare and open. No mirrors. She doesn't want to see a bit of herself, not until things are different. She has faith that they will be.

But in the new room she has trouble sleeping. She falls asleep, then wakes soon after, tugged back up into wakefulness by a sense of solitude and drifting. The room is bare and high-ceilinged. She lies awake into the night, finally sleeping during the last few hours of darkness. Then she gets up to go to two classes at the college and to Fay's. Sometimes she sleeps during the afternoon, but it is hard now to sleep at Fay's. Iris had not noticed how much of Fay's furniture is broken: dressers without handles, a cracked toilet tank, wobbly table legs. And it is dusty, grimy, smelling like spoiled food. Some afternoons she sleeps at Queen's, before Queen and Emory come home and before she has to go to work. It's a good place to sleep, clean and snug.

And at Queen's there is not the constant, exhausting possibility that Owen Moon might walk through the door.

Gratefully she lies flat on the old bed built by Queen's great-grandfather, the freed slave Dave-Nero Jones, who is in the South Carolina history textbook; who at nineteen and still a slave built the bed and carved his name in the back of the headboard. Later he got rich from feed stores and insurance, and bought fancy English furniture, mahogany inlaid with satinwood, chairs with clawed feet. But his possessions have been all dribbled out now, the land sold as heirs' property, the furniture spread across the country to descendants in New York and the South and various military bases. Queen's bed is the best of what's left, because of the curlicued name dug into it, as if Dave-Nero knew that one day the bed would be and he would not. In the dark cobwebbed shadow against the wall his hidden signature is what gives Iris heart. She can lie there and think not of the buckling linoleum behind Fay's stove, or the stink of Randall's mattress (all that he left behind), but of Dave-Nero. Nineteen and living a life not his own, he was sure enough of his worth to put his name to his work and let it stand for him. Did not even have a wife yet, according to Queen, so it was not love that set him to cutting the pine, but a trust and a longing. It is easy to sleep in his bed.

From the bed she has a clear view of the children in the picture frame. While she drowses, dipping into sleep and back out, she can open her eyes whenever she wants and see the children. They are the whitest children in the world. They look right back at her. Their mother stands behind them, crooked, as if she were about to topple into those red flowers.

Queen fusses sometimes. "What good has Dave-Nero Jones done me?" she says. "Time marches on. All of us is still maids. We each got a stick of his furniture and this lesson: it's no matter what one poor nigger manage to work up to a hundred years ago. Where is it now? And I ain't talking about money necessarily."

"I thought you liked working for that lady," Iris says.

" 'I don't mind' is what I said. I didn't say, 'I like it.' Who would like it? Get up out of that bed now, girl. You done wrinkled my spread and my shams. Go home and feed your mama and them old men you taking care of."

"Queen, did you ask today?"

"No."

"Why not? Queen, you promised."

"Tending a white girl's babies is not a job for you."

"Why not? I'd be good at it. I hate waitressing. The cook is white trash, Queen. I don't want to go back there. You said you'd help me."

"Iris, helping you is what I'm trying to do. To tell the truth I did say something to her and she said she would talk to the children's mama."

"Why didn't you tell me?"

"'Cause I'm still not sure I want you doing that job. I have minded children before, and housework is a hundred times better. If you are like me, anyway. I was always watching out for kidnappers. You mind rich white folks' children and you got a big responsibility, looking out for danger. Doing somebody's housework, you might break a glass or something and she'll get mad, maybe even let you go; but that's the worst that can happen. On children, the story's different."

"Nothing would ever happen to those children if I was watching them. Nothing could touch them."

Queen is shaking her head, hanging her uniform in the closet. Her white slip is a dazzling surprise; it is huge, like a sail. "Working for people isn't like working in a sandwich shop, you know. For one thing, you work for the lady of the house, not the man, so you can't ever tell what is really going on. You will hear her tell people you are family; and then she will say, singsonging, 'Lord, Queen, I can't see how I can pay you the minimum wage out of my little house-money allowance. Can you work for two-fifty?' Or say, 'I just don't understand these Social Security papers. How the government expect me to figure all this out? And anyhow, Queen, you wouldn't never see none of these payments coming back to you. Let's just forget all this paperwork.'"

"I don't care about that."

"Why you want to mind another person's children, any-

25

way? You got to love the babies, and they love you too awhile, at least till they get to school. Then they forget. They don't have no more need of you, they are gone."

"I don't see how that's any different from what they do to their parents. Children are all temporary. Come on, Queen. When will she let you know? When can I find out?"

Queen sighs. "She done let me know. Said Miss Alice might could use you. You can call her." Queen's voice is tired. Iris jumps out of the bed and hugs her, embarrassing Queen.

"Let go. I got to change my shoes."

She sits on the bed to put on her house shoes, old brown scuffs stretched to the shape of her wide feet. On television those same feet and shoes are on *Tom and Jerry,* shuffling around a kitchen or chasing a cat; but a body never shows connected with the feet. Iris sees Queen whole, the mattress sinking under Queen's weight, no cartoon but a real, loved, blessed body. Queen is sliding the shoes on, she is deciding something; and Iris knows she can't count on the baby-sitting job until Queen gives her approval, even if the job is available. Queen settles her feet into the shoes and slaps them down flat on the floor.

"Well, I guess you'll be happy to quit that sandwich man. All right, then."

"Thank you," Iris says, wanting to hug her again, but seeing the time has passed for that. Queen's face is troubled with something else.

"You see Emory now you've moved out?" she asks, not looking directly at Iris, buttoning her housecoat.

"No," Iris says.

"Or heard any from Randall?" Queen says, as if not wanting to leave the first question standing alone and growing big in the silence.

"No, and won't."

Queen looks out the window. "Everything goes into thin air," she says. "You can't *hold* it."

Sitting on the porch railing in the late afternoon, with his legs folded underneath him Indian-style, there's Emory waiting for Iris when she gets back to the rooming house.

26

"Oh, no," she groans when she sees him, even though the sight of him is the best part of her day. He sits relaxed, like someone without worries. He has a sense of balance. "Can't I go somewhere without you materializing?" Iris says.

Emory grins. He has on his elephant vest, purple cotton with reflective metal elephants hanging off. He's like a circus man. His eyelashes are terribly long and black; Iris has to turn away from them. Sometimes they break her heart.

"Your mother's lonesome," Iris says. "She doesn't know where you are spending your evenings."

"She knows," Emory says. "She just wants me home. Talked to her this morning. It is you she's worried over, not me. What is this new job she says you're getting?"

"Just baby-sitting. Grandchildren of the lady Queen goes to."

"They live in a big yellow house on Rutledge?"

"How did you know?"

"Same house you've been sneaking past twice a week for about a month now?"

"God Almighty, do you watch me twenty-four hours a day? I can't believe it." She throws her books on to the porch. "When do I get to go somewhere by myself?"

"Anytime you want to."

"I want to now."

"Okey-doke." He smiles.

"I can take care of myself, Emory. You don't *have* to follow me. I'm better off alone, anyway."

"That isn't true. You're better off with me."

"You don't know. I'm strong now." Last year she was not strong, and for her weakness had to spend three months in a hospital. She wants Emory to know it will not happen again. "I'm different now," she says.

"How different? Because you moved? A room changes you?"

"Yes! A room changes everything!"

He studies her face. She turns away from his eyes again.

"Look, I want the job because I can't take the sandwich shop another day. I can't," she says.

"Why don't you quit the sandwich shop? What's wrong with just going to school for a while?"

"I need the money."

"You didn't before. Fay never objected to feeding you out of her check."

"Fay feeding me?" She looks up in mock surprise.

"You know what I mean. What do you need money for?"

"For my room. I need it to pay rent. Okay? Will you leave me alone now?"

He gives up, sighs—same sound as a sigh of his mother's, hurt—and jumps down from the railing. But what can she say? He wouldn't understand what it is that makes her always send him on. It is things he has never seen—the trembling hand stuffing dollars into a purse; bruise flowering dark across the cheek; thin string of blood threading the eye-white. What can he know of those things? He's been Queen's all his life, and he's never been scared by love, never seen the damage.

"You're on your own, then," he says.

"I'll still see you at Fay's some," she says. "I'll still see you when I come over there."

He is on his way down the steps.

"Emory. Where have you been spending your evenings?"

He waves.

"Emory!"

He has always been able to disappear fast.

Nelson's room, 2-B across the hall, is an unsanitary mess but has the only telephone in the house. Iris forbids locked doors. "We live together," she has told them. "Which means certain things." She steps around the dirty clothes on the floor, a spilled can of foot powder, Nelson's cherished organic gardening magazines. He could garden organically right on this floor, she thinks. She'll have to get in here and clean everything out. She dials Mrs. Reese's number. Let it work, she prays. Let it all work.

The voice of the woman who answers is softer than Iris thought it would be. She expected a no-nonsense voice, a Charleston lady's voice, but this one isn't that. Iris can predict people from fragments of them: from handwriting or photographs or voices. This one sounds like an unusual person, someone kind of floaty, maybe a musician. Iris recalls the picture, the woman standing lopsided in the flowers, her eyes startled and on the very edge of a frown.

"I didn't think I needed someone," Mrs. Reese is saying, "but I might."

Is that a yes or a no? Iris says, "I could be there every day after about one o'clock."

"Suppose I come talk to you about it," Mrs. Reese says. "Over here?"

"If it's all right," Mrs. Reese says.

"Sure, fine," Iris says. Anything. She has nothing to hide. Her room is clean. Things are starting to go her way. Looking down into the street she sees no trace of Emory in his usual spot behind the oleander.

Three

S*omething is wrong with her,* Will Reese thinks after talking to his wife. He can hear it over the phone, a somnolent flatness in her voice. She has always been detached but now she is farther out than ever. Maybe he ought to do something about it. He can't think what, though.

His office is a dark suite in the recesses of a suburban medical complex, with new furniture and wall-to-wall carpeting. He let Claire redecorate it last year, when she first started acting sad. She ordered sofas for the waiting room, a glass coffee table, big green plants that must have come out of a rain forest. She put pictures of his family all over the place, his daughters in a clear cube on the desk, Alice and the girls together on the wall in a series taken by the hotel photographer at Sea Island, happy tanned Southerners on vacation among the bougainvillea and hibiscus blossoms. Claire said women like to see pictures like these in the gynecologist's office. He watched her hammer the little pins into the wall, then adjust the frames. Her touch in those days, even when it was not on him, animated his senses.

But the office remained dark, too cool and soft under his feet. He hates air conditioning and carpeting, but there is no avoiding them. The building has windows only in the foyer, and even those don't open. The whole Southeast is air-conditioned and carpeted now. People can pretend they are in Ohio. Will remembers his father's office, where the hot summer air blew in through open arched windows, and men's voices rose from Broad Street below, hailing each other, yelling parts of jokes across the street.

He still has his father's desk, a tall rolltop with two humps concealing an inner sanctum of slots and drawers, shelves and cubbyholes, a panel perforated to hold ink bottles, grooves for pens, tiny holes where his father once kept Life Savers and silver. Will showed Claire one day how the secret compartment springs open when you push a wooden lever under the desktop. After that he left love notes there for her. The last note is still in there, in fact; he put it in months ago, but she never took it out. He lets it sit; every few days he nudges the lever with his knee and the door pops up; he sees the note like a folded white bird still on its nest. He has forgotten what it says.

He loves the desk. Entering his office he always sees it first thing. It has the forlorn, ghostly look of a player piano, a riderless horse. After talking to Alice on the telephone, he sits at the desk, not making a move toward work. He dreads Claire's sadness, stalking him in the corridor. He stares at his family on the wall, and then at his favorite Japanese print on the opposite wall: one line that is a mountain pierced by another that is a branch. And from these windowless rooms, with the new swivel chairs, the IBM Selectrics, glass tables and plants and vinyl sofas, the world made by those two sure lines is infinitely distant. There's not a chance of grabbing hold of that limb and clambering over the edge into the silent stretched-out vastness.

He made a lot of money last year. Things are slower now, but they'll pick up again. He is good at making money, it turns out to his surprise. His father was not; his father was not even interested in making it. In fact Edmund Reese seemed satisfied with less all around than most men require: a surveying business of marginal profitability; an unheated house where the floorboards slanted southward and the windows were out of line; and a wife who seemed, even to her own son, empty-headed. What did he live for? A man has to have a treasure in his heart, whether it is a god or an art or a love, something he can turn his inward eye on as consolation for the rest. But Edmund had no god. He was an old Episcopalian. And his work was nothing but a pleasant pastime, chosen over banking to allow him time out-of-doors. As for love, who was there for him to love, really love?

Sure, he'd have to have been *charmed* by Marcella when he saw her first. She was a country girl, uneducated, and heart-stoppingly beautiful. The wedding photograph shows a girl slim as a boy, the only girl in a dark photograph of men lined up on either side of her, not standing too close to her because of the way her dress swirls out at the bottom in a pool of white satin on the dark floor. So perhaps Edmund was taken by her then. Grant him that: a young man's ardor, if not love. But it can't have grown past that stage. The woman was too flimsy to support a major love.

No. Edmund Reese lived out his life without ever explaining himself. He never told his son where his treasure was.

But here is his desk, nevertheless, the desk of a man with secrets. Will runs his hand down the scroll-shaped side panel, staring into the open front, impressed with the irony attached to the furniture of the dead. It is a paltry legacy, less than worthless compared to the *man*—yet, being all that's left, it takes on a relic's curious potency. He presses the secret lever and takes out the last of his love notes to Claire:

> All other things to their destruction draw,
> Only our love hath no decay.

Had he really believed that? Just as well that she never took it. It is a lie, no truer for the man who wrote it than for Will. Love rots.

But the poetry itself! That has staying power. At Chapel Hill he started out as an English major, before he changed to pre-med, before Edmund died. Snatches of poetry sometimes surface in his brain now, like timbers of a long-sunk wreck. He and Danny Cardozo used to read poems out loud in Danziger's and drink beer. Plenty of Betas were English majors in those days, and custom still tolerated the reading of poetry in public. Danny can still remember whole poems. Will can remember only fragments; he is haunted by parts and pieces. Sometimes the fragment is so small as to be without words at all, only the shadow of a poem falling across his brain. It is as if his memory, leaking power, makes a strange compensation: he can't remember the poem but remembers keenly having forgotten.

Last week he was doing a cesarean at six a.m. after a sleepless night. Martin, the OR nurse, said, "You look like shit this morning, doctor."

"No sleep," he said. He let her think he had been working, when actually he had been home in bed, rolling over, punching his pillow, hearing every noise in the street. He was glad when the alarm went off and he could give up trying to fall asleep. In the middle of the operation he looked back at the patient's face, which was thin, fallen to one side. Her neck was long, uncovered, stretching out from a thin bare shoulder, upper arm as slender as a child's, and limp. He was struck by that arm; he seemed to recognize it. He studied it. From somewhere in his head came the lines of a poem:

> When her loose gown from her shoulders did fall
> And she me caught in her arms long and small . . .
> It was no dream: I lay broad waking.

"Doctor?" he heard Martin calling to him.

"Who is this, anyway?" he demanded.

She read him the patient's name, a young woman whom he had seen only twice before. He delivered a squirming muscular male child and its webby blood-rich placenta. He wanted to do more for her, but the operation was over. He sewed her up; the nurses wheeled her out. He would see her again, but by then she'd be awake, taking care of herself, hardly needing him.

He had Cardozo paged, without response. "Get him on the beeper," he told the desk, in a voice that made the girls move fast.

Thirty minutes later Danny called in. "Reese? What is it?" Danny said, worried.

33

"Listen. What's this: 'And she me caught in her arms long and small. / It was no dream: I lay broad waking.' "

There was silence at the other end. Then Danny said, "You're shitting me."

"I'm not, I'm not. I can't remember. It came to me in the OR and I know I know it. What is it? Do you know?"

"Do you know where I am?"

"No."

"Calvert's Exxon. That's the only public phone on Wadmalaw Island, and it's seven miles from the blind I was in half an hour ago."

"I'm sorry."

"And I'm wet. For Christ's sake, Reese, I thought this was an emergency call."

"It is. Do you know or do you not?"

Danny took a long breath. "Thomas Wyatt."

"Wyatt?"

" 'They flee from me that sometime did me seek . . .' "

"Wyatt. Birds or something, that used to eat out of his hand, don't anymore? And his girl is gone?"

"You got it. Now if that's all, I'll be moving on. I've got two good old boys back there waiting for me to explain why I dove out of my blind just when the teal flew in."

"Sorry. I thought you were probably still in bed."

"But that didn't stop you either, did it. You sure there's nothing else now? No floating quatrains you got to nail down before rounds?"

"That's it."

"Take it easy, Will."

Right. It's tough to take it easy when shards of metaphysical poetry are flying at you and the women all around you are sad. Their sadness is oppressive, a general gloom raining down over the world. It is not just Claire and Alice. They all seem sad—his patients, the nurses, the women driving Volvos through the streets, with sunglasses on their heads and sadness in their faces. What can you do when the women are like that?

He had tried to rescue Claire from sadness, and failed. She had been an OR nurse, one of the best. Fast, sharp. He knew her only by her last name, Thibault, pinned over her left breast. Then she began hanging around the patients after surgery, talking, listening, looking them in the eye. She talked low as they came out from under the anesthesia so they would not think they had died: they could hear Claire promising safety. Suddenly in the space of a week three bad cases came up one after another like cannonballs with her name on them. An eleven-year-old girl died in childbirth. A young woman had breasts, throat, and shoulder removed. Siamese twins were born and one lived twelve hours longer than the other. Claire spent the night in neonatal, stroking and mumbling and crying over the bruised yellow thing. They hospitalized her, and Will stopped by her room to offer her the office job. She accepted. It gave her a chance to take things easy for a while and recover her strength. She seemed happier. She fell in love with him.

Now she sits at her desk out there, probably painting her fingernails, sinking into sadness. He hasn't even seen her yet this morning but he can sense sadness brewing past his door.

He wishes she had friends. Her mother is dead, her father senile in the Presbyterian Home. It is too bad that she has no girlfriends, but somehow fitting. She could never go giggling down the corridor with Michelle or Cindy, she isn't the type. There is a dignity in her loneliness, but at the same time it puts a burden on him. He has the whole responsibility of her. And she wants a future. Maybe that is what they all want, love that does not rot but lasts into the future. Unfading, unshrinking love, good as Sea Island cotton.

Sooner or later he'll have to get up from his father's desk and venture out to see her. She wasn't there when he came in, and he has been hiding ever since. He closes Edmund's desk, pocketing the dead letter.

"Claire?" he calls out. She isn't at her desk. But she has never been late. Cindy and Michelle are always late. Some days they don't come in at all; they call in and tell Claire they have a cold or cramps or trouble with their husbands, and she commiserates, giving them advice and then covering for them, skipping lunch to do their filing or billing. She never misses work, doesn't get colds more than once a year, never has cramps, has no husband.

Car trouble? She lives on the peninsula and drives out to the office complex in her old Volkswagen. If she had a flat tire she wouldn't have the first notion of what to do. If she had a wreck—he sees the little red car flattened between trucks, traffic jammed and bottlenecking on the bridge, cop cars everywhere.

He calls her apartment. After six rings she answers.

"I'm not coming in today," she tells him.

"Are you sick?"

"No. I'm taking the day off. I need to rest up."

"Are you sure you're all right?" he asks. "Can I bring you something? Candy bars or coloring books?"

"No, nothing. I'm going to sleep."

"Maybe I'll drop by this afternoon and check on you."

"No. Don't do that, Will. I look terrible, I feel terrible, you don't want to see me. What I have is probably catching."

"You said you weren't sick."

"I don't have a fever. I'm not throwing up. Define 'sick.'"

"Well, how do you feel terrible?" he says.

"I feel terrible, that's how."

"Okay."

"I'll be in tomorrow. Tell Cindy to finish the insurance and water the ferns."

People do sometimes change, of course. Habits, allegiances, dreams are all alterable, but only under extraordinary pressure—like great love, fear, grief. More often, people don't change. A girl who has never missed a day of work does not suddenly decide to stay home in bed, for no good reason.

Cindy and Michelle come in together, their voices high and carelessly mingling. They are young, and yet they are both married. They wear things in their hair, colored combs and barrettes in the shapes of poodles and rabbits, and their eyelids are phosphorescent blue. Their girlish voices and girlish decorations might suggest that they are

36

not sad. But after they put away their bags and get their mugs of coffee and sit in their swivel chairs, a grimness sets into their faces, especially around the mouth. Their lips are tight against their teeth. And to Will, watching from the corridor, they are sad girls with no joy in their lives.

In the evening he drives home, passing the corner where he could have turned to go to Claire's. He is in the wrong lane, can't get over in time to make the corner.

He turns onto his own block and sees his house still there, a heavy, monumental house of stuccoed brick. The gates are tall wrought iron. Beside the porch, ligustrum and pittosporum grow up thick and dark green, nearly black, lining the driveway. Houses like this can't be built now. The wood is heart of virgin pine, impervious to rot and termites. The trees that are used for lumber today grow so fast they are soft and pulpy, and houses built from them will not last like the old ones of slow-grown timbers. The brick walls of his house are two feet thick. It has survived fire and earthquake and hurricane. It is as thick and solid as a fortress.

But his children are thin.

As he pulls the big old Oldsmobile, a '76 Delta Royale, into the driveway he sees Beth and Marcy looking down at him from behind a column on the second-floor porch. Beth's thin arms reach through the balustrade, grabbing air; then they disappear. Were they reaching for him? In the kitchen, water is running, dishes clattering. The sound is a common enough sound for six o'clock, November, his house—but it nudges his memories of childhood the way a dog's bark at night or piano music through a window sets off a charge deep in his brain. A house with a woman and children in it at dusk is frightening to the man who draws near and hears the muffled voices, those dishes being washed. The pure domestic horror of it rings down his spine.

Four

After his father died, Will decided that North Carolina was a better place than South Carolina. North Carolina was dignified and masculine, intelligent. It had mountains, a good university town, a lonely remote shore. South Carolina after Edmund's death seemed fat and flushed, oppressive. Will stayed in Chapel Hill during his vacations instead of going home. He got out of English literature and into pre-med. He convinced Danny to do the same. "We've been kidding ourselves," he said. "How are we going to make a living on this shit? Teach poetry in junior high? Coach the chess team for extra pay? We've got to move fast, Cardozo. Think of something." The next day they changed majors. The switch meant two whole summers of classes in chemistry and biology, but Will was not eager to be anywhere else. It suited him fine to have to stay in school longer than expected.

During his junior year he had taken Alice out occasionally. She was a freshman at Hollins, and he drove up to Virginia three or four times to take her to a steak house where she ate next to nothing and then they'd sit in the dorm parlor and watch television. The idiocy of the situation did not disturb him. She was a girl he knew from home, and he was comfortable with her; it was worth the long drive. She wasn't easy to talk to, she generally sat quietly through the meal and through the TV shows and let him talk. She was aloof in a shy way, studying all the time, not particularly interested in lovemaking, what little of it he had attempted, but more than tolerant. One night he looked at her in the light from a yellow porch bulb at the restaurant, and he fell in love with her. He noticed beauty in her face. Her brownish eyes were deeply kind, her brownish hair soft and gently waved back from her temples. He had the distinct feeling that she was threatened. Right then he reached for her, scaring her with the sudden movement of his arm.

"What is it?" she said, looking around quickly. She thought he was trying to warn her of something about to fall on her. He managed to turn his gesture into an attempt to button her coat. She was cold, the coat was not lined. Her fingers were freezing, while his own were almost hot. He marveled at her metabolism. He could not live without her. Taking a dismal room at the Hotel Roanoke, he swore he would never be parted from her. Alice was fond of him, but it was partly out of concern for his academic career that she agreed, finally, to transfer to Chapel Hill. "At the end of the semester," she said. "If you promise to go back now. You've missed a whole week of classes!" (For it was *he* then who thought only love mattered, and she who argued the exigencies of practical life, like class attendance.) During the rest of the autumn he spent his afternoons finding an apartment, repainting its two rooms, caulking the tub, collecting things he thought she would like, such as a smoking-room ashtray on a pedestal and a fringed lamp shade. He moved out of the Beta house and slept alone in the apartment, staying to one side of the bed. A week before she came he bought two coffee mugs with names on them, "Alice" and "William." They sat together on the kitchen table, "Alice" facing "William," ceremonious and anonymous as the first-named lovers in a ballad. When she moved in she left behind a math scholarship at Hollins, and her father never forgave her.

She was cold all winter. He kept the gas heaters high, actually afraid of losing her to the cold. He bought an electric blanket to keep her warm. Finally spring came, and she could sit out in the sun, which she loved. She was there when he came home, cross-legged on a striped rug in the grass, reading math. The air was fresh and tinkling with the faint glassy sounds of faculty children's voices. "How do you read math?" he wanted to know. "How does it turn out? What happens after the part about derivatives?" But she couldn't explain to him what she was working on. Her white peasant blouse drooped in front to show the bony plate of her breastbone. Her hair touched her shoulders. He thought it was shocking that the plain sight of her could wrench his heart the way it did. The faraway children were an added influence. "Marry me," he said, taking the book out of her hand.

"No," she said. "It scares me." She picked up the book.

"What aspect of it scares you?"

"The loneliness." His face must have shown surprise, because she laid the book face down in the grass and looked at him. Her face changed, as if she had only just then seen something about him that might be worth having.

"But then I'm always lonely," she said. "When I'm by myself I don't notice it so much. Okay. Let's get married."

But his feelings were hurt. "Okay" wasn't what he wanted to hear. This was marriage, not a football weekend. This was *history*. He tried to point that out. "By marriage I mean the real kind. Permanent marriage."

"I should hope so," she said.

"But why are you so offhand about it?"

"I'm sorry," she said. "I'm not, really." She took a joint from her pocketbook and lit it, right out in the yard. "It's just that I always thought I'd live alone. You keep making me revise the forecasts." She smiled and held out her hand to him. "I'm glad," she said.

"And when we get married, no more grass."

"Oh, come on."

"No, I'm serious." She got it from math people; he was surprised they even knew about it, the men with their slide rules and short-sleeved shirts, the women plain and thick-ankled. Alice was the only handsome human being in the department.

"Chromosome damage I do not want," he said. "I expect fat, healthy, symmetrical children."

And marriage suited Alice, Will found. She grew even more beautiful, though she had no idea of it. Her thin face took on a glow, her eyes seemed to darken, after she married him. He watched her in fascination late at night while she worked at a table next to the bed. She worried that the light would keep him awake. No, he said; but it would, that was the whole point—he wanted to stay awake and be able to see her, the hair slipping forward, the forehead pinched up in thought, the mouth taking slow, regular drags on her cigarette. The smoke went under the fringed lamp shade and funneled back out at the top. She worked in her slip. She was both boyish and girlish. Her breasts were more nipple than round flesh. Late, near one or two, she would lean back in the chair, smoke one more cigarette, and change into a nightgown. When she finally put out the cigarette and turned off the light and came to bed, he pretended to wake up, and took her in his arms. Making love to her, he always had the feeling there was something just beyond his reach.

He changed himself for her. She loved music, liked to have something playing all the time, whether it was Mozart or Mick Jagger. She liked it going even while she worked, while they talked, while they loved. But music had always distracted him and made him nervous. He couldn't grasp the pattern of the sonatas or the lyrics of the songs. Still, he didn't want her to form any alliance that excluded him, so he pretended to listen along with her. For her sake he even grew to like a few things. He liked Tchaikovsky, a Russian, and he liked James Taylor, a North Carolinian.

All along he sensed that he was too deeply involved in this marriage. He blamed his father. Edmund's obituary had said, "Surviving are his widow, the former Marcella Stalvey, and one son." That sentence had alarmed him. It yoked the two survivors in a bereft future. So he did not go home for Christmases or summers, and when Alice stepped into the yellow light from the bug bulb he fell into an obsessive, exclusive love. It had to be that strong, had to be everything. It had to be more than it was, actually. The marriage was not made of Alice and William but was a hard bright metallic nugget located just through and beyond his wife, and he pushed toward it, crazy to get at it. That's what that was, the thing out of his reach: the marriage itself.

It was unmanly the way he fussed over her. When she got pregnant he followed her around the house to make sure she was not going to trip on something or faint and fall, and though Alice herself never got morning sickness, Will's stomach was queasy.

Then one afternoon he came home to find her in bed. She was four months along but had not slowed her pace, still stayed up late despite his objections. "I'm glad to see you're taking this seriously," he said; he grinned at her and sat on the side of the bed. "You'll need sleep."

"I'm losing it," she said.

"What?"

"I'm starting to miscarry. I've been bleeding for two hours."

He jumped for the telephone.

"I already called," she said.

"But you should be in the hospital."

"The doctor said just lie still. He said if it happens it happens." She unfolded a paperback book on her stomach.

He went about the apartment straightening up, emptying ashtrays, reshelving books, sneaking a look through the bedroom door when he could without letting her see how frantic he was. He brought her some tomato soup and Oysterettes for supper, but she wouldn't eat. Her pain was getting worse. "Please take an aspirin, at least," he pleaded.

"I can't do that. You know they have no idea what aspirin does to the fetus."

"Yes but, ah . . . honey, you're miscarrying, so it won't . . . make a difference. You know?"

She looked at him cruelly. "We don't know that. We don't know if that's what's really going to happen." Then her face turned white with the pain.

"I'm going out for some codeine. You're in bad shape."

"No!" she gasped. "Don't! Don't go." She reached out for him as he pulled on his jacket.

"I'll be back." He ran. There was a drugstore three blocks away. He ran with her colorless face before him, its blood suddenly drained by the shock of pain. It made him think of his father and how quickly death could come upon an unsuspecting heart. Of course she was not in danger, he knew that, he kept repeating it to himself as he sped down the sidewalk. What kind of doctor would say "If it happens it happens" and leave ordinary human beings to deal on their own with a terrible event?

"Alice, I'm here," he called as soon as he was back, slamming the door and running to her. She had pulled herself around in the bed so that she was half-sitting, half-lying against the headboard, trying to encircle her pain, her head and knees drawing together around it.

"Is it worse?"

Her eyes were blank. "Yes," she whispered, then screamed.

"It's nothing, don't worry! It will be over. Alice! Don't be afraid, I'm going to help you!" He ran to the bathroom and filled a tumbler with water. He had trouble with the childproof cap on the bottle; he pressed down and turned but the cap kept slipping past the grooves it was meant to catch on, so he set the plastic bottle on the floor and stomped on it. The tiny white tablets scattered across the floor. He scooped one up and ran to the bedroom. Alice swallowed the pill and gulped water.

"I feel better already." She looked at him gratefully. He knew the pill could not possibly work that fast. He knew that the sudden end of pain meant that the fetus had been expelled. Alice relaxed. He helped her to move back down into the bed.

"I think it's all right, Will," she said. "Maybe it was something else. I think the baby is going to be all right." She fell asleep.

He knew it was not all right. Now what, was the question. He could not leave it up to her. She would not be able to handle it. He stroked her long thin arm for a while. Her skin was cold from the evaporation of sweat. He covered her with a blanket. Then he gathered her up close to him, cuddling her in his arms. She mumbled. He rubbed her legs, her stomach. She was sleeping as only one can sleep who has outlasted pain—not a normal sleep but an extraordinary, deep, healing sleep. He felt between her legs for the sanitary pad and unhooked it, slid it out.

He couldn't tell much. The fetus was less than the length of his finger. It looked normal, but without lab work there was no way to tell whether it had been long dead or not. He could take it in tomorrow and have it checked. But where would he keep it till then? In his palm it was barely visible inside its dark bubble, but he could see its shape, its whiteness. He had to flush it down the toilet. There was nothing else to do with it! He was angry, and struck his head against the bathroom door, and cried. He had had no choices in this; it was worse than his father's death, when at least he had alternative courses of action to take. He felt his life begin to cloud over, as lives must at a certain stage when there is nothing to do but what has to be done.

In the morning she was happy. "No pain," she said. "It's okay."

"No," he said, cupping her face in his hands, kissing her forehead. She understood. She never asked for the details. He made sure she was hospitalized for the next two miscarriages.

It dawned on him that the loneliness of marriage, the thing Alice had so feared, starts out of the love itself, which can never deliver on its promises. He gave up certain hopes he'd had, of Alice and William as progenitors of a whole new clan, the North Carolina Reeses. Alice gave up her work. Eventually they moved back to South Carolina, to the flat tidal lowcountry, where, when Alice finally became pregnant again, Marcella brought over honey in warm milk every night, which she said would make the baby "stick"; and God knows what made the difference but nine months passed, and a girl was born, his serious Beth.

So North Carolina, which he had looked to almost as to a promised land, turned out to be only an interlude in his life, and he ended up where he began. The children were born, and though he had nothing against daughters, that's what they were, and not likely to change his life as he'd thought children might. His wife had turned vague and timid, a Phi Beta Kappa in math unwilling to drive a car! And his work, which in North Carolina had promised to be a second love when his first faltered, has become a business, simply one more ob-gyn office with air-conditioned, carpeted, silent rooms.

Coming into the kitchen he doesn't notice immediately that the woman there is his mother, not his wife. She stands at the sink, her back to him. Then she turns, and he realizes it is Marcella. He has not seen her washing dishes in years; it is like catching her at something at which she would rather not be caught.

Her eyes are bright and excited. She reminds him of a Katharine Hepburn character, beautiful but with a screw loose, not trustworthy. He doesn't trust her answers to the simplest questions, such as "What is the date?" or "Is it raining?" She is good at fooling people; but she doesn't fool him anymore.

"Where's Alice?" There is no longer a need for formalities between them, like hello, how are you. Other men become more polite toward their mothers with age, but he has gone the other way.

"Alice," she announces, "has gone out to interview a prospective baby-sitter."

"What are you talking about?"

"I gave her the name of a girl who's looking for a baby-sitting job, and she went to talk to the girl. She asked me to stay with the children until she comes back."

"And when will that be?"

"Oh, soon, I expect. The girl lives around here somewhere."

"Since when has she needed a baby-sitter? Beth is in school every day and Marcy goes twice a week."

"She needs one. Take my word for it. She needs to get out more. This girl can come afternoons."

"It was your idea, then."

"No. It was Queen's idea. Queen knows the girl, and suggested Alice might want to use her. The girl is white," Marcella hurries to explain. "But Queen says she is very nice. Queen seems to take a protective interest in her."

He goes into the living room, knowing she will follow him. She can't help it. He casts scowls at her, which she does not notice; he will have to tell her outright to go home.

But when he starts to, she begins talking at the same instant, and she prevails.

"Duncan wants very much to have you and Alice over for dinner," she says.

"Fine."

"When will you come? You couldn't come the first time. You couldn't come the second time. So I want you to set the date. When are you available?"

"I don't know," he says.

"Then will you talk with Alice and let me know?"

"Fine."

"Don't forget to tell Alice." Marcella's fingers are incredibly long, tapering down over the back of a velvet chair. One of them traces a path through the pile of the fabric. Her hands are always moving, as if independent of her thoughts. And it is not only these insignificant movements that are made without thought; even her major actions are often not considered in advance.

Suddenly he is struck by an idea. *She* isn't sad. She is the only woman he knows who is not sad. The others, whom he tries to please and cheer, are sad; and she, whom he ignores, even insults, is happy.

"Duncan has a new project he wants to discuss with you," she says. "A theme park on the river." She watches him for a reaction, which he does not provide.

"I'm asking a favor of you, Will," she says. "This time don't argue with him."

"I might not be able to help myself. I can't pretend to agree with him."

"But at least don't be rude. Don't be unkind," she says.

"Be dignified, you mean. Respectful."

"Yes."

"When he builds something dignified and respectable it will be easier for me to treat it with dignity and respect," he says.

"Will, this man is my husband. I've been married to him for six months now and you have yet to carry on a civil conversation with him."

"You are free, Marcella, to marry anyone you choose. I have nothing to say about it."

"Of course you don't. That's not the point."

They fall silent, not looking at each other. He is not ashamed of turning his back on her and leaving her alone in the room. She is almost not his mother. She was never meant to be a mother; some women are not. It just took him a long time to figure that out. Now she has finally gotten herself a new life: new house, new job, new husband. There is no proof left of her link to him.

She is a realtor now. In her second year with Dixie Homes she sold a million dollars' worth of real estate and met Duncan Nesmith, married him, moved into his fake plantation house on the Battery—all as smoothly as if it had been ordained for her to do so. And perhaps it had been. Duncan gave her a Cadillac with a license plate that says REALTY. Duncan is a land developer.

What Will has against Duncan is not that he married Marcella (Will holds Marcella responsible for that, a marriage that he interprets as a last-ditch effort to stave off the boredom of age); no, not that he married Marcella, but that he came from Ohio. Ohioans love what they think is the South. Boiled shrimp, debutantes, the Civil War, —they're gaga over every bit of it, fueling the tourist industry in Charleston and Savannah and New Orleans and every town that has a plaque or a monument. Who knows why. Maybe they are close enough (a river's breadth from Kentucky) to know a good thing when they see it, or maybe the combination of industrial decay and bad winter weather is driving them south. And now they are not only vacationing here. They're buying condos. They're staying year-round and investing in real estate, restaurants, inns, banks; buying up farmland as if the South were some non-English-speaking banana republic crying for development in the image of Ohio.

And they're sneaky. They operate out of Atlanta with dummy corporations, so you think you're selling the family place to young men from Georgia . . . you hate to sell, but it's part of the New South, right? But the New South is Ohio warmed over. No one will know until Ohioans have insinuated themselves into key positions in the business community, and it will be too late. And Duncan Nesmith is their leader. Land that Will's father used to measure, marsh and mud flat, woods, coast, swamp, is falling to Duncan Nesmith to be filled or cut over, skinned of all real growth, the virgin cypress, the tangle of honeysuckle and jasmine, and then *landscaped*. With plants that didn't even grow here in Edmund's lifetime. Dwarf juniper! Spruce! There must be vast nurseries in Akron and Dayton raising strains that will transplant south.

They aren't even Yankees—the old enemy. They're good guys. Americans.

In front of the television his two daughters sit, bending their torsos forward as if drawn by a magnet, up and out toward the screen where the Brady Bunch's father is kissing the Brady Bunch's mother while all of the Brady Bunch look on. They are trying to smooth out some difficulty so that the household can run happily again. Beth and Marcy don't see him. He stands behind them and watches the show. Then Marcella comes and stands behind him.

To tell the truth, he is interested in the program and wants to know what the Brady Bunch is going to do about the snakes one of them has hidden in a cage under the bed. But he can't watch with Marcella there. He turns the set off. The girls don't even look at him. Beth reaches out to turn it on again.

"Hold it," he says. "I'm home."

"So?"

"What happened today?" Usually they insist that nothing happened. They did nothing. Mommy did nothing. He imagines their days when he is at work as a series of long empty mornings making a silent, hollow childhood for them.

"Mommy threw the dolls away. I don't care, though. I didn't love them or anything. They were dumb," Beth says.

"I care," says Marcy. "I want Tiffany back. Tiffany had on her wedding dress. Now she is burnt up."

"I didn't even like Crystal and Heather. But Tiffany was Marcy's baby," Beth says. He sees their faces begin to redden toward tears, and he is helpless. He knows Marcella is watching him to see what he will do.

"You do something here," he says to Marcella. They are

her grandchildren; she ought to be able to console them or do whatever it is they need.

The bed in his room is unmade. In the middle of it is a full blue enamel ashtray. Ashes have smudged the sheets. He checks the butts: Golden Lights. At least she hasn't gone back to Marlboros. He empties the ashtray and rinses it in the bathroom sink, then changes the sheets. But he must have pulled a single-bed sheet from the closet by mistake; after he gets two of the contoured corners on he sees the sheet won't reach to the other side of the bed. Alice doesn't keep the sheets in any order. They are all jumbled into the linen closet. He knows he could organize the house better than she does. He would even enjoy it more than she does. He could take care of the children, too.

Maybe, though, he should not have left them with Marcella. She is not very good with them; she can't put herself in their shoes, she doesn't have the imagination. He finds the three of them settled in a big chair, Marcella reading *Sleeping Beauty* with Marcy in her lap and Beth straddling the arm. He had forgotten the princess is not the only one who sleeps. The whole castleful is conked out—guests, servants, dogs, dead to the world. When they wake up they seem not to know that a whole lot of time has gone by.

After the story Marcella has nothing to say. The script has run out.

"I guess I'll go," she says.

"All right. Thank you."

Her hands flutter up to her hair. Has she seen Katharine Hepburn do that?

"I'm parked around the corner," she says. "You'll have to walk me to my car. You heard what happened last night?"

"What?" Marcy says.

"I'll walk you," Will interrupts.

"Even old women have to be careful," she says.

But she isn't old-looking. She has creases at the corners of her eyes and mouth, and some loose skin on her neck that she tries to keep covered with a scarf, but she doesn't look old enough to be a grandmother. He finds her youthfulness embarrassing. She ought to be more wrinkled. With older patients he is sometimes surprised at the firmness of breasts and abdomens that should be slack and wrinkled. There are also young women whose bodies are prematurely old, but of the two types the more astonishing is the old, unwrinkled one.

He follows Marcella into the street. Maybe he shouldn't leave his children alone in the house, even for the few minutes it will take him to walk to her car and back. Maybe he ought to lock the door.

"Will they be safe by themselves?" Marcella asks.

"Of course," he says.

In the fast-fading sky, chimney swifts sail between buildings, so many of them that their high chittering is continuous, almost unnoticeable, like a ringing in the ear. They are nervous, gathering in huge flocks as the date of migration approaches, a vague tension mounting in their brains until in a week or two something will snap and they will go, *get out of town.* Near the corner two long-haired girls in high heels are leaning together against a house, laughing the low sisterly laughs of unmarried girls, jumpy and oblique.

It seems to him that his mother leans toward him, her shoulder brushing against his. He steps away from her. If she did lean toward him he can be sure it was not in a spirit of intimacy or affection: it was because she saw those girls. Marcella is a mimic, involuntarily. If she sees two people leaning against each other, she will lean, too, not having the resources to act or speak in a whole, independent manner. She has to get ideas from other people. This may be the reason he has never trusted her. He can't tell what of her is borrowed and what is genuine, her own.

She touches his elbow, then grips it tightly.

"Look!" she whispers.

"What is it?"

"No, don't look. Just keep walking." She pushes him by the elbow, around the corner, and then lets him go.

"I wouldn't believe it if I hadn't seen it," she says.

"What?"

"You didn't see?"

"Goddamnit, what? No, I didn't see," he says.

"Those girls."

"What about them?"

"They were men, dressed up like girls. Transvestites."

"No, they weren't." He opens the door of her car.

"They most certainly were. One of them had his wig on crooked. I don't think they're dangerous, do you? They just like to dress up?"

"I really don't know," he says.

He hates her car. After his father died, the old Plymouth sat unused in the garage. The battery went dead. Marcella said she didn't want it, even though it was a beauty, in great shape. Will tried to tell her it was still a good car. She kept it for five more years without once driving it. Finally, without telling him, she sold it to a Filipino cook in the Navy.

"Good-bye." She waves and puts her mouth close to the window as it is going up. "Don't forget—" And the window shuts off the sound of what he must not forget. He watches the green car move off down the street, and he knows how her mind works: as carelessly as she drives. No wonder she isn't sad. Nothing is complex to her, there are no folded corners of experience that are mysteries to her. At the intersection she turns on her lights, and REALTY flashes out above the bumper.

The noise of the swifts subsides as they head for home, to the chimneys where the remains of last spring's old twig-nests are still glued by saliva to the bricks. Taking over the skies now are the bats. He can almost hear their tinny, blind voices in Marcella's brain.

And could transvestites harm his daughters? They are gone as he comes around the corner, and he doesn't know which house they might have come out of and gone back into.

He could live in a safer place. He could live downtown near the Battery instead of in this ambiguous zone between rich and poor. Marcella keeps finding houses for sale in better neighborhoods, but he won't move, he has set his family here. "Courting disaster," Alice says.

He had wanted a family. Unmarried and childless he was loose in time, fatherless, mother-threatened. After he got his family, his sense of orientation and stability improved, but at times now, and increasingly often, a new, dizzying suspicion grabs him and spins him: the suspicion that the stability is false; that he will round his corner one day and there will be no house; and worse, that he will be glad to see it gone.

There is still enough light on the porch to reveal a difference in color between the deck-gray wooden floor and the white columns, banisters, and ceiling. The porch is empty, a corridor from the street to the black leafy yard. His house is entered sideways, through a door to the east.

"Bedtime!" he calls.

"Mommy isn't home," Marcy says.

"She's probably in the Piggly Wiggly," Beth says. "Sometimes she gets lost in there, she thinks she's in Harris-Teeter instead. But then the mayonnaise or something isn't in the place she thought it would be. I know where everything is in both stores."

"Good for you, girlie."

He helps them undress and step into the bathtub. They are so thin he averts his eyes. At one time he wanted lots of children, a family big enough to boom through life, absorb its own difficulties and spring back from trouble robustly. Small families are feeble. But in a big family, affliction and grief are less destructive; they get diluted. If he had not been an only child, for example, it would not have mattered so much when he refused to go into his father's business. Another son could have done it. Another son could have done all that he had failed to do.

He wanted to have the children his father had not had. But Alice's body would not yield a big family, reluctant at every stage. Three miscarriages. And the bodies of his surviving children don't promise fecundity. They are too thin. Against their knobby shoulders and ribs, his hands look large and grotesque. He washes their meek, bent necks; the soap slides in rivulets down their backs, over the shoulder blades that are like wings, over the bumps of their spines, and he rinses them and lifts them slack-limbed and dripping out onto the bathmat. They stand still and let him towel them dry, as quiet and compliant as orphans; they raise their arms into the air as he slips their nightgowns down over their heads, then tucks them into bed with the sheet and blanket gathered up under their chins. They sleep together in an old sleigh bed that used to be his mother's (when she remarried she bought a new bed, king-sized, with stereo in the headboard) and he tells them the sleigh will carry them into sleep.

Will never asked, but he assumes his father died in this bed. The body was already at the funeral parlor by the time he got home from Chapel Hill, and the house was cleaner than usual, there was a ham on the dining table—a ham!—and a black wreath on the door, which he removed and threw into the leaf pile out in the yard; and the only person he wanted to talk to about the death was the dead man.

Where was he when it happened?

In his bed. He had come home for lunch, and after he ate, he felt a discomfort in his throat, or his arm or chest, he couldn't tell. He said he thought he ought to take a nap. Then he went up to his room. He lay down and loosened his tie and died.

So quickly? Just like that?

Yes.

Alone?

Yes.

What did he think?

He thought, So that's what it was, the long pain.

He had felt it before?

His whole life.

Thus in dreams for a year his father appeared, every night and then with waning frequency, but always with a similar message, a detailed account of the moment of his death, followed by a riddlelike hint that the details were insignificant.

After the girls are in bed, he leaves the hall light on for them. If they wake up in the night they like to see that they are still in their own house, the sleigh has not really carried them away and stopped too soon, like a carnival car break-ing down before getting out of its tunnel, leaving them alone in untested darkness. This way they wake and see out to the hall, the familiar wind of the stair railing, the grand-father clock, the open door into their parents' room.

He could never bathe them every day; it is too sad. Better to always see them dry, clothed, immortal.

The Dukes of Hazzard is on. What are other people doing now, in the lit dens and living rooms and bedrooms and kitchens of the town? Are they all watching *The Dukes of Hazzard?* Cardozo, for example. A man who lives alone is free to do anything at eight P.M., while normal men must watch television. Cardozo can drink, go out on the town, fuck nurses. But when Will telephones, Cardozo's phone rings without an answer. Will has not been able to reach him all week, not since the Sunday-morning cesarean, that girl's long neck and drooping arm, the lunatic call to Danny for help. Yesterday at the office he picked up the phone without seeing the light was on; someone with an ironic voice like Cardozo's was on the line. "How is—" it said, but the line went dead. "Who was on the line?" he asked Claire. She shrugged. Michelle's husband, Cindy's husband. These were men he preferred not to become familiar with, short, burly Navy men. One wore a knit cap. The other one had a tattoo, but also a fluffed-out hairdo. He didn't understand them. Every afternoon they waited outside in vans for their wives to get off work. He had never liked mesomorphs. They favor men's cologne and have no capacity for irony, shouldering their way through life as if it were a crowded sports event.

If it's warm outside, Cardozo may be sitting by his pool. He says he sits by the pool at night and watches women undress in the windows of the apartments. Will hasn't been out there since the day he helped Danny move in. The place was so depressing he could not go back. Danny didn't seem to mind it. He talked up the pool, the swinging life-style. Will drags a kitchen chair out onto the porch. Rocking back on two of its legs, he watches the night. A bat rides low through the garden, under the overhanging oak limbs and the shaggy crepe myrtle branches. Across the wall a dog whines, quiets down, whines again the way dogs do when, try as they will, they cannot help their sorrow—it will come out. Now and then a thought of Alice shoots into his brain, but he dodges it. He will wait for her, but he will not think about her. He remembers part of a puzzle he used to know:

You are going somewhere—a city, a town—where everyone is either a liar or a truth-teller. You come to a fork in the road. A man approaches, a citizen of the town. You may ask him only one question in order to find out which road leads to the town. What do you ask?

He can't remember the solution. It is a riddle that he heard from his father when he was thirteen, and his father wouldn't tell him the answer. It was a challenge. "You figure it out," he said. "Bring me your answer when you've got it." Two days later, Will walked down to his father's Broad Street office. "Let's see," said Edmund, sitting sideways at the prodigious rolltop desk, bending over the boy's written solution.

"That will work," he said slowly. "Yes, that will work."

He never said it was the *right* answer.

For years Will thought it was the sudden nature of his father's death that left him with this terrible feeling of inconclusiveness, as if his father had been taken away before completing the work of fatherhood, leaving behind an unfinished product. He blamed his father's untimely death for all his own shortcomings, for his unsureness and his perverseness; all of it was Edmund's fault, for dying.

At nine o'clock Alice's car pulls up at the gate, headlights catching the dark leathery leaves of the camellias at the end of the driveway. Will waits in the dark while she opens the gates. She drives in, turns off the headlights. He still doesn't move or call out when she walks back to close the gates, which clang shut with the heavy ring of iron against itself, then shiver briefly on their hinges. Alice does not see him.

She walks to the steps, fifteen feet from his hiding place, and opens her shoulder bag, holding it up to the light from the streetlamp; takes out a cigarette and a lighter. A small flame puffs up under her face, illuminating her jaw, the cigarette between her lips, and, as she bends into the flame, her gentle eyes, her smooth brow. She hikes the bag back up onto her shoulder, leans against the railing, and blows smoke out into the dark yard. The sadness of all other women pales in comparison with Alice's, he thinks; she could be the source of it, infecting the others, spreading female melancholy like a drift of poisoned smoke winding into the night. A contagion of sadness.

What she does next takes him by surprise. She hums a tune, something he has heard on the radio but cannot name, and it makes him furious. She still knows the rock groups, the names of the singers and the words of the songs. He doesn't. He hates to hear her sing; that kind of song makes him feel old and stodgy.

Five

She sees him, of course, shrunk back against the wall, shadowy but unmistakably Will. The shape of his head, the set of his shoulders are a pattern she could recognize and love out of a crowd of shadows. When he does not speak she understands he is hiding to watch her. Let him. She is wearing new clothes. Maybe he will see her in a new way.

For some reason she dressed up to visit Iris. She put on a long-sleeved silky blouse with an attached bow at the neck, a navy skirt, stockings, the fish earrings. A doctor's wife. That is what the girl would be expecting. And it is living up to baby-sitters' expectations that keeps households civilized. So she took her car, even though the girl's house was only blocks away.

It was a mistake. As soon as she backed out of the driveway, she knew: the car was wrong. She remembered driving to look for Claire, the last time she took the car out, sneaking past the office, past Claire's house, not finding Claire or her car, then aimlessly taking streets that Claire would have no business on, letting the car have its way. She looked carefully at each band of tourists, each trio of secretaries, and especially each couple—a man helping a woman cross against a red light, a boy and girl sauntering with their arms crossed behind and their hands in each other's hip pockets. Of course not one girl was Claire but each girl had something Clairish about her: the tourist squinting into her canvas bag; the secretary in patent-leather heels and full skirt; the woman grasping the man's sleeve, afraid he might be rushing her into danger; the entwined teenagers. Alice stared at them. Suddenly she realized she had driven six blocks automatically, without thinking, without really looking. She could not remember stopping at all, though she was sure there had been a stop sign at Calhoun and Smith. Regaining her senses, she swung left into a narrow street and hit a car head-on. It was a one-way street; not her way. Luckily the other car had stopped, and she herself had been driving so slowly that the damage was slight and all to her car. The black man whose Ford she hit was glad to let it pass without an accident report. She gave him fifty dollars. The wreck was minor, only a meeting of fenders, but she could still hear it now, months later, the *blam* and the pieces of her left headlight dropping onto the street. She'd said to the frightened black man, "I'm never going to drive again." "It ain't anything," he said quickly. "It is," she said, starting to cry; "it's horrible." The cars sat at an unusual angle in the intersection, mouth-to-mouth, as if in a kiss gone terribly wrong. Water or gas or something dripped from under her half-blinded Peugeot. "It ain't anything!" he insisted, already getting back into his car. "Wait," she cried, and then, seeing he had no intention of waiting, she pulled out her wallet and handed over all the bills in it. Without a word he took the money and left her alone in the street, maneuvering his car deftly around hers and disappearing down Calhoun. How could he leave her there? She stood for a while by herself, her hand on the warm hood, deserted by her own victim. He should have stayed, she thought, instead of leaving her there with half a wreck. He had robbed her of something.

The suddenness of the accident—not its noise or the shame of it or her foolish behavior—was what stunned her. That everything could come to such a dead stop! She wouldn't take that chance again, even if it meant giving up cruising for a sight of Claire. She did not drive again for half a year.

Now, on her way to meet Iris Moon, she was afraid of going too fast. The car moved ahead at the slightest pressure of her toe on the accelerator. She took her foot off the pedal altogether, and the car slowed. But only as velocity approaches zero does the chance of a wreck also approach zero. By the time she reached the block where Iris lived, her breathing was shallow and her hands were wet. She parked and sat for five minutes in the car before she went in.

On the porch an old man sat in a green metal lawn chair, bouncing back and forth on the tubular supports. Pink skin and rash bumps showed through the white fur on his face. His thin little body pumped the chair at the rhythm of a heartbeat, making the smoke from his cigarette zigzag upward. When Alice stepped onto the porch, his eyes were on her like snake's eyes on a bird, hard and meaning business.

"No rooms available," he squealed, rocking faster.

"I'm here to see Miss Moon."

"Miss Moon!"

"Yes."

"That's far enough. Don't move one step closer. You and your fake earrings."

Alice kept her distance, trying to read the mailbox labels behind his head. The old man was swinging his legs back and forth. His stare reminded Alice of that of a man who once exposed himself to her on the Battery, sitting on a park bench with his legs spread and his pants open, watching her carefully to see her face when she noticed—which was not immediately, because she was puzzled by the look of concentration on his face, as if something about *her* had caught his attention, like a button undone on her blouse. This old man in the lawn chair had the same look. He swung his legs and stared at her ears.

Her eyes dropped downward to what he was showing her. He had no feet. At mid-calf on each leg the skin was folded and neatly tucked over a stump. The stumps were naked and pink.

"I wish you could see yourself in a mirror," the man cackled. In his lap a cat's tail flipped up, long and yellow. The tail, which had been coiled neatly around the cat, now lashed out and dropped down over the man's knee, ending each slow swing with an ominous twitch at the tip.

The man kept his eyes on Alice. "You her mother?"

"Oh, no. I'm a neighbor."

"You ain't taking her away, taking her back?"

"No."

Then his eyes released her. With his head back, he panted, stroking the cat. The cat shifted position, recurling its tail up into a ball with the rest of it. The man put his head down close to the cat and whispered, "I see you down there in that little cat body." He did not look up again.

Alice opened the screen door and went into the hallway. The house smelled like catfood. A hand-lettered sign on the wall said: NO SMOKING IN BED. UNPLUG TV'S AT NIGHT (FIRE HAZARD). NO NOISE. REMEMBER OTHERS.

A door opened. Someone stuck a head into the hall, a bald, roundfaced head with small features huddled in its center. It raised its eyebrows.

"Iris Moon," Alice said.

The head nodded toward the stairs and watched her go.

She saw that plaster had fallen from the ceiling over the stairwell, revealing thin wooden slats and thick beams. There were two doors on the second floor; the front room would be the better apartment because it would get more light. She knocked. The girl who opened the door, letting sun into the hallway, was beautiful.

She was not thin. Her stomach was rounded, her face full. Her hair was thick heavy hair, brown, and her eyes were brave. Her mouth was wise. A scar thin as a thread creased the upper edge of her top lip. Alice felt immediately old. Her leather shoes, her stockings and skirt and blouse were the getup of an old woman; Iris wore bright red plastic sandals, jeans, a soft yellow T-shirt. Her breasts were small, but her nipples showed like beads.

"I'm sorry I don't have a chair," Iris said. Alice sat on the low mattress. Her knees came up toward her chest. Iris said she had seen Queen's pictures of Marcy and Beth.

"Have you had any experience baby-sitting?" Alice asked.

"I raised my brother, Randall, and sometimes I take care of my nephew when my sister leaves him with us."

They settled the questions of schedule and payment. Iris would go to school in the mornings, then to Fay's, then to Alice's in the afternoons and maybe weekend mornings.

"Your room's nice," Alice said, thinking of how she might make her own resemble it. If she got rid of her draperies and the rug, some of the furniture—the Eastlake dressing table and wardrobe, the chest of drawers, all the old dark pieces out of the Reese family history—maybe she could make her room as open as Iris's. There was so much air in this room! It left no space for furniture of the kind that crowded Alice's room. Her own bed made her short of breath, its high headboard looming black above her like a wide-winged night bird. She never filled her lungs in that bed. Iris's bed was a mattress on a metal frame with wheels. Alice lit a cigarette.

"I thought you would smoke," Iris said. "I could tell you're a smoker."

"How?"

"You're thin," Iris said. "A married woman who isn't fat, you can be sure she smokes. The divorced are thin without smoking. In the Laundromat, anyway; that's where I see people."

"I don't like smoking," Alice said. "I've tried to stop."

"I got Jacky to stop. The old man outside? I think I know the secret."

"What is it?"

"Jacky saw his feet die. I told him when I moved in here, smoking was bad for him, him being seventy-six. But nobody quits anything just by being told to. Then one night in February Jacky passed out on the sidewalk. I found him in the morning. His feet were white. I always thought gangrene turned things black, but I saw his skin when they took his shoes off, and it was so white it looked bright, frozen bone-white. The doctor that did the operation said anybody as old as Jacky couldn't recover fast. If at all. But it's been nine months now, and he's doing good. I took him off tobacco and alcohol. Up to then he was alone and life didn't really *register* on him. When he lost his feet, and I was around to see the stumps, then it hit him. I gave him good food. He's never complained."

"I thought I saw him smoking just now."

61

"Lettuce cigarettes. I found these lettuce cigarettes for him. I don't think he likes the taste, but he likes people to think he's still a smoker. He transfers the artificial cigarettes into a Winston pack. It's a matter of pride."

"So lettuce is the secret?"

"No. The secret is when it hits you."

"I see."

Iris's face was deep and serious. Alice was afraid Iris might say that if she'd let the Lord into her life, her need to smoke would vanish forever. Iris had that look. But evidently Jesus was not what she had in mind. Think about losing your feet was probably what she meant. Meditate on those stumps until you see they are yours.

Iris was not like other teenaged girls. Her voice and expression and gestures were free of the coy hunger that usually flickers in the eyes of girls that age. She seemed to have skipped over adolescence into adulthood, saving the child's generous nature from the ravages of teenaged narcissism. And Iris had none of their skittishness. What could they be expected to do in case of emergency? But Iris looked like she could be counted on. If she could handle this—nursing a dying man back to health, at age seventeen —she could handle anything.

"Don't you have a kitchen?" Alice said.

"No. Mr. Rambo's apartment has a kitchenette. I cook in there, and we eat in there. I'll have to go down soon; they get nervous when I'm late."

"I've got to be going, too," Alice said.

"Why don't you eat with us?" Iris said.

"Thank you. But my mother-in-law is with the girls. She isn't used to spending more than a short time with them."

"But your husband's home by now."

"Yes." Alice looked at her watch.

"Stay and eat supper. The men will like having company."

"I don't know. Jacky didn't exactly take to me."

"Oh, Jacky. Jacky is afraid my mother or my father will come take me away. He says a child should be allowed to live alone. The parents don't own it. I tell him my parents wouldn't argue with that. But he's still scared. Please stay for supper. He'll see you're not a threat."

"Well, I guess I could stay awhile. I can help you cook."

"No need to. It's leftovers."

They went downstairs. Mr. Rambo turned out to be the bald-headed man. He let them in.

"Mr. Rambo, here's Mrs. Reese. She'll be joining us for supper, so get another chair."

Mr. Rambo raised his eyes surreptitiously to Alice. The flesh hung from his jaws like a bulldog's. His little eyes and mouth were nearly lost in his face, stuck on in a pinchy bunch like a Mr. Potato Head.

"He's a quiet one," Iris said. "Aren't you, Mr. R.? He *can* talk, of course, but he's a thoughtful man more than a talkative man. Let's use the real plates, Mr. R., since company's here. And here's Nelson, right on time."

Nelson, a thin stoop-shouldered man of about fifty-five, had come in without a sound. His hair was in a ponytail and his feet in tire-tread sandals. His face skin was tight and glossy, as if maybe some of it were grafted from another part of the body. He kept rubbing a finger over his short mustache.

"Nelson, tell Mrs. Reese where you work," Iris said as she heated a pot of greens.

"Agricultural station," Nelson said, sliding into a chair, popping a grape off the bunch in the middle of the table and into his mouth.

"Tell her what you do."

"I'm a cantaloupe breeder."

"Nelson experiments with seeds. He invents new cantaloupes by mixing pollen."

"That's interesting," Alice said.

"Mr. Rambo, you can get Jacky now," Iris said, shifting another pot onto the burner, scooping up forks out of a drawer. "Nelson, paper napkins and pour the milk. Ask Mrs. Reese if she wants milk or tea."

"Tea would be good," Alice said.

"Nelson gave me a singing teakettle." Iris held up a yellow kettle on which plump birds sang out quarter notes in looping streamers. Nelson, pouring milk into tumblers, gaped at the columns rising pink and yellow and green in the fluted plastic, then stole a quick, proud look at the tea kettle.

Mr. Rambo carried Jacky the way a groom carries his bride, one arm under the knees and the other under the shoulders. Iris held the door as they came in, and Mr. Rambo put Jacky in a chair at the table.

"Collards, picnic shoulder, sweet potatoes," Iris said. The table was a dinette not much larger than a card table. To fit on five plates Mr. Rambo had laid two at the corners, and he and Iris took those.

"Tell Mrs. Reese where you work, Mr. R."

The big head rolled upward toward Alice.

"At the Senior Citizens' Center," Iris said. "He's good with elders. He takes Jacky down there with him, on the bus, and he stays on to help with arts and crafts. What did you make today, Jacky?"

"Bird feeder."

"Where is it?"

"I don't know. He carried it." He jerked an accusing thumb at Mr. Rambo, who got up from the table and rummaged around in a corner of the room, then set into the middle of the table a plastic laundry-bleach jug with one wall cut away.

"Jacky, it's perfect! Where will we hang it?" Iris said.

"It won't work," Jacky muttered.

"Of course it will work. We'll put stale bread in it. We can hang it on the porch."

"I thought here would be better," Jacky said, pointing at Mr. Rambo's front window.

"Do you think so?"

"Because of the cat."

"Oh, the cat. Yes. We'll hang it in the window here and then we can watch the birds while we eat," Iris said.

"I can get seeds," Nelson said.

"Birds don't like cantaloupe seeds," Jacky said.

"They can learn."

"They won't."

"You never saw a cantaloupe seed, I'll bet. What do you know about cantaloupes and birds?" Nelson said.

Iris said, "We can try them and see what happens, can't we. Bring the seeds tomorrow, Nelson."

Alice watched the three men eat. They held paper napkins in their left hands under the table, sat up straight, cleaned their plates. Sometimes they glanced at Iris. The scene was familiar. Of course. It was Snow White's household. Dwarfs, ugly and alone in the woods, despairing of ever winning love, resigned to their own company; and along comes a girl fit for a prince, taking over their lives. What will they not endure in order to keep her? No wonder Jacky was hostile when Alice came. But now that he saw she was not taking Iris away, his eyes had softened.

Nelson washed the dishes; Mr. Rambo dried.

Iris stood behind a chair. "I'll be working for Mrs. Reese, starting tomorrow," she said. The two men at the sink turned to stare at her. Jacky's eyes rolled cold onto Alice. "I'll be baby-sitting her two little girls every afternoon. For me it will be much better than Sub Heaven." She looked at them and they looked at her.

"You know I hate Sub Heaven," she said.

Jacky spat onto the floor.

"What do you think you are *doing?*" Iris said. "What in the world do you think you're doing? I refuse to believe you did that on purpose, Jacky. You've had an accident, I think. Now you'd better clean up your accident." She handed him a paper towel. He glared at Alice.

"Right now," Iris said.

He lowered himself out of his chair and onto the floor. He rubbed up the spit.

"Mr. Rambo," Iris said. "It's time for Jacky to go to bed now."

"It's only nine o'clock," Jacky cried in dismay.

"But you're tired. You wouldn't have had that accident unless you were tired."

"Nine o'clock," Jacky whimpered. "Nine o'clock! And I was captain of my own trawler. A seagoing man, in bed at nine o'clock."

"You weren't no captain," Nelson said.

Mr. Rambo backed out of the room. Jacky's stumps bumped the doorjamb on the way through.

Then Nelson's face turned white and he dropped a fork. "I forgot," he said. "The mail came for you, Iris."

"What mail?"

"A letter."

"I don't get mail. I don't have a mailbox."

"They put it in mine."

"Who knew I was here?" Iris said sharply.

"I don't know." Nelson pulled an envelope out of his shirt and handed it over to Iris. Without a pause she slit it open with her knife and unfolded a letter. She was a fast reader, Alice thought. After only seconds of looking at it, she dropped the creased white sheet of paper onto the table.

"Look at that," she said. No one picked it up. "My father," she said. "Says for me to drive on down to Florida. Gives directions how to get there!" She laughed.

"Are you?" Nelson said.

"He knows me so well. Doesn't he know I don't have a car? Don't even have a driver's license? You're looking at the most useless invitation in the world, from someone who knew it, too. *He* wasn't taking a big chance."

After supper Iris walked with Alice out to the street. "They're afraid," Iris said on the way. "But they'll see, I can go work for you without abandoning them. And they'll learn to do for themselves. That's what I want them to learn, anyway."

In the street two girls were strolling arm-in-arm. They looked out of place, old-fashioned. Two girls linking elbows, walking out—in this block, at this time of night? There was nothing to see; there were dangerous people around.

"Hey, Iris," the girls said. Their voices were boys' voices. Iris said hello back, as if they were not out of place at all. "Lou, Sandy," she said in greeting. Lou and Sandy walked on by, and Iris didn't look at them after they were past. Alice saw then, Iris was a godsend. Not in the way Queen was a godsend to Marcella. Not like that, for domestic assistance, but for her different point of view.

On the car radio "Desperado" carries her home without a thought for automobile accidents. The driveway gravel crunches under her heels as she walks back to close the gates. The gravel is actually ground oyster shells, bleached by the sun, broken to a pebbly grit. Even in the night it makes a white path. She had held off smoking in front of Jacky. Now she lights a cigarette and hums the song.

> Desperado,
> Why don't you come to your senses
> You been out riding fences
> For so long now . . .

and lets Will watch her smoke, and lets him hear her. She sees him. He thinks she won't notice him there, lurking black against the gray wall.

As if she could ever not notice him, given half enough light and any vision short of blindness.

Six

One time Alice saw a woman in Burger King sitting in a booth with two children, the woman about thirty with her hair hanging flat in frizzed hanks as if she had not brushed it that day, and the children bouncing on the plastic cushion of the banquette. Without saying a word the mother slapped the little boy on his bare thigh. The slap was loud enough to make people turn around and look, but the boy did not cry. He slumped down in his seat until his chin was level with the table top. Then the woman lit a cigarette.

From across the restaurant Alice stared. She could see in the woman's movements—the lighting of the match, the first hard drag—this woman would rather be dead than in Burger King eating French fries and drinking an artificial milkshake, with bedraggled hair and noisy bouncing children. This was a woman who would never quit smoking; not now, not at forty, when her voice deepens to the pitch of a man's; not at fifty, when it will rasp and bubble with phlegm and people standing next to her in the checkout line can hear her breathe.

Now, according to Iris, Alice ought to conjure up just such a vision of her own future—her own breath diminishing, her own lungs rotting. She tries, standing out in the night with her husband's spying eyes on her back. But the vision won't come. It is like trying to call up a dream, or invoke a muse. What comes when you call can't be the real thing, because the real thing comes only unbidden.

He is still watching her. She wants to sit down on the steps and cover her face with her hands, rock back and forth, cry—all in hopes that he will come to her. But the risk is too high, he might not do it. Then she would look crazy.

Once she overheard a conversation between two businessmen waiting for an elevator. They were holding briefcases and wearing suits. She had to come up behind them and wait. She expected their talk would be about business deals, the transactions that men make between themselves to keep the world moving. But one was saying, "I've got to find out. If she's really psychotic, I'll leave her. But if she's faking it, I'll stay." Alice would have said it the other way around, but now the truth of the man's words is clear. Will would leave if he thought she was crazy.

She slings her pocketbook over her shoulder and turns back toward the porch. She pretends to catch sight of him, cocks her head. "Will? Is that you? What are you doing?"

"Taking the night air."

He comes after her into the house. When she turns on the kitchen light, out of the corner of her eye she sees two cockroaches dart into a crack under the refrigerator.

"Where'd you go?" he asks, opening the refrigerator door. "Do we have any more salami?"

"It's wrapped up in the butter compartment. Didn't you eat?"

"No."

"Did the girls eat?" she asks.

"I guess so. Marcella was washing dishes when I got here."

"I went to interview a baby-sitter."

He peels a disk of salami from the stack, rolls it up like a cigar, and pushes it into his mouth.

"Going to get a job?" he asks.

"No."

"Have a beer." He holds a bottle of Tuborg out to her, the only one left.

"No, thanks. If you think this is a bad idea, I won't do it."

"I don't even know yet what the idea is," he says, chewing.

"This girl is going to come over every afternoon to baby-sit. She's good with children."

"What will you do?"

"She's better with children than I am."

"Oh, come on. You're great with the girls. You do everything you're supposed to do, and you do it well."

"Today I threw away their dolls."

He sits down. Chewing, chewing, then drinking the beer. "I heard something about that," he says after a swallow.

"You're doing that on purpose, aren't you."

"What?" he says.

"Making noises with your mouth while I'm trying to explain something."

"Not at all. Tell me. Why'd you throw out the dolls?"

"They were obscene."

"Dolls?"

"You know which ones. The sexpots. I couldn't take it any longer. What happened to baby dolls?"

"You did the right thing," he says.

"I know you don't think that. Don't say it just to placate me."

"I'm not. I agree with you. It's fine. And fine with me if you want a sitter. But don't do it because you think you aren't a good mother." He holds his hand out toward her. She takes it.

They undress in their own corners of the bedroom. She watches him empty his pockets out onto the dresser, snap off the watch that measures tenths of seconds. Chin raised, he tugs at his tie, slides it through the collar with a smooth pull. He lifts his wrists chest-high to unbutton the cuffs, tosses the shirt into the hamper, quickly unties his shoes and slips them off, setting them on a wire shoe rack in the closet. She pretends to be looking in the mirror when he stands in front of the closet, but she can see him unbuckle his belt, unzip his pants and step out of them. Methodical, businesslike. In white underwear, he ducks his head to hold the trousers chin-on-chest while he slips a hanger under the legs and clamps it on. Everything is smoothly removed; everything is easy for him! The undershirt is old, stretched out thin and soft, lifting away from his back the way a football player's jersey floats loose in September practice. She has watched the high school boys play near the Battery, with their shoulder pads and cut-off shirts. It is the loose cloth over the hard-muscled skin that she thinks of now when he walks past her. She wants to touch the shirt, the worn white cotton, more than anything in the world.

He closes the bathroom door behind him.

On the dresser are his stacks of coins, scraps of paper, a rubber band, and a paper clip—it is pretty much the same pocket litter a little boy has. She never checks her own pockets. Anything left in them stays there until it drops out in the dryer—a key, a child's plastic barrette, a book of soft, well-washed matches, crumbling. She has never in her life been a good custodian.

She unfolds one of the notes. "Dr. Cardozo called. Call him back at 3." Claire's handwriting is fat and round but not cute; there's a graceful twist in the final upswings. Alice could never make a 3 like Claire's. That 3 is lovely, brings tears to her eyes. She opens another note:

> All other things to their destruction draw,
> Only our love hath no decay.

The hand is Will's: small, cramped, nearly illegible.

So they're still going strong. No decay. Well.

And still writing love notes? Oh, still?

It's a bad sign. She had begun to think time might work to her advantage. Will might tire of Claire; Claire might move away, might fall for a Navy man. She had begun to think that her own failure to take action might prove the smartest strategy of all, and if she could only last long enough he would come back.

But "no decay"!

She is in bed when he comes out of the bathroom, and she lies still as he settles in. He begins night on his back, stretched out straight, his arms at his sides. Later in deeper sleep he will bend away from her like a thermocouple, drawing his knees up, pulling his forearms in. He falls fast into sleep; she does not. She had trouble with it even as a child. She would lie in bed and pray for sleep to come.

Sometimes she would try to start her favorite dream, in the vain hope that dreaming would bring on sleep.

The favorite dream was a dream about sleep, a dream of moving closer and closer to sleep's ease. It began with a house, which she entered on the first floor, where a large fast-moving family greeted her, lots of children, children's noises, and food—the mournful smell of cooking, the noises of cooking (fat spitting in a pan, stew bubbling, meat searing), and the family begging her to stay, crying, "Eat with us!" But she was on her way to another part of the house. On the second floor the rooms were cleaner and quieter. Adults lived there—people who were only distantly related to one another, or merely acquaintances. The furniture was plain and bright, tightly upholstered in polished cotton. Somewhere on the second floor was a hidden staircase to the third floor, but it was hard to find. Sometimes it might be in a coat closet. Sometimes behind a bookcase. And it might appear to go down instead of up. While she searched for it, the people who lived there followed her, whispering, "What is she looking for?"

Sometimes in the dream she never found the staircase. She woke up feeling dislocated and confused. But occasionally she found it. She climbed the steps and stepped out into a large, elegant room, where light streamed in through floor-to-ceiling windows, past brocade draperies drawn back in heavy, still folds. The sofas and chairs were a deep brown velvet, thick and rich, more like fur than fabric. Sitting before a piano near a window was a girl who did not move or speak, alone in the room with the music she was about to play; the air quivered with the possibility of music, but the room's silence was as mossy and deep as its velvet, and closed her in a trance.

Now this was a dream she loved. She dreamed it hundreds of times during her girlhood, but as she grew older the staircase got harder to find in the dream. Then the dream itself got hard to find. It would not come to her. She could think it out, awake, but the feeling was not the same. The waking dream did not move her heart.

After Will has been asleep half an hour, his long breaths regular and soothing to her like ocean waves, compensation for her own shallow panting, she shakes his shoulder. The curve of it is hard, rounded off like a ball, not bony like hers. The undershirt slides over his skin like satin on satin. His eyes open up.

"I love you," she says. His eyes are open but he isn't awake. Maybe her words will sink into his subconscious. If people can learn French from a record while they're asleep, maybe he can learn this. But his eyes close again.

After she lost the house dream others came and recur now but they are static buzzers, never leading to music or beauty or sleep. Their seed is not ecstasy but error. There's the dream of twins: Will is twins, and the one she married by mistake is the wrong one. Seeing the old, right one, she recognizes him as her true love. But the wrong one, to whom she is married, is polite, well-meaning. How can she set things straight?

In another dream she has to go back to school. A mistake has been discovered in her transcript, invalidating her degree, and she has to take a basic math course. But she has lost all her understanding of math, the numbers are nonsense. Suddenly it's time for the exam, and she sits hopelessly pondering tennis balls thrown in parabolic curves, swimming pools filling up with water, trains traveling toward each other at increasing rates of speed.

She was born the only child to parents who had not expected any children, after ten years of marriage. So she had all their love, but it was calm and restrained. As a rule, no one fought or sulked except when her mother lost her temper on occasion. No one hugged, or mentioned love. Love was like a child who'd drowned. Its ghost was the most important member of the family. Every morning her father read philosophy in his study for two hours before going to the newspaper office. Her mother sewed for other women, not to make money but because she was good at it. She made dresses from intricate Vogue patterns with fifty pieces, with facings and interfacings and hand-rolled hems, dresses out of imported Irish linen or antique French lace, lengths of fabric so fine they demanded to be made into something extraordinary. Elizabeth specialized in wedding dresses, making new ones and restyling old ones. One of the first she ever made was a candlelight satin gown with a train, for Marcella Stalvey's wedding to Edmund Reese. Marcella had come to town with nothing, not even knowing where to buy what she would need for her marriage into a prominent family; and Edmund's mother had asked Elizabeth not only to make the wedding dress but to help Marcella shop. There was not much wealth in the Reese family, but there was a history back to the Lords Proprietors and a need for satin wedding dresses, monogrammed sheets and towels. Elizabeth showed Marcella what to buy. She had taste, she knew what was right and taught what she knew to the tall, pretty country girl.

Was that coincidence, that their mothers came together then? Or when Elizabeth's steel scissors cut into the thick creamy satin for Marcella's gown, were forces set that would gather strength and eventually join the children of those two women?

But we are not joined. We only touch, Alice thinks. Why should she believe that because Elizabeth designed and fitted and sewed Marcella's wedding dress, this marriage was meant to be? Nothing was meant to be. Coincidence is no signal. Pattern is not meaning. But they are all she has to go by.

In spite of living in a house full of tempting silks and the thin rattle of brown tissue, the fabric-covered buttons and rolls of steel pins, Elizabeth never made a dress for herself. Alice did not realize this until one afternoon she came home from school and found her mother standing in front of the mirror in a mint-green chiffon gown, the bodice draped Grecian-style, the skirt falling softly over Elizabeth's hips and legs to the floor.

"It's just right," Alice said. It was. The color and the misty fabric and the natural line of the cut seemed made for Elizabeth. But she said, "It's not for me," and took it off, and Alice realized that none of the dresses that Elizabeth made were ever for herself. She didn't ask why. She knew only that, for some reason, Elizabeth did not consider herself the kind of woman to wear the dresses she made for other women. She loved her work, could lose herself in it and stay up all night to finish a dress, but she was never proud of it and didn't teach Alice how to do it. Nor did she teach her the things she taught Marcella, about sheets and towels and tablecloths; she never talked to Alice about those things. It was Alice's father who taught her; from him she learned to love not silks and linens but the bindings and gold letters of old books, the mottled endpapers and gilt pages. Her father took her to bookstores and to the library with him on Saturdays, and in the evenings while her mother sewed, Alice and her father read. It must have been the quietest household a child ever grew up in, with reading and sewing the only entertainment, and no noise of children.

Will was an only child, too. Maybe that's what drew them together. They recognized in each other the old loneliness, as well as a selfishness that demands more than all the available love. Maybe that is why they married.

But my mother made your mother's wedding dress. You can't leave me!

Last summer they went to Sea Island for a week. It was the only beach resort Will would go to, because it is old, not one of the new ones. He will not go to those, the developments that have eaten away at the coastlines of the Carolinas. "Who's building them?" he asks. "Interlopers. Turning our real places into artificial places; making marshes and ponds into golf courses and pools, and selling our land back to us for two hundred thousand dollars a lot."

She suggested Sea Island, where Southerners have been going for generations, to the quiet old hotel and its flower-filled courtyard. His parents had been there once. He said all right. But when he got there he didn't like it. He didn't want to play golf or tennis, didn't want to go to Plantation Night or take the Beach Train Safari. He hated lying by the pool. After two days of it he began to leave the island during the day and drive to nearby historic sites. Alice took the girls down to the pool. They were good swimmers. Alice could watch the children and at the same time watch the other mothers around the pool. She wore sunglasses; no one could tell when she was looking at them.

The women were her age or younger, with children who still needed tending, but Alice didn't strike up any conversations. The women were blond and tanned and wore gold jewelry into the pool, earrings, bracelets, necklaces, rings, gold glinting and winking against their skin as they came up out of the water. How did they get their hair so corngolden, too, their bodies so sleek? Droplets of water stood on their shoulders like bright tears; they wrapped themselves in thick hotel towels and cried out words of encouragement to their swimming children. Some men were there but it was clearly a women's place. The men sat back in lounge chairs, wearing white Sea Island trunks, watching their wives with affectionate pride. As if a man could ask no more than to watch his ottery golden wife dive into the Sea Island pool and come up at his feet, shaking off water, her gold chains tangled across her collarbone, and his suntanned children pumping their fat legs through the water in her wake. From his chair under the umbrella he might see the world as beneficent, forgetting he saw it differently back home in Atlanta or Memphis or Winston. The children will jump in again and sink and pop back up, buoyant as inflated beach balls.

Will couldn't stand this sort of thing: the pool and the women, the yellow umbrellas. He drove out to Bloody Marsh, where the Spanish were defeated and turned back, kept from moving north to Savannah and Charleston. He drove to Fort Frederica, the first English settlement in Georgia, of which nothing now remains but the brick outline of each house in the ground, like a life-size map laid out under the giant oaks at a bend in the Frederica River. He sat on the riverbank and got sunburned. "Those are real places," he said. "This"—the pool, the women, the yellow umbrellas—"is a fake place." Every day he grew glummer until by the end of the week he was morose and would not eat the food that was already paid for. She worried about him, but she could do nothing when he got like this—her attention made him worse. She suggested they could leave a day early, and he turned on her.

"Don't pretend to care about me," he said.

"But I do care about you."

76

He clammed up; he went out to the fishing dock and did not come in for the seafood buffet or the bingo game. Finally, after Beth and Marcy were already asleep, he came back to the room and went to bed.

That night she woke up from a dream, hearing a low sibilant sound like whistling. She opened her eyes and saw him lying on his side in the other bed, facing away from her. At first she thought he was mumbling in his sleep, but then she could see the white telephone cord running from the phone over his shoulder. He was talking on the telephone, the receiver under his neck, his upper body hunched over and head bent down. She couldn't make out his words; he was whispering in the dark, bent protectively over the telephone, the covers pulled up almost to his head.

In the morning he was in good spirits. He ate waffles and shrimp and eggs and honeydew. When they checked out he chatted happily with the cashier, bought a handful of silver-covered mints for the children. He noticed a photographer pinning up yesterday's photographs on the bulletin board.

"You missed us," he said, raising a hand to the man. "And now we're leaving."

"No trouble," said the photographer. "I'll take you now and send you the proofs." The photographer was blond; he doubled as a lifeguard in the afternoons. He winked at the girls. His pants were an alarming shade of green.

Alice shook her head.

"Come on," Will said. "It'll be a reminder of the trip. We might not be back here for a long time."

"Come on, Mommy," Beth said.

"I don't want my picture taken," Alice said. She knew what she looked like—someone at the edge of catastrophe, someone already flinching from a blow that had not yet been delivered.

"I want it," Will said.

"Let's do it in the courtyard," the photographer said, gathering up his equipment. They followed him out into the green garden, dense with red and pink and orange flowers, things like hibiscus and bougainvillea that don't grow even one state farther north. Sea Island is inside

77

another zone, where semitropical plants can get the heat they need to put out those colors.

"Let's have the Mommy here." The photographer took her by the shoulders and moved her into a bed underneath a vine heavy with blossoms, one piece trailing down beside her head. Her heels sank into the well-cultivated soil.

"And the pretty girls. You can hold your mother's hand, or her skirt here; that's it." They moved toward her.

"And the Daddy."

"No. It's perfect the way you've got it now. Don't ruin it," Will said. He stood behind the photographer while the pictures were snapped, and Alice did not have the strength to call him into the photograph. Her heels went in deeper until her feet were flat. A wide-open red flower brushed her ear, and birds called out across the tile roof above, in a wild mix of creaking whines and sharp chucks—grackles, long-tailed and black with flashes of green and purple like colors in black oil. Ugly birds, worse than crows.

The photographs came in the mail a week later, showing a handsome, healthy woman and beautiful children, bloom-ing. The photograph was the kernel for a dream that started then, in which her children were not her own, but wraiths of the children she had lost, the real children.

When Will is snoring lightly, Alice gets out of bed. The windows are open. The white gauzy curtains stand away from the sill but do not flutter, the air behind them steady and night-cold. The girls might be chilly; she should close their windows. She finds Marcy and Beth asleep against each other, arms laced, legs crossed. Alice untangles and separates their limbs, smooths their nightgowns down, pushes hair away from their foreheads. Their skin is cold. She closes the windows and searches in the linen closet for a light blanket but can't find one, the closet is too much of a mess. So to keep them warm during the night she gets into bed between them. Before morning comes she has waked up five or six times, roused by the unfamiliar deli-cious embrace of weightless arms, a cheek pressed against her back, a hand under her breast—small bodies digging in close to her own; for warmth, for comfort.

She has forgotten most of the formulas and theorems she once knew. All that's left from her major in mathematics is the memory of a crazy sort of landscape where each new advance made holes open up in solid ground, made previous rules into nonsense. The longer she studied it, the more beautiful and the less real it became, until finally she let it go. It was too seductive, a world of the mind, quite the opposite of what she had thought it would be. She hoped marriage might anchor her better. And it was strange how instantly the mathematics vanished from her head. Riemannian geometry, the double infinite rapport, discontinuities and singularities—all the things that used to occupy her for days on end vanished without a trace when a child whimpered. That milk should spring to her breasts at a baby's cry was an event and a puzzle far more compelling than all the math. And sometimes with children asleep at her sides she recognizes old feelings (wonder, surprise, the delight of the lone explorer) and knows she is getting at what she was after with mathematics, anyway.

Seven

Iris's hair grew long again when she was in the hospital last year, because she couldn't get hold of any scissors. Before, she cut on it every morning, snipping the wisps that stuck out, keeping a straight-edged line across the base of her skull like a protective helmet.

Scissors were allowed on the unit. You could ask for them and use them with a staff member present. But Iris's doctor had left orders that she could not cut her hair, so they wouldn't give her the scissors. Dr. Packer said she had to face up to the possibility of long hair. She was there only three months but even in that time her hair grew almost to her shoulders. An abundant, magical growth, richly brown and shining. "What do you put on it?" a nurse wanted to know. "It's what you eat, not what you put on it," Iris said. "Good food makes good hair."

"You are what you eat," said a crazy woman, and another one said, "You are what what you eat eats." In her whole first two months these were the only intelligent remarks Iris heard spoken. Nothing the doctors or nurses said made sense. She concentrated on growing her hair out. She began to like it as it grew, especially the way it would swing free when she moved her head. It grew so fast it seemed to be making up for lost time, as if it had been waiting for this chance.

Three months was the limit you could stay on the unit.

If you didn't get well by then, you went somewhere else. To a private hospital if you were rich, the VA if you were a veteran, and State if you were poor. State was bad. Most patients would get well if they could, rather than go to State. Even the worst off in Iris's unit knew they didn't want to go there. As they neared the three-month limit they began to walk taller, dress more neatly, keep their hair brushed, talk politely to the staff.

Iris didn't care. They told her about the wards, the zombies, the ones crouching naked in corners. Secretly she wanted to be with them. It was her doctor who was determined that she would not go there, and it was he who began to get anxious after two months.

"Get well, Iris," he pleaded with her, holding her hands in his little skinny ones. "Get well so you can get out of here and start your life."

That was the one helpful thing he said to her, the first thing that caught her attention. *Start your life.* Because she had assumed that her life was over. She was sixteen years old but in her mind she was thirty, fifty, ninety. Even before she was taken to the hospital, picked up off the Laundromat floor by an ambulance driver and driven to the emergency room—even before that day, she was old. She was taking care of Randall and Fay, doing all the cooking and housework, paying the bills by walking once a month to the power company, the phone company, the waterworks, twenty-nine blocks altogether. The women who took her money said how nice it was of her to run those errands for her family. At home she ironed, washed, swept out; Fay stayed in bed most of the day. Owen had been coming home at a rate of once a year, and Fay would start getting out of bed when the season came in which chances of a visit from Owen were on the rise, but when it got to be over a year Fay grew short-tempered and jittery. Randall was not a child a sister might love; he was mean and unpredictable. Feeding him was something she did because he was her brother—just as you'd be obliged to feed a dog even though you were certain the dog harbored no love for you and would just as soon be wild in the woods and probably *would* be, one day.

81

There were two good things: school and Emory. School was a haven, clean big classrooms with metal windows and green shades, teachers to tell everyone what to do, a lunchroom where the brown trays were sometimes so fresh from the dishwasher they were still warm and damp. Inside her desk she had a zippered clear vinyl pencil case and four sharp pencils, a pack of clean white notebook paper with its delicate blue lines the color of blood veins under skin, and a felt-tip pen that wrote bright red and knife-thin. She was the only white student in her class. Sometimes others would start the year, then leave to go to Christian schools. In the lower grades the black children were her friends, but later they left her alone. One day a white teacher from the school came to the apartment and left Fay an application to a school run by her church, but Fay was against church schools, she said, and lost the paper. Iris didn't care. Sometimes she imagined herself the only person in the classroom, in spite of the noise around her; her desk and the space near it made a world, separate, inside the bigger, noisier world. The school library had copies of *Family Circle*, and she read these at her desk during recess, copying out recipes that sounded like things Fay might eat.

She had been walking to school with Emory ever since second grade. When she was in the second grade Emory was in the first, and Queen asked Iris to walk him. She showed him how to cross streets; she waited for him after school was out. He was like a little brother, a good one. By and by, as they moved up through the grades, it was Emory walking Iris, taking care of Iris, though he was still shorter. He taught her not to be afraid. Sometimes children gathered on the corners, and Iris wanted to cross the street to avoid the bunch of black boys pushing each other back and forth, but Emory showed her how to walk through, how if you walked steady and didn't look at them, and best of all if you were really *not* afraid, then the cluster would break open and let you pass. Emory had a lot of trust.

More than trust, he had love, for people and things and events, and it could not be contained in his wiry, jumpy body, but overflowed into his pictures. He was smart in all subjects but best in art; the teachers put his pictures up on the walls, the principal framed one and hung it in his office. One time they were walking home and came upon four older boys blocking the sidewalk with bikes. One called out something that made the others laugh. Then a bike tire was jammed up against Iris's leg. Bits of stone embedded in the treads pricked her skin. Bikes were on all sides of her. She couldn't see Emory. The boys were still laughing. Then she heard Emory cry out, "Tandy, look at me now, I got to see your ugly nigger face." Behind them Emory was crouched on the sidewalk, sketching quickly. "He drawing you, Tandy," a boy said. "Yes, I am," Emory cried, and there was Tandy's head in a square of the sidewalk, ugly and big-lipped and insulting, but magical in its likeness to Tandy. The boys moved away from Iris and jeered at Tandy. "Draw me, can you draw me?" one said. "Watch out, you'll be the next," Emory said. He motioned to Iris to go on without him.

After that, people thought she was under Emory's protection, and Emory was as untouchable as a conjurer or a priest, so they left her alone. Maybe that was how word got back to Fay. But it wasn't true. She was under no one's protection and never would be. She would take care of herself. When Iris was sad Emory would clown around and cheer her, and she might wake up in the morning to find her sidewalk covered with colored-chalk sea oats and sharks and gulls and sand dunes, a pastel shoreline rolling to the street. But she was on her own, and he was on his.

Emory was going to make his way. He didn't expect any opposition, either; he always trusted that a path would open up, and Iris knew it would for him. Dave-Nero Jones was in his blood.

One afternoon Iris came home from school and found Patrice and her Tommy in the kitchen drinking Cokes.

"Where'd you come from?" Iris said, letting her books down with a slap on the kitchen table, not exactly pleased to see her sister. Why couldn't Patrice drink the Coke out of the bottle instead of putting a straw in it? Patrice had these habits.

"Well, look at my tan, doesn't that say Florida to you?"

Patrice was twenty-one. She had on a sun-back dress and white spike heels but she looked worn out.

"How'd you get to Florida?" Iris asked, with resentment because Patrice was always going somewhere ever since she went to live with the aunt, while Iris was stuck with Fay. Patrice had been to Six Flags and Carowinds and Myrtle Beach, places people go for fun. Now Florida.

"I got there. Went with friends. Came back alone, ha-ha. Anyway, guess who I saw."

"How should I know?" Iris couldn't even remember the name of the man Patrice was married to for six months, or the name of the one she went to Myrtle with last year, much less the latest love.

"Come on, guess," Patrice said.

"I don't know anybody in Florida."

"You know this particular person. You know this particular person very well."

"Abraham Lincoln," Iris said.

"Do you have to always be facetious?"

"I'm not, he's at Disney World. He's the only person I know in Florida," Iris said.

"Owen."

"Owen what."

"I saw Owen in Florida. I was in this town getting groceries in a Winn Dixie. I came out carrying two bags, pushing Tommy in the stroller, when this car veers into the fire lane, the guy jumps out and calls, 'Hey, Patty.' Nobody calls me Patty but him. It was him. He *lives* there, in St. Cloud, Florida. I mean he has a *family* there, a job and a family, in a real house. It was a cute house, with a carport and a little porch. Not in a real good section, but still . . . It wasn't a mobile home. It wasn't a project. He said he's an electrician. I don't know when he turned into an electrician, but that's what he said, and making good money at it."

"Did you tell her? Mama?"

"Sure I told her. I came over soon as I got back. Can you believe it? He really—"

"Where is she?"

"—lives a regular normal life. I always thought he was moving around all over the place—"

"Where is she?"

"Back there. In her room."

Fay was in the bed with the sheets pulled up to her nose, her eyes closed. She wouldn't open them, she wouldn't speak or move. Iris patted her head. "Mama," she said. "Mama, I know you've had bad news. But don't worry. You know what I think? Open your eyes so I can tell you're listening to me." But she didn't open her eyes. Tears squeezed out from under her tight lids and ran down each side of her head to the pillow.

"Honey, Patrice saw somebody else down there," Iris said. "Listen, it couldn't have been Owen, because he said he was going to be in Burlington, remember? He had a job lined up in Burlington. Remember? So it couldn't have been him. Somebody who looked like him. Patrice's eyes are bad, and don't forget, she hasn't seen Owen in four or five years. She's never here when he comes. Now snap out of it. Right now. I mean it."

Fay opened her eyes, then narrowed them again the way she does when she is suspicious.

"She went to his house. She saw his wife. His *children,*" Fay said.

Then she closed her eyes again.

Iris ran back into the kitchen.

"I don't care what reason you make up," she said to Patrice. "But you get in there now and tell her you were wrong. Tell her you didn't go to his house. You didn't see any wife or children. You didn't even see *him* for sure. You tell her now, Patrice. Right now."

"Don't be ridiculous. I *did* see him."

It was not hard to reach out and pick up the little paring knife from the drainboard, or to hold it out toward her sister: the knife was not a threat, but an explanation, showing Patrice why she needed to do what Iris asked.

"Do it now," Iris said.

"Jesus Christ, okay. Okay." Iris followed her and listened to make sure she did it right. Patrice had no practice talking to Fay. She didn't know how to guide Fay's listening the way Iris did.

"Tell her you were drunk. She'll believe that." Iris

watched through the crack of the open door. Patrice's story wasn't very good, but Fay did open her eyes. Then Iris went into the room and said, "See, Mama? Now you get up, I'll fix your hair for you. Want to look in the mirror?" She picked up the long-handled mirror on Fay's table and held it toward her. Slowly Fay reached out a hand and held the mirror sideways up close to her face, sliding her eyes way over instead of turning her head to look in. Then she dropped her hand and the mirror hung in the air, inches off the floor. She closed her eyes. Iris took the mirror before it could fall out of Fay's loose grip.

"You two deserve each other," Patrice said, and slammed the screen door behind her, pushing Tommy's squeaky stroller down the sidewalk, her sharp heels clicking over a flock of delicate white seabirds wheeling down the pavement in a blue-chalked sky.

Fay didn't get out of bed. Not even to go to the bathroom; she messed her own bed.

"No, Mama!" Iris scolded, her own tears coming. "No! That's very bad. Oh, I can't do this, Mama. Don't make me do everything. Can't you get up? Can you get up just for a minute and let me put clean sheets on the bed?" But Fay didn't move. Iris rolled her to one side of the bed and changed the sheets right under her, and changed her nightgown.

There was no place for her to go for help. It was all right to go to Queen when she was eight and her mother disappeared, but now she was sixteen and Fay was, after all, still here, not gone away or anything. It would be wrong to get help from Queen. She wrapped the dirty sheets and the nightgown up in a bundle and went to the Laundromat. It was late afternoon, when people were starting to fix supper, so no one else was there. The Laundromat was clean except for a couple of empty Tab cans on top of one machine and an ashtray on another, traces of the morning crowd. There would be another crowd in at night. The Laundromat was one of Iris's favorite places. Women came here to make things clean for their families. They folded clothes and chatted and swapped advice about food and laundry products and husbands. It was a public place but its uses were private ones, so people who found themselves there together were in a way related. Iris thought of the loneliness of rich people who have their own washing machines, doing laundry alone in big kitchens, and she wondered if they were lonesome.

Usually Iris washed her sheets and then carried them back wet to the project clothesline, to let the sun dry them white and crisp. But now the Laundromat held her. She didn't want to go back to the dingy kitchen and dark hall, the tiny rooms whose cardboard walls were ballooning inward. When the washer light went off she took the sheets out and pushed the dripping bundle in a wire basket down to the bank of dryers at the far end of the room. She put in four dimes and watched as the sheets tumbled gracefully and slowly behind the glass door. They would stick to the side of the drum up to the top of the roll, then fall and climb again, fall and climb again. Stooping in front of the machine she could feel its heat leaking out toward her, and she held her hands down to catch it. Then she began to make out the shape of a face in the dryer, the face of a child spun out of white whirling muslin, as if spinning matter might generate spirit the way Aladdin rubbed up his genie. She stepped back and watched.

At home there was nothing for her but Fay, nothing but Fay forever, and Fay getting worse every year, almost an infant already. She dreaded Fay's teeth falling out, one by one, and Fay refusing to get dentures. Then Fay would have to be fed mashed food with a spoon. And even the pretty face that kept Fay happy now would not stay pretty forever, and the wide forehead and flat cheekbones that were its mark of beauty would someday be only strange-looking. Already Iris could look at Fay and see her face taking the shape it would have in old age.

In the dryer she saw a better face, the pretty child, the mirage.

She noticed after a while that the dryer had stopped, maybe had been stopped for a long time. She watched it to see if it might start up again. When it did not, she had to use all her power to move through the six feet of space to the machine. Her body was heavy and tired, and she thought, *I can't carry myself another step into this life.* Inside the drum the sheets were hot, Fay's white nylon nightgown was limp with heat. She gathered the laundry up to her neck to collect the warmth, and she laid her cheek against the bundle as if it were a giant, soft pillow. Then in a corner of the room, as far from the street as she could get, she laid the warm laundry down in a nest, a round cozy clean bed as warm as an animal's den, and she curled up in it.

"You know it was your own face," her doctor said later.

"It was the face of a child," she said.

She knew what the doctor meant but he didn't always know what she meant. At first, after Emory found her and called the ambulance, she was like someone thought dead but not really dead. People spoke around her and she heard them but could not answer. Later she was more like someone in a dream; she understood everything, but when she tried to speak, unusual words came out, unplanned sentences, not having to do with her thoughts. It was not till the doctor said she could start her life that things began to match up again, the world and the words and the thinking. Then she began to be able to choose her words, so that he could make sense of them, and she kept back the ones that upset him because they didn't match the topic of conversation, just as in school she had learned to underline the topic sentence of a paragraph and cross out the sentences that didn't stick to the topic. Occasionally she felt sorry for this doctor. He had the job of making her normal. If he was lucky he might make her appear normal but otherwise the job was hopeless. She could make him happy or sad by the way she acted.

"Poor you," she said to him one day after musing on his predicament.

"That doesn't sound like something you'd say," he said.

"It isn't. The genie said it." The doctor winced. Iris had been in the hospital two and a half months.

"The one in the Laundromat?"

"Yes."

"Is it in you now?"

"Yes."

"I see. And sometimes it speaks for you?"

"The genie is growing the hair."

"Aha." He tried to compose himself, but he was by nature a nervous man; she could tell that he was terrified, by the way he took a deep breath and smiled toward her. Suddenly she felt sorry for him. She almost cried for him. This was a man who did not deserve to be frightened; he tried so hard to do his impossible job. She wished she had not said the things that made him fidget and drop his shoulders disconsolately.

"Listen," she said. "Don't jump to conclusions. I don't mean the genie is sitting inside me, separate from me, or anything like that. I mean there's a spirit of new life. You said I could get out of here and start my life. That's what I want to do. Get a new start."

"Good, Iris. Good. Isn't that good?"

"Yes."

It was good, and after she said it, it began to be true. She had never thought of it before. Why not begin again as if she had never had this false start?

Maybe the doctor arranged it, but later that week Fay paid her first visit. A nurse came into the dayroom and touched Iris on the shoulder, saying, "Your mother is here." Iris did not doubt the woman's word, but she immediately drew back from the touch and from the news. She was afraid of what Fay would look like. At first she had believed Fay would die, left alone like that. What would she eat? And it would be Iris's fault. Iris had stayed in the hospital knowing full well that she was needed at home. She had told her doctor, "My mother will die without me."

"Get well and go home, then."

"No."

But Queen and Emory had come to visit, and Queen said, "Fay is doing real good. She looks fine and is getting up every morning, watching after Randall. No need for you to worry." But Queen always said no need to worry. Queen would say no need to worry even as a hurricane bore down because she knew Jesus would take care of you, and if he didn't you didn't deserve to be taken care of.

So when Iris went into the visiting room, she expected to see Fay in a wheelchair or a walker, toothless, worn down to nothing. Instead, there was Fay laughing and playing cards with a colored man near the window, looking like a woman Iris had never seen before. Her hair was blonder. She had on a lavender long-sleeved blouse so pale and thin you could see the straps of her bra and slip on her shoulders. Her makeup was faint, just pinkish instead of caked on dark, and she had put on weight. Her cheeks didn't hollow in like a skeleton's.

"You look pretty!" Fay said in surprise when Iris came in. "Your *hair.*"

"You look pretty," Iris said. Each was shocked by the other's looks. And pleased, after the shock.

"What did you do to your hair?" Iris asked, touching Fay's new hairdo. Fay always liked to be touched. Iris remembered Fay used to ask her to tickle her arms.

"I dyed it and got it styled," Fay said.

"I'm letting mine grow."

"I can see that. Wasn't I right? Your father will see how pretty you are."

"Is he home? He isn't home?" Iris said.

"No, not yet. I think he'll be coming soon. He always comes in the spring."

"Where's Patrice?" Iris asked.

"I don't know where Patrice is. Don't talk about Patrice now. Talk about you and me. You and me and your father."

Iris was sent home ten days later. Dr. Packer was a happy man when he shook her hand and gave her a going-away present, a soft red leather wallet that folded in on itself, with a cardholder and a change purse and a thin rectangular mirror hidden inside. When she opened it she could not help seeing a slice of her face in the tiny mirror. "Thank you for the hair," she said, and though that was not exactly what she meant to say, it was something that he understood.

"Promise you'll never go away again," Fay said, brushing Iris's hair in the kitchen.

"All right."

"I knew it would be like this," Fay said.

"What would?"

"Your hair. I knew once you gave it a chance it would be

90

thick and brown. It's Owen's hair. I mean, look at this pitiful mess of mine. You're lucky you didn't get this." She stepped in front of the mirror on the refrigerator door and brushed her own thin pale hair.

"Oh, yours. Yours is beautiful," Iris said.

Fay took a second look. "Well, it was what he used to like. Owen liked blondes. The Florida woman is a blonde. Not a natural blonde, but I don't think he can tell the difference. I saw her, you know."

Iris said, "When?"

"He brought her here. A couple of days ago." Fay looked at Iris. Iris did not speak.

"He brought her here," Fay said.

"I heard you."

"She stayed in the car while he came in, but I could see her pretty clear. Enough to see the color of her hair. I asked him was it her, and he said yes."

"What did he come for?" Could he have heard that Iris was sick? But that would not have brought him. He had not come to the hospital.

"To tell me. So I wouldn't count on him."

"And he's married to her?"

"Yes. He's married to her. Nell." Fay looked back into the mirror. Iris stood up behind her and touched her arm. They were like women at a funeral, exhausted, burying hope, acknowledging at last the world's worst, yet in that instant already reweaving their hopes and dreams. Fay sat down, and Iris took the hairbrush and brushed Fay's hair. The bristles slipped through the fine light strands as if through silk, following the skull's contour from brow to crown, then into the air, dropping the hair in drifts.

"He said he would come back," Fay said, "even though he couldn't promise when."

"I know he will," Iris said.

"His life has taken him where he didn't plan on going. That can happen."

"Sure," Iris said. Fay must have had a reserve of strength that Iris never knew about before. She had gotten through this meeting with Owen, and the final truth about him, without help from Iris. *Let her have whatever she needs now,*

Iris thought. The remnant of a flag; a dream of a dream.

"He'll be here for Easter, I bet," Iris said. "He likes you in Easter colors."

"You're right, he does. He likes this blouse, it's Eastery purple and he said it was nice."

"It would look pretty with a skirt the same color but a shade darker."

"I don't have one."

"Let's look for one. Let's get you some new clothes to go with your new hair color."

And so Iris started her life. On the outside it looked just like the old. She still took care of Fay and Randall. But she was no longer old inside, she was brand new and growing. Emory made the whole back sidewalk under the clothes-lines into an arc of colors blending from one into another, bent like a bow about to shoot. He told her Iris was the name of the painter's paints. It was only a matter of time.

Things went her way. Now she's all set—the room, the college classes, the baby-sitting job. She has a full head of hair and a spirit. The strength she found in the Laundromat is toughening her in secret like a pliant stem turning slowly strong until one day it is hard wood. The children are better than she hoped for. What is it about them that pulls so strong? Not just their smallness, not their looks. But the courage!

Looking at the doctor's wife, Iris was certain that Alice Reese was not a good mother. She pictured it just as a clairvoyant visualizes a certain event without knowing all the details. Iris could see Alice Reese in a large room, with the children in need of some sort and calling for help while their mother sat smoking a cigarette, paying no attention. Of course, Iris had suspected something all along, from the photographs on Queen's dresser; yes, the little girls were clean and prettied up, in their appliquéd and mono-grammed clothes—but year after year they stood together looking into the camera alone. No mother appeared with them until the last one, which was a posed vacation picture, not to be trusted.

And look at the house. The girls' things are never put

away. Beds are unmade when Iris arrives in the afternoon. Today she spends an hour sorting through the laundry, taking out the children's clothes; she irons and folds them, then reorganizes the dresser drawers and tucks away the little pants and tops and sweaters in neat stacks.

The final proof, the clincher, is that in spite of the Surgeon General's firm warning and Iris's hints as well, the mother keeps on smoking. A mother who smokes doesn't deserve children.

Iris can see in the little girls' eyes how they long, as she used to, for someone to come take them away. Half the time she dreaded it was Owen who would come, but the other times she dreamed of someone who woke girls by kissing them and took them far away from their parents. Oh, if someone had stolen her early on—or maybe if she had been adopted right out of the delivery room—then her life would have been completely different.

But she does not dwell much on ideas like that. What's the point? She hopes to forge ahead into the future instead of wishing for a changed past the way Fay does. And so she turns over in her head the germ of her plan: to take the Reese children away with her. Who knows where or how, without a car, without money, without (now) a friend (and Emory would never have helped her do it, anyway). But she is in no hurry. Time is on her side, after all. Every day the children put more trust in her. They are as easily won as little animals starved for food. She brushes their hair.

"Now, Miss Reese, how shall we do your hair today? Do you want the purple rinse and the frizz?"

"Oh, no!"

"How about the golden frost and the Cinderella Special?"

"Yes!"

One day she got as far as the bus station with them, not with anything specific in mind; she took them for a walk and, without planning it, drifted to the station. They read the cities' names on the fronts of the buses: New York, Washington, Atlanta. But the excitement Iris expected to see in the faces of travelers was missing. Everyone there was black. They sat in orange bucket seats bolted to the floor, looking already exhausted from a journey not yet begun.

Marcy pulled Iris down to whisper in her ear, "Is this the station for black people?"

"No, it's for everyone. Everyone who wants to go someplace on the bus." But most of the passengers didn't really look as if they wanted to go. Iris wished she could tell them to cheer up, think of the highways to come, a new city one day ahead. Things will change, she promised the travelers as they boarded the bus for Washington, D.C. Though they glanced from the windows down at Iris without interest, she was full of hope for them.

"Would you like a bus ride?" Iris asked.

"Not me," Beth said.

"Me either," Marcy said. They shrank back when the bus made its turn out of the station, looking too long to make the corner, engine churning, brakes whistling. But it got out, and roared up the street. Iris felt suddenly abandoned. She turned back to the waiting room, where a boy was playing a video bomb game, and two women sat surrounded by stuffed and overflowing paper bags, their luggage.

"Let's go home," she said, and the girls were glad to follow her out.

She got an armful of old *National Geographic* magazines out of the Reeses' basement. Some issues had articles about different American places. She showed Marcy and Beth downtown Houston; a Seminole reservation in the Everglades; Seattle, Washington; and a fishing village in Connecticut with the promising name Mystic. The three of them sat together on the floor and flipped pages, looking for somewhere they'd like to go. Iris wanted Mystic.

"Montana," Marcy said, holding up a picture. They all took a look.

"Pretty but too cold," Iris decided.

"Yeah."

"I got it, Cincinnati," Beth said.

"Not bad," Iris said, tilting her head. "Okay! Cincinnati wins. Look at the zoo it's got. Look at the river."

When they heard Alice coming they quieted down right away, as if they'd all agreed ahead of time to keep her out of this, when really they had not. It was something that was understood.

In the evenings Iris goes back to her room satisfied. She reviews the day and tallies each gain she's made, like a girl trying her best to land a certain boy, except that what she is after is the love of the children. That's all, right now. Just trying to make them love her; and that's not against the law, is it? What's so bad about that? Then she realizes she is arguing with herself as if half of her were Emory, accusing her, and the other half Iris, defending herself. Ha, she laughs. She is pulling him along with her in her head, even after she asked him to leave her alone.

Eight

In a white jumpsuit Claire bends in her swivel chair toward the files, her behind full and perfectly framed in the open back of her chair. To get closer she stretches her legs out in front of her, anchors her heels in the carpet and drags the chair and the rest of her along after. Will remembers moving a dinghy through the marsh in a similar way, throwing an anchor out ahead and pulling up to it. He stands in the doorway a minute to admire her. Some women can do anything with their bodies, even something awkward, and have it turn out to be graceful. It's the innocence of dancers. Maybe it comes from her nearsightedness. Nearsighted people are generally trusting, unsuspicious sorts who move without calculation.

She casts off from the filing cabinet with a toe and swivels to face him. Her contact lenses have helped her see better but they haven't changed her habit of squinting. Every morning when he comes in she looks up with a blank, squinty stare, then breaks into a surprised smile of recognition, as if she never expected to see him.

"Good morning," she says after an instant's pause of bewildered squinting.

"Good morning." Already his brain is in gear, working to get her into his private office in the back. Five minutes ago he was all for business, with no such deviousness in mind. But a lock of short black hair curls flat behind her small ear. Her eyelids look damp. After she smiles she closes her mouth to hide her teeth, which she thinks are too big. It is this awkward grace, her embarrassment, that stings him. Sometimes she seems very young, vulnerable.

"You have an appointment with Dr. Cardozo this morning," she says.

"He called?"

"You're supposed to meet him at eleven."

"I know what he wants. Business talk. He's got something up his sleeve. Why are you sitting there like a doctor? I don't like the way your hands are folded. *Prim.* Let's go get some coffee."

"Cindy isn't here yet. I can't leave the switchboard."

"Turn it off," he says.

"No. You might miss a call."

"For Christ's sake, all I want is five minutes over a cup of coffee."

They walk back through the empty carpeted corridor to his room. Inaudible footsteps make him uneasy, make him feel like a cat burglar in his own territory.

"Why did we have to carpet everything?" he asks. "What was wrong with Miratile, like in the old office? They said brake fluid wouldn't harm it. Boy, you could hear your feet on that stuff."

"Right. It also looked like you were someplace that had to get hosed out every day. This is more comforting to the patient." She pours a cup of coffee from the coffeemaker. He reaches around her from behind to unzip the front of her suit; manages to get the zipper down far enough so that her breasts, slung loosely in a narrow ribbon of a bra, tumble out.

But she twists away from him and zips herself back up again with a terrifying finality. He is a man abandoned on an island, oceans receding around him.

"I need to talk to you," she says.

"No talking."

"This is different. This is important. For once you've got to talk to me."

"We've been through it all before, Claire. It was unpleasant. Nothing's changed. It will be unpleasant again."

She tears off the top of a pink Sweet 'n Low envelope and pours the fine white granules into her coffee. "Yes, it might be unpleasant again," she says.

So once more he will have to tell her that what she wants can never happen, that a normal life with marriage and children, Christmas and insurance and wallpaper, isn't in the cards for them. He will have to confess that he knows he has ruined her life. And will keep on ruining it, past reclamation.

"All right, we'll talk. Not now, though, okay?"

"Why not now? No one's here. This is the only time I get to see you unless you come to my house. And it's been two weeks since you last came over."

"I'll come. I'll come tonight. How's that. You can cook your shrimp dish." She's a good cook. She cooks complicated dishes in her tiny kitchen, and they eat on a pine gateleg table, drinking the wine he brings, eating as slowly as possible, making love afterward.

"No, I'm not going to cook."

"You mean we aren't going to bed."

"I mean I'm not going to cook, but right, we aren't going to bed. We're going to talk."

"Okay."

"Okay."

She shifts the articles on his desk, switches the photo cube with the penholder, nudges the memo pad back toward the cubbyholes, then brings the rolltop speeding down in its track, clattering home.

"I'm going back out now."

"Okay."

A sad woman can trigger disaster, and Will doesn't want disaster. All his life he has feared it: something bad from the stars—catastrophe, cataclysm, calamity—all those ancient words for flood and earthquake. He has never had a disaster. He thought his father's death would prove to be one—it seemed one at the time—but life for everyone except his father went on. And went on in pretty much the same way it had gone before. He has had only false alarms, never a true disaster, and yet he has always feared it. Now the smell of it is in the air. Claire wants to talk.

The first false alarm, his first whiff of disaster's possibility, came when he was six, the day he began the first grade. School scared him: the thick, unwieldy crayons, the sudden and repeated alarms of bells, the unsmiling gray teacher whose upper arms shook with ominous fat, the chattering, loud children. But the real terror came when he got home. He had survived the day, he was safe, he had been a "brave boy," as his mother had told him to be, and he was laughing with relief when he reached his block and saw his house. He called his mother as soon as he was within earshot, eager to answer her questions and remake the horrible day into a pleasant one, for her. She wasn't there. He looked in every room. He had never been alone in his house before. Suddenly the brave boy was in tears and panic-stricken. He rushed to her room, to her dresser, and opened each drawer to see if she had taken her clothes. They were there, her underclothes white and folded in tissue paper. Her dresses were still hanging in the closet, thin ghosts of her. Then he knew something had happened to her, someone had taken her away. He thought of the vegetable man who came every day in a truck, an old black man who, though he seemed kindly and gentle, might be poor enough to hold his mother for ransom. When he telephoned his father's office he could hardly say the words, he had to repeat them: "Something has happened to my mother." He thought his heart would stop, its thumping was so fast and heavy inside him. Had she told him to be brave because she knew something terrible was about to happen? He was in his bed when his father came home, but he could hear the several phone calls his father made, and by the time Edmund came to his room, Will knew it was a "false alarm," as his father said, and that he had made a fool of himself.

He heard his father chastise his mother when she came home.

"The boy was terrified. He was shaking. How could you do such a thing?"

"But I forgot. I forgot he would be out early on the first day." Their voices drifted up to him as he lay stiff in his small bed, his brain already forming a resolution for life: to do without her.

"How could you forget your own child?" his father had asked her.

So that chance of catastrophe passed. She had not left, had not been abducted; she had been at the grocery store. Maybe disaster no longer comes as a fire or flood or any single stroke of ruin, but is instead a creeping, insidious thing—a decay. Things go bad, but slowly; things degenerate, rot.

Cardozo is waiting in the doctors' lounge.

"What do you say, boy," he says, extending his hairy hand, a golden paw. "How's it going?"

"How've you been, Danny."

They sit at a card table littered with Styrofoam cups. Coffee is beginning to leach out of them in droplets clinging to the sides. The room is stuffy. The windows don't open, and the air conditioning is turned off.

"Got a buck Sunday at Marshfield. Twelve points," Danny says.

"Don't tell me."

"Hell, how can you be an ob and not hunt? It's expected of you."

"I'm too old, I guess, Dan'l. What's up?"

"You think over my offer?" Danny says.

"I thought it over. I still don't want to do it."

"Don't want to do what? It isn't doing anything more than changing your sign. That's the only real change. The suite next door to yours is empty; I could be in it by Thursday, and we bust a hole through to connect them up. I move my furniture in. We share call, patients, equipment. We get a big tax break."

"I don't want a group practice. I want to be by myself," Will says.

"You sound like Greta Garbo. It isn't a fucking *group*, it's you and me. Say it. You don't want to practice with me."

"I don't want to practice with you."

"Why the hell not?"

"I don't want all that duck crap all over my office. Duck lamp shades."

"All right, Willy. All right. I get you. You don't want your Japanese prints crowded out." He has built a tower of Styrofoam cups. "The Japanese would never have appreciated something like Ducks Unlimited, would they."

"What are you after, Cardozo? You don't care about tax breaks. What's this all about?"

"Okay, I'll tell you. I'm not in what you would call good shape."

"Physically?"

"Physically, mentally, financially, emotionally. Sexually. Spiritually. What else is there?"

"Is it Carol?" Will says.

"That's the financially. She wants more money. There's some trouble with the kids—minor, but trouble. They're both in therapy. Carol wants to make sure they don't suffer separation anxiety; gotta keep those self-concepts intact. But it's been three years now. They ought to be out from under it. Oh, they've got the best shrinks in the Southeast. We were always modern parents, me and Carol. Enlightened, I think you would call us. We did Lamaze, we did Leboyer. Then we did divorce."

"Lay off yourself. It's over with now."

"But there's more. Let's see. Too much booze. Also I lost a shitload of money on a land deal that flopped. The worst is that I can't gargle anymore. I've lost confidence, and you can't gargle without confidence. I panic right in the middle of the gargle and swallow the Listerine."

"You're leaving out something," Will says.

"I am? What?"

"Your secret conversations with Claire."

"Come again?"

"I picked up the line and heard you. What's she telling you? That I'm skipping appointments? That I nearly fucked up that cesarean? You've cooked up this scheme with her, haven't you, to save me."

"No. I cooked it up by myself, to save myself," Danny says.

"Let's just keep things the way they are, okay?"

"Can we do that?"

"Jesus Christ, what is it with you, Cardozo?"

"Friend, it isn't with me. It's you. Martin said you buzzed out in the C-section. She thought you had been drinking. I know that isn't it. Now tell me what it is. Claire says you're losing patients."

"Spelled T-S or C-E?"

"Look, you used to be good with women. You got all the primiparas in town; the word was out that you took time, you understood. Now it sometimes seems you plain don't like them anymore."

"It's true. I don't," Will says.

"Why not?"

"They haven't lived up to my expectations."

"Oh," Danny says, rolling his eyeballs to the ceiling.

"Come on, you've got to know how it is. I mean when I started I was young! They were young. You could tell from all those women having babies that life was going to be something, you know? They were having babies. If that isn't optimism, nothing is. Now I have some of the same patients. I see them every year. They're starting to clot and spot, they're scared. I'm not there to deliver babies, I'm there to look for signs of disaster."

"But you deliver babies, too. Women are still having them."

"Women are still having them. But the point is, they aren't mine."

"They never were."

"Oh, yes, they were! Every goddamned one of them was *mine*. I could see that girl, a girl my age, lying there panting, and in the days before they started letting husbands in she was all mine. I was the one urging her on, I was the one saying "Breathe!" and "Push!" and she'd sweat and cry and strain, call my first name, and I'd answer with hers. I'd watch her face going red, and I'd talk that baby out of her, talking to her the whole time because she was mine. I was responsible for her. I wasn't going to leave her until the child was born, right into my hands at the same instant she went limp. Jesus, it's the quickest change I ever saw, from that biting-down travail to that limp joy. I'd hand over the baby. And she'd know it came from me. Sometimes I cried. I'll tell you, Danny, I don't have a single patient I call by her first name now. Even some I used to, I call Ms. now."

"And in the C-section?"

Will sighs. "In the C-section, I looked up and saw the girl, searching for her face the way I used to, but of course she was way under—just laid out there for me to open up. Like a package of baby. No hollering, no names, no joy. Which isn't new. But she looked different. To tell you the truth, she looked dead as a doornail. I don't know what happened to me."

"Claire thinks you need a partner."

"So she did put you up to this. Well, report back to her that I said it was none of your business what I do, in my practice or anywhere. None of your fucking business. And not hers either to spread around town."

"I'm not exactly around town." Danny dismantles the tower, cup by cup. Danny has aged. In the last few months his looks have changed. He was always a boyish-looking man; people thought him younger than he really was because of his sandy hair and his unmarked skin. But Will sees wrinkles not just at his eyes and mouth but down his cheeks as well. Right down the middle of his cheeks, two harsh lines.

"Okay, Willy," he says.

"I'm sorry about Carol; and Dan and Julia." (The children. They've been gone so long it is hard to remember Cardozo as a father.)

"No sweat. Things will shape up. Call me if you change your mind about my offer." He pushes the door open with the outspread tips of his fingers, and is gone, loping down the hall in red-rubber-soled saddle shoes.

The first rift between Danny and Will had come when they were twelve, and Danny found out that his great-grandfather was a Jew. Joseph Cardozo arrived in Charleston in 1781 from Portugal, built up a pharmacy business, and married the governor's daughter. She raised her children as Episcopalians, and he gave money to the Episcopal church, which in one year even listed him among its members. But to prevent misunderstanding among future generations, Joseph Cardozo in a codicil to his will renounced "all connection, real or reputed, to Christianity" and required that his heirs do the same. They did not, and forfeited a sizable inheritance.

But something came down to Danny when he was twelve. Till then Will and Danny had been best friends in the ways boys in the South can be, paired off as a couple through childhood, so that when people thought of one they thought of the other, and said the names in a breath: Will and Danny, Reese and Cardozo. But suddenly Danny drew back. He read books about Jews for a year and wrote in a notebook. It looked as if a Jew grew up inside him, and Will envied that secret self. It gave Danny a strength that stayed, though it was not always visible. The Jew in him could keep an ironic eye on things, see past trouble; could preserve a distance and a dignity even when things went bad—land deals and marriages, for example.

Will's own genealogy is a dull succession of generations that has left him no spiritual legacy. As a boy, he wished for Danny's Jewish soul. He longed for a heart like the one his friend was getting, an unstoppable pump that would not falter. Danny might appear to be in trouble, but he never really is, he has this secret strength. Now, though he's lost fifty thousand dollars in a golf-course scheme and his ex-wife is suing him and he lives without furniture, these are minor details. The man is complete. Self-destructive to some extent, but whole enough to take it.

The partnership offer was a rescue mission. There is no other explanation.

They used to hunt together: ducks, quail, squirrels. They were young doctors, married but without children, and there was something fine about going out from their homes in the early still-dark hours, each man knowing the other had left a marriage bed and a woman's warm limbs for this cold dawn. They had hunted together as boys, too, but the best hunting came in those early years of marriage. They talked very little then, drank some but not immoderately. They did not kill much game. Then slowly the talk and drink increased, the killing increased, they went after bigger animals: turkey, deer, feral hogs. Finally Will said no more deer or hogs. Then no turkey. No squirrels. Eventually no doves or partridges. His last hunt was a duck hunt with Danny three years ago in an abandoned rice field on the Santee. They sat facing one another in the blind, each with his knees apart but almost touching the other's, their hands dropped down between their legs. It was cold. The broken dikes impounding the wetlands looked like ancient earthworks built in a design that could be seen only from a spaceship; but he knew the dikes were built by slaves in an expense of human labor greater than what it took to build the Great Wall of China. He began to feel uncomfortable. The sun still had not gotten up over the horizon but its color was already on the marsh like a slow flood tide. The rice field, which had been a gray shadow, turned white, pink, yellow, before settling into gold-green. He began to think something was essentially comical about two men with guns huddled in a thatched box waiting for ducks. Here was the same heartrending stillness that used to dazzle him, the marsh at dawn hazed and unsuspecting seconds before the shots and the panic—here it was, same as ever, and yet it was now only an old ritual of old men, played out for the sake of what it used to be.

"Carol's had it with me," Danny said. "She's gone. I deal with a lawyer from now on."

"No kidding," Will said. He saw Cardozo's eye fasten on something in the sky, over Will's left shoulder.

"Coming in over the north dike," Danny said. "Teal."

"Blue-wing."

"We weren't concentric. We had different centers. She says I'm nuts—it's in the divorce suit."

"No," Will said. Neither man looked at the other.

"Yeah. I have to fight it because it means I couldn't see the kids. If it gets into court, would you testify? Here they come." Danny shot into the flock just coming over their heads. Then Will shot. His duck fell awkwardly, not straight like a dead bird, but still flapping a wing. It flapped again in the water, drifting into the cattails. He marked its spot. He would have to wade out to get it, then twist its neck. Danny shot again.

"Would I have to say I think you're sane?" Will said.

"That's the general idea."

105

"I'll perjure myself, for a friend." One flying duck was circling back. *Don't be a fool, don't come this way,* Will thought. He could see the bird's confusion; not knowing where the danger was, it had veered from its path to turn back, and this course would carry it directly over the blind once more. Will shot straight up. The bird blew two feet higher into the air, then dropped straight down into the water, a yard from the blind. Shot fell down around them like rain, making blips in the water and clicks on the pine flooring of the blind. Will's eye itched, and a gnat flew into his ear with a tiny whine and tickle.

"Her proof of my insanity is that I won't give her a divorce. That I claim I still love her. I'm not facing reality." Danny sighed. "It was a surprise to me, you know? A surprise. Things go along and go along, marriage and practice and children, and then *kablam!* it's all in jeopardy, everything's on the line at once."

"That's not true. It's only the marriage."

"Maybe. We'll see." They drank some more bourbon. Six wood ducks came in on the west side, their harlequin markings caught by the sun. Two fell when they were shot, but the rest hardly wavered in their flight, just lifted a little higher and away toward the next field.

"We need a damn dog. I can't remember where the first four ducks are," Danny said.

"Let's pick them up now. The gnats are bad, and it's getting late, anyway. We won't see many more."

"You can't tell. Wait awhile," Danny said. Will's stomach was churning from the shock of straight bourbon. The sun began to heat up his head and neck, and the haze over the field lifted like a scrim, revealing the world to be much brighter and more clearly delineated one part from another than he had thought it was. The dead birds were already beginning to decompose, the microscopic tissues breaking down, the organs stopped, juices souring, as they drifted with the breeze on the water's surface, making paths through the yellow sludge of algae and duckweed. Across the field in a dead pine, a great blue heron spread its broad wings, then flew off across the dikes. Will gazed after the slow, strong wingbeat, the careful curve of neck, the long legs trailing.

Danny fired twice at some teal that were out of range. "What do you think, Will," he said.

"About what."

"All this."

"All what." But he knew, he knew. He did not want to talk about it; talk like this was self-indulgent, pointless.

"Carol. All that," Danny said.

"You'll pull through."

"Yes, but what did I do wrong? I mean here we are, you and I, we've lived almost the same life, grown up together, med school together, everything, but now I've made a mess of it and you haven't. And I didn't even know I was doing it. Christ, I didn't even know. If she had said something, I would have changed whatever it was she didn't like, you know?"

"What was it? Why'd she leave?"

"She thought I didn't love her, she said. I did love her, but she said it wasn't a deep love, it wasn't deep enough to make up for the rest, the bad parts. Does that make sense? I loved her. It wasn't enough. She took off. Now I say I want her back because I love her. She says it isn't enough to come back to. God." He was drinking his bourbon from the bottle now. There was not much left, so Will knew they would leave soon.

"So what do you think?" Danny said.

"I think she was right."

"You do? I didn't love her enough?"

"Well, did you?"

"Shit, I guess not." Danny put the bottle down and looked out over the yellow-green field, the yellow-green water. Tears filled his eyes, then ran down his face.

"Let's get out of here," he said. They untied the rowboat and set off to look for the fallen ducks, following the black wakes through the scum. They found all but one, the wounded blue-wing. Its trail led into a clump of cattails too dense to get into with the boat.

"You want to put on the waders and go after it?" Danny said.

"No." It was the first time in his life he had ever left wounded game in the field.

"Me neither. Let's go."

That night, through lawyers, Danny told Carol she was right (he was crazy, he didn't love her enough, she could have all the money and his children too), hoping this belly-up display of love would bring her back to him. Instead she accepted the terms and moved into a Harbortown Villa at Hilton Head. Now she plays tennis and poisons his children's hearts against him.

Will eats lunch in the hospital cafeteria, then drives back to his office for the afternoon appointments. Days are too long.

Now Claire is doing her nails. This is the only woman he has ever known whose fingernails look like the ones in magazines; such fingernails are possible only for unmarried, childless women. Filed to a curving point, they are painted salmon-pink, a color he doesn't much like, but he likes it on Claire's nails. He likes to see her doing them with the little set of tools: orangewood sticks with different-shaped points, cuticle scissors, dips and creams, and the slim, long-handled brush. She concentrates on the work, bending over her hands, painting each nail slowly, meticulously.

Once, a year ago, he watched her do her toenails in bed on a Saturday morning. She clipped them, her knees pulled up under her chin. He saw the white band of underpants between her thighs. Her toes lifted up to meet the clippers in her hand. Then she held out the bottle and her foot for him to paint. The nail on her little toe was so small it was only a spot of pink. He knew as he touched it, touched the soft instep, the heel, the tendon like a tight string, that he would not in his lifetime see this happiness again; it was the still zenith of his time on earth. In the room all objects—the radio, the dresser and its tilted mirror, the thin white towel hung over a chair—were as they should be, instantly complete. Nothing could have been added or removed.

Rooms, mornings, women to come would be less than this.

And so it proved. Now Claire paints her fingernails at the reception desk. Her back straightens. His heart is a shambles of its own making.

"Shall I do the other hand?" he asks, coming up behind her. She squints at him, smiles, says no.

"What have we got?" He looks over her shoulder to the appointment book under her fingers. "Mrs. Jenner canceled?"

"Yes. She didn't say why."

So there are only two appointments for the afternoon.

"I have an idea," he says. "Where are the girls?"

"Cindy's on break. I sent Michelle out to get coffee filters."

"Let's cancel these two patients and spend the afternoon at your place."

"You can't cancel them. They're already here, waiting. Mrs. Donato was a twelve-thirty appointment. You're twenty minutes late."

"Just go out and tell them I'm caught up at the hospital in an emergency. Reschedule them for next week."

"No," she says.

"Why not?"

"You can't do that."

"You don't want to spend the afternoon with me?" he says.

"No, I don't. You're coming over tonight, remember?"

"Six o'clock," he says. "Okay. Claire, let me ask you something. Have you and Danny been talking about me?"

He knows from her face they have. Claire can't lie.

"What do you mean?"

"In the future, I'd appreciate it if you'd keep the details of my practice and of my private life confidential."

He steps out into the waiting room, courageous as a gladiator. "Good news, ladies," he announces. "I can't see you today because I've got to run over to the hospital for a delivery. Baby couldn't wait. If you'll see the receptionist she'll give you another appointment." They will be glad, after all, not to see him. Women dread these visits. As they should.

Claire is angry and won't look at him when he passes. So he locks himself in the back office. He didn't really want to spend the afternoon with her, anyway; he just didn't want to spend it with the patients.

He sits at the desk. He draws a picture of a stickman at a crossroads—a tatterdemalion who can neither find his way nor ask for help.

Nine

There are certain animals, usually small, scraggly creatures, that don't build their own homes but take over the abandoned burrows of other species. *We live like that now,* he thinks, *making our pitiful nests in these grand houses, dwarfed by the high ceilings and enormous rooms; the cornices and ceiling medallions and wainscoting are mere curiosities to us now.* Claire's place is a carriage house behind a tall Victorian mansion that has been cut up into twelve apartments. Will parks his car on the street and walks back down the unpaved driveway, under the leaning, scrawny trunks of Japanese plum trees.

No one will notice him. Or his car. No one will come to a window and say with suspicion, "Who is that guy?" because strangers are familiar here.

The Japanese plums grow right up out of hard gray dirt and a rubble of brick, stucco hunks, mortar chips. The plants that thrive in this town are those that don't need rich black soil, plants that can find nutrients in the mixed ruin of fallen walls, burned houses. Japanese plums are tough trees. The long, serrated leaves are stiff and make a clatter when he walks through them. So what if anyone hears? The apartment people don't know him, even after three years. Still, the rattle of the dry leaves disturbs him.

In the early-evening shadows some of the apartment lights are on in the big house. Through a third-floor window he can see a refrigerator. Surely anyone with the bad luck to live here must count on someday living somewhere else: in a house with the refrigerator on the ground floor, things in the normal places. No one could think of this place as a permanent home, but would always have to be trusting in something better coming up.

Once this whole house was the home of one family. Is this how things fall apart, then? Not in sudden collapse, but by slow fragmentation. Houses turn into apartments, estates into subdivisions. We can't sustain the things we used to sustain: dynasties, clans, big families; we can't even maintain their monuments. Statues are losing their noses, tombstones their letters.

Growing up in an old city, you learn history's one true lesson: that history fades. Nothing sticks together for very long without immense effort. His own strong house is in a constant process of disintegration. He calls workmen to come repair the roof, paint the porches, replace sills; but even this work has no permanence, it will have to be done again in four or five years. Is this noble activity for a man? Patching, gluing, temporizing, begging for time?

Near his back door a lump of stucco fell from the wall after a heavy rain, leaving a round wound of exposed deep-brown brick. The bricks are still solid but the mortar between them is a fine powder that he can gouge out with his finger. Now he has to decide how far to go with the repairs, whether to tear off more stucco and find out how extensive the damage is, even take out bricks and re-lay them, or just cover up the wound and try not to think about what's underneath, as he must do with some patients.

Claire's carriage house is nicer than an apartment. It's small but at least it is a house with its own walls and roof. He has a key. He lets himself in and calls her. The shower is running upstairs; she doesn't answer. Her philodendrons and ferns are all bunched up in a semicircle around the small bay window. She used to have a cat, but when it died she bought more plants instead of another cat. He looks closely at the philodendron; he touches one of the leaves. Claire actually shines them, rubbing each leaf with wet cotton. They seem to have a sharp green smell after they've been rubbed.

Or maybe that is his imagination. There is something here, something like a scent, that makes his hair stand on end and makes poetry fly into his brain. He likes to walk in and see her unmatched oak chairs, plants huddled together, the thinning Oriental rug, the strange way light streams into her windows without lighting the dark, shadowy corners of the room. Everything here is thin and clean and private as a closet. There is no evidence of a man; it is a single woman's place, and being in it is like being inside her thoughts. He is the only man who comes here. He knows the place well. Here's her forlorn bookcase, the titles reading like a list for a desert island life: *Norton Anthology, Outline of Western Thought, Lives of the Composers.* She actually reads these books because she's sure everybody but her is thoroughly familiar with Verdi's life or the categorical imperative or Theodore Roethke. Nobody knows this stuff, he tries to tell her. Even if they heard of it in college, which is unlikely, they have forgotten it. But she's unconvinced. She stays up late reading Janson's *History of Art,* which she can hardly hold up at a readable angle. Now, looking over the neatly arranged shelf, he realizes her life with him *is* a desert island.

He sees a new book, a slim red volume, wedged down there between two paperback Shakespeares. He takes it out, leafs through it. Poems. *Love's Meter,* "an anthology of the greatest love poems in the English language." Why did she buy this? He puts it back on the shelf but not soon enough: it has spoiled his reverie, the sense he had of being a familiar intruder. He never saw that book before. It is one he would have chosen for her. But the day when he gave her love poems is gone.

The cramped kitchenette is so small they always bumped into each other when they cooked. He used to stand behind her and bother her while she worked, press against her behind and reach around to touch her breasts while she was chopping parsley. The little refrigerator and stove are so old their white finish has deepened to a rich cream. He loves this kitchen. Its diamond-paned cupboard doors reaching to the ceiling, its deep old sink and mismatched faucets—it is like the good old kitchens, not the new magazine kitchens. He grew up in a house with the same refrigerator in its kitchen for twenty years, same stove, sink, breadbox, can opener on the wall. Now a kitchen isn't good for more than five years, the styles change. You had to have harvest gold or avocado. Then those were out and some new color was in, coppertone. Stainless steel. Almond. His mother's new kitchen is almond, with an island in it, and in the island a processing center, with attachments that screw in and chop or slice or grate your food. Cuisinarts make people think life is eternal. Marcella whirring up a puree in that gleamy dazzly almond kitchen has not an inkling of what really is the end of all that preparation. But here— here in Claire's dark old kitchenette a shiver of recognition dances across his shoulders, the rich dark thickness of time moving toward an end.

He unpacks the bag of food that she has left out on the counter. Her groceries are pitiful, a quart of skim milk, a big can of V-8, celery, Cup-A-Soup envelopes. But then down at the bottom he finds a package of two thick filets and a basket of unblemished white mushrooms. The first good sign of the day. His spirits soar. She used to love to cook and eat with him and then make love.

He hears the shower turn off upstairs; the pipes rumble behind the walls of the kitchen. She dries herself inside the shower stall so that water won't drip on the wooden floor of the bathroom. Then she wraps the towel around her waist and steps out carelessly, not even thinking of her breasts. If he were there she would be self-conscious. She thinks her breasts are too big. He knows how she moves. Slowly. When he hears her bare feet on the floor above him, the soles of his own feet itch, just as they did when he was a boy climbing a roof or a tree, and the itch was a combination of exultation and fear. Then her footsteps stop. Maybe she is bending forward, shaking out her curly black hair, her breasts jiggling with each toss of her head. She twists the towel around her head, straightens up, and (he's seen her do this before, he is not making it up but remembering now) arches her back, her hands resting behind her hips, elbows bent. He knows how she moves.

But it is reverence for his old passion that brings him

here now, not passion itself. He is hanging around the way pilgrims haunt the site of an old miracle, not hoping to see it again really but honoring it, needing its memory. The first time he slept a whole night through with Claire he kept waking up in nervous agitation, like a man who has a rash. His brain ticked with the continuing knowledge that the woman next to him was an unfamiliar size, a new shape. Her feet kept touching his; Alice's never did. After the fourth or fifth waking he pulled her underneath him and made love to her again, as a kind of certification. In his arms, half-asleep, she was moving with him, making a soft, loving noise, and he was ashamed to be thinking of Alice. Why, when he could go for days hardly remembering her existence, would she come to him then, shaking his heart? He could not forgive her that immanence. To spite it he made a harder, rougher kind of love to Claire, and it took hold of him. He couldn't stay away from her. After that first night here, his life seemed new, *he* seemed new. He was crazy. What risks he took! Once he spent three days here with her, telling Alice he was in Colorado. Claire used to laugh at him, surprised by his delight and its depth. Her own was something different. In the act of lovemaking she was agile and undistracted, dolphinlike, arcing above him in that night ocean with an abandon he did not know a woman could be lost to; but immediately afterward her mind flooded with irrelevant thoughts, memories of child-hood, worries. She rolled away from him and gasped, "Oh God, my father's birthday is tomorrow," or, "What can I do about the bats?" The attic of her house was full of bats; some had gotten in under the eaves and reproduced. You could hear them scratching around, tweeting up there. But he would stroke and rub her legs until her fretting subsided and she could stretch out and doze or sleep. Then she was like a cat, close to purring. He could see that he made her happy.

She didn't seem to mind, back then, the position this love put her in. Perhaps the danger wasn't visible then. She didn't seem to mind when he told her she would have to be a brave girl (he used just those words, in a joking way) and not press him for what he could not give. She understood, and only once had she disobeyed: after an abortion. Danny Cardozo made the arrangements and did the abortion in the hospital. No one knew, not even the OR nurse, who thought it was a diagnostic D & C. He wanted to stay with her, but he couldn't do it again, witness the death of a child of his; and he couldn't explain that to Claire or Cardozo. He was frightened by the apparent tendency of his life to replicate its own past. How many times would love bring him the loss of a child, the grief of a woman whose bravery mocked his cowardice? He waited in the doctors' lounge, then drove her home and sat in a chair next to her bed while she slept off the Pentothal.

When she woke up he touched her cheek and pale mouth. Her eyes were still big and woozy. She said, "I love you." Her mouth was cracked at the corners, the skin dry and split. Her face was discolored, with hollows under her eyes as dark as if she had been hit.

She said, "Come on, say you love me. You do." She reached up to his ear and held his earlobe and tugged at it. He leaned down and kissed her forehead. She laughed. She said, "Sometimes it's not having a baby that locks people together." She was right. He had already felt it, driving her home, as she sat rigid on the seat next to him and her fingers, folded over the armrest, were white from gripping it so hard. He helped her down the driveway and inside, got her into bed. When she played with his ear, he pulled back. He saw her stretched out, her soft blue nightgown, her breasts overfull, sloping outward. Her bare feet stuck out from the nightgown; her toes, he realized, were very much like his mother's, long and fingerlike.

"Tell me you love me," she said.

"Don't."

"I was thinking about you. My main thought was, what a waste. I know you love me, Will, I can tell you do. You touch my arm and you stare at me and you get sad when I'm not around. You want me to sit in your lap. Last month when I had that bad cold you were so worried! It was just a cold!"

"I know."

"I'm not asking you to leave your family or something earthshaking. Just to say you love me."

"You're exhausted, Clairy." Her looks frightened him. Her eyelids were swollen and her eyes had the deep wet shine of fever. Her hands moved across her stomach.

She said, "One time we stayed up all night and slept the next day. You wouldn't go. Then I kept saying, 'You'd better leave,' and you'd pretend to be asleep, you wouldn't let go of me. You wouldn't leave. You said you couldn't leave me."

"I couldn't."

"Then please. Oh, it's so *easy.* It isn't hard!"

She sounded so sure of it. And probably he did love her. The difference between love and no love is slight, anyway. People are fooled every day about whether they have it or not. So he picked up her hands and leaned down close to her.

"I can't do it!" he cried out in anguish, surprising her, surprising him. . . . He was thinking of the depletion of his resources. For Alice the passion lasted, say, five years, for Claire one year; and with that record he could look forward only to meager affairs, matters of months, weeks: pitiful spurts of passion.

"Don't ask me to. I can't." He turned away from her, knowing she'd cry now, and then what would he do? She cried easily. When the cat died she cried for days—it had crawled up into his car engine one night to get warm, and when he started the car something broke the cat's back and flung it out onto the pavement. She blamed him for it. She cried when patients miscarried; she cried when she saw *Kramer vs. Kramer.* One time he found her crying in the office because she had been thinking about Alice and said she knew how Alice would feel if she found out he was unfaithful.

But that night as he stood looking out of the low window onto the dirt driveway, and the leaves scuttled across the ground like crabs, and a child had been lost, that night she did not cry.

He had sat by her bed until midnight, without ever turning on the lights. The sun dropped low, colored the sky,

117

set; the room grew dark slowly. They listened to the news and sports on the radio. Before he left he gave her a Demerol, and set another one for her on the table next to a glass of water.

That night was more than a year ago, but something about this darkening evening has reminded him of that one. The leaves in the wind, the dark house—it is time to turn lights on but he is reluctant to do it, he wants to see night come.

He could have been wrong about the pilgrims. Secretly they do hope for a return of the miraculous. They only pretend not to because they don't want to get their hopes up; they don't want to make fools of themselves.

Her footsteps cross the floor again.

He knows why artists have always loved to paint "the Bath." When is a woman ever more desirable? Warm and pink from hot water, her skin is tight, soap-scented. Tendrils of her hair are wet. Her face is clean and childlike and sure of privacy. That's the one common quality of all the bathers of Renoir, Degas: the woman is preoccupied, she bends, trusting her solitude, intent on some detail of her bathing—and all the while the voyeur lurks with his palette in the shadows, peeping. In the quiet instant just before violence he savors a pure guilt, all his own, none hers. Between what Degas's crouching bather thought and what Degas knew, what a world there was, and half an explanation of love.

He would wish it that way now—he would climb the steps without making this creaking noise, which certainly alerts her; he would like to sneak up on her. But as he comes up through the stairwell he meets her eyes, locking onto his as if they had been trained to the exact spot where he would emerge, waiting for him. She has on an old velour robe that has lost its shape, faded unevenly from purple to dull red. She's shaving her legs. Toward him from the opening in the velour rises one long naked leg, its foot resting on a chair.

"You're late," she says.

"I wanted to surprise you."

"You did." He can see to the top of her thigh. The slender length of her leg takes his breath away. She leans over and shaves her calf.

"You do that without soap and water?"

"No. I shaved in the shower but I missed a spot."

"Here?" He moves to her side, touches her ankle, rings it with his thumb and finger, just above the anklebone. She tries to pull her leg back but he holds it tight. He has her off balance.

"Untie your robe," he says.

"No. Let me get dressed now."

His left hand moves under the robe. She pulls back in earnest one last time, but then his hand reaches her belly. He lets her foot slip from the chair, keeping a grasp on her thigh to hold her foot just off the floor. She unties the robe without taking her eyes from his. Then he lets go of her in order to step back and see her. Behind her the light of her small lamp fails to reach to the spot where they stand; there is only a glow in the corner. More light comes from the window, the reflected pink of a sun already below the horizon, the rays glancing to clouds and bending back to earth, to neck, breasts, hips. Someone in the yard could see. If he were she, he would not allow it; she permits him to endanger her.

"You're pink and gold. Look." He pushes the robe back off her shoulders, and uncurls her fingers from the handle of the razor.

Her eyes are closed.

"I've loved you a long time," she says.

"Years and years."

"Longer. I loved you before I loved you." She turns to him, leans into him, and the twist of the body into his is familiar, a recognizable instant in the turn; she should stop here, they should make love. But she keeps on turning and is turning away from him, out of his grasp completely. She is pulling on the robe, tying it tight around her waist, tough as a nurse again.

"I really have to talk to you, Will."

"Let's hear it, then." He should never have let go of her, he should never have let her regain her balance. She turns on another lamp, pulls down the window shade.

"This is going to be real hard," she says.

"Why don't we skip it, then."

"It's serious."

"Are you pregnant? Say so right away if you are. Christ. I can't stand stalling, Claire. Say it."

Tears fill her eyes, her nose turns red, exactly like when the cat died.

"There are worse things than being pregnant," she says.

"Well, I don't want to go through it again."

"We didn't go through it the first time." She tries not to cry but the words bring sobs out with them. "Anyway, I'm not. But I want to be. I don't want to waste away."

"Is that all? Is that what we have to talk over? Is that it?" But she is crying too hard to talk. He says, "I'm sorry. Claire, I am sorry. Listen," he says to comfort her. "Don't be sad. I know how you feel."

"You don't."

"Yes, I do."

"I'm going to get married, Will. Danny and I are going to get married."

A man can lose his leg and not know it. His brain can't handle the enormity of the loss. At first Will hardly hears what she says, it makes so little sense. Then his sense of direction fails, he feels his face turn hot.

She takes a green dress from the closet and underwear from the bureau drawer. The underpants and bra are iridescent white, shiny. They're new.

"What do you mean?"

Her voice breaks, her lip trembles. "We're going to get married."

"You and who?"

"Oh, please. Please, Will." She's still holding her clothes. "I love you. But this is the end of it. I came to some kind of end."

"And in stepped the good doctor Dan."

"I can't talk to you about him."

"No, I guess not."

"Don't be bitter. He's been worried sick about this, he really has, he doesn't know what to do. He tried to get you to go into practice with him. He doesn't want you to be left alone."

Will sits on the edge of the bed.

"What is it?" she says.

"How long have you been seeing him?"

"That doesn't make any difference now."

"The hell it doesn't! It makes all the difference. How long?"

"Look, I said I would not discuss him with you."

He leaps from the bed and grabs her by the arm, so suddenly that she gasps.

"Tell me," he says.

"I—we've been friends for maybe a year."

"Friends."

"Yes. That's all. That's what we've been."

"But you did hide it. You deceived me."

"Deceived you?" she says.

"Yes! You deceived me. You betrayed me. Both of you."

"Let me go."

"Oh God. Yes, I'll let you go. I should have let you go sooner."

"Will, I have to get dressed."

"Go ahead." He turns away while she dresses behind his back. Silently he conducts an inventory of her furniture: the bed, the dresser, the chairs. He loves her furniture. He doesn't want to give it up.

Especially not to Danny. Claire bends toward the low mirror on her dressing table. She puts lipstick on the way a little girl might, slowly, squinting her eyes, and the whole action, usually unattractive, is endearing.

"Why Danny?" he says after a while.

"He's nice to me."

"That's a reason to marry him?"

"Yes. He's that nice. He loves me, he likes how I am. He thinks I'm pretty."

"I've always thought you were pretty."

"He says it."

"I said it."

121

"Twice. The first time was the first night you slept here. The second was when I went home for my mother's funeral and you felt sorry for me. I looked terrible. So what, anyway. You don't want to marry me. But just for the record it was only twice. You are very mean, you know." She says it without malice, it's a simple statement he can hardly argue with.

"Danny's mean, too," he says. "Danny's just like me, Claire. Is that why you're going to marry him?"

"He's not like you at all."

"He's like me in all the ways that have driven you crazy."

She looks at him sharply. "You're wrong. He cries for me. Can you imagine that? He cries out loud asking me to marry him, saying he can't live without me."

"I don't believe you."

"Is it so incredible?"

Of course she would be impressed by that. A man who weeps for a woman either loses her immediately or binds her to him forever, depending on what kind of a woman she is. Claire is the kind who, having lived her whole life unaware of the possibility of men's tears, is utterly won by them when they come.

"He's cracking up," Will says.

"Get out."

"I mean it. He told me. He's having all kinds of problems."

"Get out, Will. Get out now."

"Listen, Claire. I'll marry you."

"Sure you will."

"I will. I want to. I can't give you up." Sitting on her bed he reaches for the hem of her dress, holds it between his thumb and fingers.

"How could you marry me?" she says.

"It's done all the time. Divorce."

"Divorce Alice? You would divorce Alice?"

Oh, don't say her name, don't make it sound so real. He would never divorce Alice. He can't even hear it said.

"Yes. It wouldn't take too long. I could go to Haiti or somewhere and get a divorce in a day."

"You would do it?"

122

"Yes." *Liar! Deceiver of women, and of the dwarfish, unspined self behind these eyes!* He lies enormously and pointlessly, yet can't confess a half-true love that might once have done Claire good.

Claire stands looking at him for a long time.

"I don't know if I believe you or not," she says slowly. "But even if I did, I wouldn't say yes. Six months ago I would have. Not now. Everything's changed now."

"Well, just tell me how the hell everything could change so fast without my knowing? I've seen you every day. If you were changing shouldn't I have had some hint of it? Shouldn't I have noticed something?"

"Yes, but you didn't."

"Okay, then, what was I supposed to notice? How was I to tell you were falling in love with someone else? You didn't exactly cut me off. We did a lot of fucking, Claire. Were you fucking him, too?"

She starts to cry. "No, I wasn't." She puts a finger under her bottom eyelash to steady her contacts, and he realizes that all this while, despite his suffering, she has been dressing for Cardozo. Those are Cardozo's goddamn steaks downstairs.

He pulls her down to the bed and wipes the tears from her face, holds her the way she likes it when she is sad, with her head against his chest, his hand smoothing her hair. He unzips the green dress and helps her take it off, and her white underwear, and after a while she stops crying; he can hear only her sharp breaths against his ear as she holds on to his neck and shoulders. It is nothing like what he wanted; it is a desperate, cornered loving, ungenerous. He zips up his pants and lies next to her. He loves her, after all, that's the ironic part. She lies naked, unmourning, next to him.

After a while he pulls the sheet up over her.

"When are you going to get married?" he asks.

"I don't know. We thought about it last Wednesday but a patient delivered early."

"Last Wednesday! My God, Claire. This isn't something you can just run down to the corner store for. You have to make plans. You have to get a license and a place to live."

"We have a license. We have a place to live."

"Not at his place. And not *here*. This place is mine."

"Oh, Will. Listen. I do want to help you, but you have to make an effort. Don't torture yourself."

"*Help* me!" He laughs.

She says nothing.

"Well, where *are* you going to live? Or is it a secret?" he says.

"We don't know."

"It's here, isn't it?"

"I said we don't know."

"Please don't use the plural pronoun. Please just speak to me as one person, just yourself if you can. I know it, anyway. I know it's here. God." He wants to ask her for a souvenir—a book from the bookshelf, a fork, a towel. He kisses her forehead and gets up from the bed.

"You need me to go now. Isn't he coming?" he says.

"Not until eight."

"It's almost seven-thirty."

"I know." She stares at the ceiling.

"I'll marry you," he says, passing her the underwear, the green dress.

"I know." She doesn't reach for the clothes. He lays them next to her, careful not to crease the dress.

He stumbles down the stairs, or at least he thinks he stumbles, falling out into the evening air, stupidly and clumsily fleeing the carriage house and its gridded rectangles of golden light, like some little house in a forest, the humble home of a woodsman and his good wife, shrinking behind him as he runs down the driveway. He is panicked at the thought of meeting Danny coming in. Claire is the most truthful person he has ever known, but he can't really believe that Danny Cardozo ever wept for her or wants to marry her. Danny will never marry Claire. Goddamn him for deceiving her.

Out in the street there is no light left, and he drives home through accomplished darkness. There may be stars, but in a car you don't feel stars. Turning onto his block he spins the wheel a fraction too far and his wheels bump up over the curb on the right; he recovers, but the jolt shakes his plans. He does not stop at his house. The lights are on in it, but they are not lit for him, and he does not stop. He telephones his wife from the office, wakes her up in order to lie to her. He spends the night on the vinyl sofa, and the room is so closed off that no external sound or light can reach him, only the rackety and shifty figures of his dreams.

Ten

"How come I don't have eyebrows?" Beth is sitting on the edge of the bathroom sink, looking into the mirror. Her feet, in pink socks of elasticized nylon so thin they show the round ridges of her toenails, are balanced on the opposite rim of the sink.

"What do you mean? You have eyebrows. Please hand me the soap. Every time I get in the tub the soap's gone," Alice says.

"I can't see them at all unless I get up close."

"Because the hairs are light," Alice says.

"But it's ugly, having no eyebrows. When will the hairs get dark?"

"I don't know. This isn't my soap." The soap is shaped like Donald Duck but all of his hard edges have worn smooth and he is now only vaguely ducklike, a yellow misshapen knob. Alice slips down in the tub until her shoulders go under, but she can't get rid of the view of her white, ugly stomach. It is a reason not to take a bath, the sight of the pallid body stretched out before her, naked and absurd. Luckily, eyes are so located that you don't have to see the rest of yourself most of the time; you can move through life without that constant reminder of your own shape.

This bath was a bad idea. A bath in the middle of the day is unsettling.

When she soaps herself, the protuberances that were once Donald Duck's cap and bill and tail poke into her skin.

Beth has pulled herself up to a perch within inches of the mirror, to study her face as if it were a picture of another person. At six she is starting to look at herself critically, starting to split the visible self off from the thinking self. A little girl at the mirror, just beginning that lifelong interrogation.

Alice spreads the old washcloth over her chest. When she was young she once saw her mother naked. She walked into the bathroom and her mother was standing before the full-length mirror, brushing her hair, which was long, down to her waist, and the color of gold-brown grass. To brush it she had to tilt her upper body to one side and let her hair fall free, and as she leaned, her breasts fell gently to that side. When she saw Alice she cried out and tried to cover herself with her hands. Alice meant to back out of the room without looking; but could not take her eyes off the beautiful long breasts, the round belly and its black tangle of hair, all doubled in the mirror, so that the room seemed full of nakedness, all white limbs and hair.

It was the dark hair that frightened her, so unlike her mother's lovely golden head, so suddenly black against the white skin.

Beth jumps down from the sink. "I want to ask you something," she says.

"What?" Alice takes the washcloth from her chest and washes her arms. Under the balding terry cloth she can feel the duck's head break off softly from its body, and the two pieces of soap roll around under the cloth. She tries to keep them hidden from Beth, but the soap is too slippery, the head falls out into the water with a plop.

"You broke his head off?" Beth says, peering into the tub.

"I didn't break it, it just came off. It's soap, honey. It was bound to wear away sooner or later."

Beth says nothing.

"What did you want to ask me?"

"I forgot."

"Oh, come on. Don't get mad. It might stick back on." She tries to make the two pieces of soap join together again.

"It's ruined. You ruin things." She runs out of the bathroom leaving the door open; a chilly draft comes into the room. The mirror mists over. Beth's accusation, like a song in Alice's brain, repeats itself with a deadly rhythm. It is true, too. She starts with good intentions. In fact, she starts with love but by and by the love gives way to something else —to the fear of losing love?—and ruin begins. With Will she started out with love.

Wrapped in a towel she makes wet footprints on the floor into her room. Beth isn't there. Marcy is sitting in the middle of the bed.

"Don't suck your thumb, sweetheart. Are you sleepy?"

"No."

"What's the trouble?"

"You know. I miss Tiffany."

"How about a bowl of cereal? With milk and a cut-up banana?"

"Okay. Count Chocula."

"We don't have Count Chocula. We never have Count Chocula."

"But I like it, I saw it on TV and I like it. You could go get it at the Piggly Wiggly."

"No, I could *not* go get it at the Piggly Wiggly."

The thumb goes back into the mouth. With her other hand Marcy twists a lock of hair at her temple.

Sometimes the talk between children and adults is sickening in its gravity, an exchange tense with misunderstanding and so unbalanced, so unequal, that it cannot be drawn out beyond a sentence or two on each side. When will they talk in paragraphs? When will they talk on her level and joke and fib? Their allegiance to the truth is disheartening.

"Don't suck your thumb." Alice pulls the thumb out of Marcy's mouth with a sucking snap.

"You are mean and crazy," Marcy says.

"Listen, miss, you don't talk to me like that. I'm your mother."

"You're still mean and crazy. I can't love you."

"Don't talk like that, Marce. We have to love each other even when we get mad. I love you when I'm mad. You're mad at me but you still love me."

"No, I don't."

"We'll get another Tiffany. How about that?"

"We could get another *doll.* We could not get another Tiffany. There's only one of a person even if it's a doll."

"Don't suck your thumb. Please, please don't suck your thumb. How long is this going to go on, anyway? Are you going to be sucking your thumb when you're twelve? Fourteen?"

"No."

"Yes, you are. You'll be sixteen years old and sucking your thumb. The men will think you're still a baby. And babies don't get married."

The sulking and fake crying turn into hot real tears, the petulance to grief, and Alice watches herself turn from tormenter to consoler. "Oh Marce, oh babe! I'm sorry. Don't cry. I'm sorry." Kneeling on the bed she rocks her child in her arms and hopes desperately the baby-sitter will come soon to save them. "Of course you will get married. Have lots of children. Of course you will!"

That is why she wanted the baby-sitter, after all. She wanted that strange girl in the house, coming into the house every day, proof of other worlds beyond this house and this family. She wants her children to see the girl; and she wants Will to see the girl. Every time Iris comes it is like opening up a room that has been long closed—letting in air, letting in light. Iris is so clear, so single-minded. Alice almost wonders if she might be slightly retarded. But the girl at seventeen is already on her own, making her way in life. She seems strong. She seems unburdened by a sense of history or home or kin.

Moreover, she has those small, soft breasts and a way of moving that suggests freedom. She moves the way Alice would like to move, for example, if she had a mind to win her husband back. If she really wanted to make the effort; but she does not. It would be too much trouble, it would take too much energy. She has none.

She doesn't eat much. She does spend a lot of time buying food and fixing it, loading the dining table with food for Will and Beth and Marcy, a balanced diet with foods from the four food groups, but by then it has ceased to be food in her mind. It is table decoration, *failed* table decoration at that. What beautiful foods she begins with, chosen with love from the supermarket shelves. Yesterday's meal began, laid out on the counter, like a lineup of perfect materials for a food artist: cold thick-fatted loin of pork; mountain apples that were small and hard and green-spotted; tiny white onions with dry loose papery covers; and heavy stems of broccoli bursting at the end into budded blue flowerets. Raw pure things, discrete, named. By the time she had peeled and diced and cooked and mixed and seasoned everything she was sick with loss, disgusted with the result of her work. Of the crisp bright broccoli she had made a mushy olive-green casserole, cheesed and crumbed. The apples were hardly apples anymore, so thoroughly had she cooked away their apple color and shape and texture; even their taste was lost under cinnamon and clove. And where were the little white onions so strong they had made her cry when she cut through their hard rings? Yellowed and slippery and bland in a pasty sauce of flour and milk. When it was all set out on the table she could only watch with growing revulsion while he cut through the sizzling fat of the roast, and the juices sparkling with miniature globes of fat dripped across the blade, down onto the Singapore Bird, her fine turquoise-and-rose wedding china with silent cockatoos perched in the spreading branches of flowering trees.

You ruin things.

Iris comes, looking tired, but then she would be, after classes and cooking her mother a lunch and walking over here. This is her second week in the house, and already she has won the girls. She won them the first day. Now they meet her at the door, Marcy taking her hand, Beth carrying her books into the kitchen. They think it is exciting to have a baby-sitter in the afternoon, a signal of something unusual in the regular stretch of their week. Iris is telling them about photographs she has seen of them in Queen's house, and Alice listens from the dining room. She is still nervous when she leaves them. Sometimes she eavesdrops on their talk. Iris describes in detail the photographs of the five previous years.

"Remember one taken under a Christmas tree? Beth riding a green caterpillar?"

"Oh, yes, that worm thing. I remember that. An inchworm with a saddle."

"I don't," Marcy says.

"You weren't born yet," Beth says. "You weren't in the picture because you weren't born yet."

Marcy puzzles over that incredible condition, of not being born yet at a time when her sister was riding a caterpillar and getting Christmas presents.

Iris says, "But I remember one of you, Marcy. I remember a picture of you at Halloween. I *think* it was you. With a Woody Woodpecker mask and a Woody Woodpecker suit?"

"That was me! I have that same suit still. Want to see it?"

"Sure," Iris says.

"Want to see something secret that I have?" Beth says.

"Yes," Iris says.

"Wait a minute. See, I have to keep them wrapped up in this napkin. Wait. Here." A gravelly handful of glass chips rolls out onto the kitchen table.

Iris exclaims, "What *are* they? They're *beautiful.* Why, look at this one, it's huge. And this one, you can see into it. It's sparkling inside itself, see? Look sideways."

"Emeralds," Beth says.

"Wow," Iris says.

"I helped her find them," Marcy says.

"Be sure to keep them in a special place so you won't lose them."

"Oh, I do. I hide them."

"That's smart."

"I'll go get the woodpecker suit, okay?" Marcy says, already on the run.

The web of love and anger is so dense between mother and child, it is never clear what thread is laid down first: the child's cry or the mother's sympathetic caress; the mother's anger or the child's misbehavior and remorse. Once Alice knew a woman deaf from birth. She had three children who never cried, even when they cut themselves or skinned their knees; even when their father or an aunt was present and could be counted on to hear and become distressed. Children are braver if their mothers are deaf or dead.

"I'm off to the grocery store," she tells Iris. "I think I'll walk and have them deliver the groceries later today, so I might be gone more than an hour." The three of them are sitting on the floor examining emeralds. Beth drops a napkin on top of the pile. Iris sits cross-legged with Woody Woodpecker on her lap.

Out in the street, people are happy, some whistling, walking briskly, all because it is a Friday afternoon, happiest time in the American week. Even the weekend is not as good as the prospect of the weekend. They line up in cars to deposit their paychecks, joking with the teller who is locked into her little cage on an island in the bank lot. Alice hates them all for their inconstancy to hope. True to it on Friday, how will they behave on Sunday? Sluggish, downcast. Making cross remarks to members of their families, going to bed early in order to escape their own troubled thoughts. Fifty-two times a year they go through the same buoyant rise and terrible decline, and for no good reason but time, the way time passes. If Alice could ever once get a firm hold on hope, nothing could weaken her grasp, certainly not the coming of Sunday night.

The walk to the supermarket takes her through the black neighborhood of midtown. It is not the way she used to go; she used to detour around the project, sticking to the business streets, or even go to another store. But Iris walks through the project every day. Alice asked, "Isn't it dangerous?" Iris said, "I don't know. I guess it could be, if you're afraid. I'm not because it's just something I've always done. I mean, if you live in it you aren't scared of it."

So Alice started walking Iris's way. The first time she was frightened, as out of place as a clown in her white-woman's clothes and her white skin. People stared at her from windows and porches, from cars. Of course they'd stare. It is unheard of in any Southern city for a white person to walk through one of these places, the old colored towns now gulped into the city and lost behind stores and hotels. The only whites that do it are insurance agents. She has seen them, young twenty-five-year-old men in cheap suits stopping at every house to collect a weekly premium. But this is not the worst of the city, it isn't Bayside, where old people don't leave their houses for months at a time, so frightened are they of what is on the street. No, this is just old colored town. The houses are painted wood, with patches of garden out front. Children hang from the porch railings and old men gather on the corners or in the yard that has a cable spool set up as a card table, surrounded by busted dinette chairs and Coke crates. There's always a game. Sometimes it is an animated game, the men laugh and toss cards or coins out onto the table, and sometimes it's sedate, a dreamy slow afternoon game under the pecan tree, so quiet the squirrels come down and creep up to within inches of the chairs, getting what nuts have been rejected or overlooked by the children.

It is a pocket of slow, warm living in the middle of town, like a world coexistent with the rest but not visible from it, not from the main traffic arteries or places white people go. *Sometimes, if you're lucky,* Alice thinks, *you can find this: a haven where you least expect it.*

The little gardens are different from white people's box-wood-and-bulb gardens. The flowers overflow, bend out onto the sidewalks, climb fences. After blooming they are allowed to die in their own beds. All the daisies are dying back, their tall stalks drying brown, their lower leaves clumping close to the ground for winter. Reedy mounds of chrysanthemum are dotted with a few last bronze buttons, a scattering of small leaves; and cannas fan out behind yellowing four-o'clocks. Occasionally a thick wisteria winds up the side of a porch, a fibrous wooden snake, ridged and rough. A big one can pull a beam down or lift sewer pipes out of the earth, nothing but root above ground and below, undiversified and therefore of magnificent strength. Its bloom is always a surprise when it comes: delicate lavendar grapelets, with a sweet smell that fills a yard.

She no longer feels out of place on this walk, now that she's done it three or four times. Some of the people are always there when she passes, some of the old ones, any-way, who stay near home. One is a woman she sees every time, a large-boned, deep-black woman sweeping her porch or her steps or the sidewalk, even the dirt yard, sweeping every time Alice walks by. The woman is near sixty and shy; her smile is the slow, embarrassed smile of a ten-year-old. Her hair stands away from her head, stiff and shiny. She raises her eyes from the broom toward Alice but does not look right at her. They will never speak, too shy of each other, but every day the woman's motions are the same when Alice comes by—the broom stops, the woman's face lifts. Alice takes it as a greeting.

Estelle, who ironed in the kitchen while Alice's mother helped ladies pick from swatches of silk in the front room, used to look at Alice in the same slanted way. Why didn't Estelle look straight at her? She knew Estelle had high blood pressure and diabetes, and that of her own six children one was killed in Korea, one robbed of eight dollars and stabbed on a Bayside street, and one fatally shot in the back by an off-duty policeman who mistook him for a suspect, when he was really only peeing against a wall. But those weren't reasons not to look *Alice* in the eye.

Later Estelle died, too. By that time Alice had grown out of love for her, the strong sense of Estelle as someone real and touching her life having sunk into memories, old smells and sounds, moments like this instant of recognition when she sees the woman, great arms sweeping, shy eyes looking just past what they seem aimed on.

And my mother didn't even trust Estelle with the silver. She counted the spoons once a week.

What will happen to all these black people, now the movement is dead, their heroes tucked away in public offices? Was the whole civil rights movement nothing but a minor disturbance in the succession of years? White people have started telling jokes again. Blacks and whites live farther apart than ever, like the double curve of a hyperbolic function, two human worlds of identical misery and passion but occupying opposite quadrants, nonintersecting. In a way, equal but separate. One day something will blow up, but Alice doesn't know whether it will be the world or the South or the Reese family. She pretends to be invisible. If she tilts her head back a bit, she can't see her feet stepping forward or her arms swinging, only the transparent ghost of her nose and a faint curve of cheek. She is a pair of eyes, a mind, moving through this black neighborhood, this hidden world almost certainly doomed. Her fingertips dropping down into her shoulder bag come to rest lightly against the cool metal of the Shrieker canister. But if she were accosted here and set off the alarm, who would come? Who would help? These people are not interested in her. Why should they be? She takes her hand off the Shrieker. Iris said not to be afraid. Children skitter down the sidewalk ahead of her, walking home from school with bookbags, cheerleading pom-poms, cans of Pepsi. A dog barks at Alice, darting out from his yard at an angle to ambush her, going down on his front paws and yipping in the middle of the sidewalk until a boy grabs him by the collar and drags him struggling and gurgling back into the yard. She is not scared. The dog's eyes are sweetly brown. He's a perfect dog.

Her father, editor of the evening paper for twenty-six years, did not believe in progress, and he was in a position to judge, doing daily business with world events on a scale that ran from fillers to headlines. All of Alice's schooling suggested the world was improving. "Trace the steady growth," the tests said, "in the rights of Americans, from the Declaration of Independence and the Bill of Rights through the subsequent Amendments and the current Civil Rights Movement." But her father said the world was not improving: what looks like progress is only change, he said. Without telling him, she held on to her own girlish trust in a trend for the better, certain, for example, that by the time she grew up there would be no more maids. People like Estelle would all get master's degrees in counseling, their children would go to medical school.

He has not won yet. She is still not sure about progress. Evidence seems to support him—these houses with sagging porches, the woman sweeping, the old men under the trees —but it's hard to say for sure what such things mean. She does know that the man who doubted progress now sits in front of his television day and night, a self-fulfilled prophecy. He should have given progress a chance. Should have hoped against hope.

Young, he had hoped. But after coming home from Princeton with a degree in philosophy he went to work at the newspaper, where the kind of hope taught at Princeton dissipated. Why do philosophers in the South so often end as newspapermen, poets as doctors? Maybe they crave what's found in pain and loss: a sense of living among other human beings. They'll give up dreams for it.

She turns the corner onto America Street, where the supermarket rises suddenly up out of its parking lot, the biggest supermarket in the state when it was built fifteen years ago, now outdone in dozens of suburban malls. Its long glassy facade is papered with ads for Tide and Crisco and canned corned beef: civilization.

Like colored town, the store is a place she likes. Who can be sad in a supermarket, with all its proof of human omnipotence? Thousands of pounds of food stacked in rows, waiting for the hungry, all of it grown and packaged and transported without a hitch. And more comes in tomorrow to replace what goes out today. When you see such achievement, you must be hopeful; every box of quick grits, every can of cling peaches is a spur to hope.

Once she did see a woman steal some pork chops. Alice didn't report her because the woman took such care in selecting the meat. She looked at all the cuts, then picked the Family Pack, the best bargain. She put the package into the top of her stretch slacks and pulled her smock down over the bulge. Alice watched from behind her cart. Thrift in theft! It won her and bought her silence.

A boy unhooks spotted bananas from the wire-and-paper banana tree and hangs up new hard, green bunches. The checkers, Martha and Doris, lean on their registers and talk. The workers here are black; they are pleasant but let you have the privacy you need to shop. These are good jobs; the store would be a good place to work in every day, clean and busy, filled with food.

The produce aisle is like a garden path, earth's plenty jumbled into mirrored bins on both sides. She wants a honeydew. The pale-green melon, smooth-skinned and nearly spherical, would have a delicate, subtle taste. She turns it in her hands. The tomatoes are bad. The season is over but these are shipped in from somewhere, small and pale and nearly hollow. She gets a bag of collards and some crookneck squash to fill the crisper, which she emptied this morning of what had been left there to spoil: a bunch of limp carrots, yellow broccoli, and a cucumber that collapsed when she touched it. How effortlessly and smoothly things go from ripe to rotten; it is nothing but a waiting game.

Always after produce she goes to meat, then dairy products, bakery, and out, keeping to the periphery of the store, where the real food is. Canning and preserving are good tricks but she likes to buy the things that still look like what they are. Reaching into the poultry case she pulls out a bagged chicken; it has the feel and heft of a water balloon, rose-colored liquid swelling the bag like amniotic fluid, cushioning the bird, its folded wings and plump legs. Into the chicken's back she sees carved, in carefully incised letters, angular like cuneiform, the words FUCK YOU, the chicken's skin receding from each cut to show the bird's pink inner flesh. Tears come to her eyes. Why would anyone want to do this to her? It is a bad omen that her hand went right to that particular chicken. She pushes the buzzer that calls the butcher out. "Look at this chicken," she says, holding it out to him.

"Yes, ma'am."

"Somebody wrote on it," she says.

He scrutinizes the chicken, turns it over and over in his hands, holds it back to read it as if it were a message. Well, it *is* a message.

"Yes'm, they did."

"I'll just get another."

"Yes, ma'am." He takes the chicken back to the butcher room. Through the glass window Alice watches him open the bag and pass the chicken over to his assistant, a boy. The two of them laugh. She is a joke to them. She sees her hands stretched out in front of her on the cart. The supermarket is huge and vast, a wasteland. These foods will never make her family healthy and hearty. This sweet milk is already turning, these eggs in their perfect shells already going slowly bad. She lets the cart pull her down the aisles.

Where is cheese? She thought it came right after milk and eggs. There ought to be a Dewey decimal system for food. She is lost. She has to let the cart pull her down the aisles.

Then she catches a glimpse of color and movement outside the store, a woman whose figure she recognizes, whose walk stops her heart like a wheel pausing at the top of an incline, then falling with redoubling speed. Claire. Dressed in white, getting into her car at the curb, the red Beetle that Alice used to hunt for on the streets. There is a man in the car, just closing the door on the passenger side; taking the bag of groceries from Claire's hands when she gets in, settling the bag on his knees. Alice sees them through a foreground of people and carts and the big ads flapping on the glass, the backward writing illegible. The man is not Will. He leans toward Claire, the man who is not Will, and she to him, and they kiss each other over the bag of groceries, in the Volkswagen, in the parking lot. The man is Danny Cardozo. Watching from forty feet back, Alice is frozen by fear, knowing immediately what she has seen and what it means, that kiss, that bag of groceries. Only lovers shop for food together.

Now she is nearing the checkout counter; the wheels of the cart roll forward, taking the curves slowly, guiding her to the end of their circuit about the store. She dreads the checkout counter, where she will have to let go and stand by herself again. Martha and Doris see her coming, but they don't move to get ready, they stay propped up against the registers like mannequins in the midst of a window change. Alice can't let go of her cart. Across the entire front of the store now, the western sun makes a wide ribbon; beyond that, the parking lot, the way home. But what has gone wrong? How can Claire kiss Danny? Does Will know? Doris turns; she must be tired, she moves so heavily and slowly, saying, "I'll take you here," as if resigned to an onerous chore. Alice is supposed to unload the food onto the conveyor belt. The sun streams and streams through the glass. On the floor big square patches of shadow are thrown down by the paper ads.

"You okay?" Doris says. Then she motions to Martha, who comes around to Doris's register.

"Mrs. Reese? Want to unload now?" Their voices fade out, come back, fade out, like a car radio going under bridges, the waves getting blocked.

". . . having a fit . . ."

". . . not like that . . . my neighbor child gets . . . can't speak out . . ."

". . . hey? hey? . . ."

"What is that she holding out . . . what . . . Lord . . ." They run, they run away from her. Who would help? "Lord. Oh Lord. Oh Lord" is what the shape of their mouths say, their hands covering their ears. The store is filling up with a long high wailing sound. The fat manager comes running. Alice remembers when he started as a bag boy. George. Now he is Mr. Smalley. He used to help her carry things out to the car. He, too, has his hands over his hears, but he lets one down to reach for Alice's hand, and he takes from it the orange Shrieker. Holding one ear he tries to read the directions on the canister. Then he twists the button on top and the wailing ceases, leaving a soft messy quiet hole in the air.

"I'm so sorry," Alice said. "It just went off. I didn't even know what it was at first."

Mr. Smalley looks at her, breathing hard. "That thing is dangerous. That thing could burst somebody's eardrum, Mrs. Reese."

People are looking at her from all over the store, coming out from the aisles with coffee in their hands, vinegar, Drāno. Martha and Doris creep back to their registers, like something Alice saw before . . . like those squirrels cautiously approaching the cardplayers, head-down. Doris rings up the food without a word. *Crazy white woman,* she must think. She punches the keys on her machine with terrifying speed, not even looking at the numbers, letting the conveyor belt carry everything under her level palm, held just above the line of food as if in blessing. Alice puts the Shrieker back into her shoulder bag. Here's a job she would like, punching the food out all day long, friends with Doris and Martha maybe, but no husband, no children, nothing on her mind but the numbers, 1.89, .69, two for .89, 1.22, and the sun through the long window all day.

Eleven

On the way home she misses the things she saw before, the gardens and children, people on their porches, the dog, the trees. An hour ago they were pumped up with life, full and dappled, everything glistening: leaves, hair, that dog's eyes. But as her mind fills up, the things around her deflate. The only sharp, real thing is what she saw, Claire and Danny and their kiss and their grocery bag.

If Claire goes, everything can go.

Maybe it was someone else. Maybe she saw it wrong. Sometimes her peripheral vision is so acute it can distract her. She might be looking right at one thing, and something else on the edge of her field of vision sparkles or shifts and she spins to catch it—a car coming, a child skating into the street, the kind of thing you need to see early to be ready for. But sometimes she catches sight of things that turn out to be not there at all when she looks straight on: what she thought was a roach or a mouse is dust on the floor, a leaf in the path. Her eye tricks her.

No doubt about the red car, though, the woman's figure, the man's head. These she saw clearly. All the way home she tries out various explanations to make what she saw into something unremarkable, but nothing works. Danny and Claire. Part of her wants to rejoice. This is what she has been waiting for. She knew, she knew it would wind down. "Only our love hath no decay." Ha. Knowing, she sat it out, waiting for the end. But this is not the one she expected; it isn't the ending anyone would have expected. What does Will know of it?

She sneaks into the house so no one will know she is home. From the back garden come her children's voices, a speckling of laughter in the background of the afternoon. For November the day is warm. Daylight Saving Time is gone, and she is not accustomed to the quick death of afternoons. This hour from four to five is more valuable now than a month ago, when it was only a middle slice of the afternoon. To the hammock on the second-floor porch, rope woven across two wooden bows, she goes now. From up here she can see the street and the driveway and part of the yard, and no one can see her. People don't look up much. They train themselves to look straight ahead for what's coming, or even down to watch their step, but they don't look up, to the sky and clouds, birds, the tops of buildings. So it's a good place to hide.

The hammock sways into the sun and back out. Even with her eyes closed she knows the difference, warmth beating over her face and arm like whatever it was that first encouraged life, fluctuating.

"There he goes, into the vines," she hears Beth say.

"Oh, no. He's after a bird. Iris, he's after a bird, help!"

"Stop him. Throw something."

"Shoo! Shoo!"

"Where is he now? I don't see him. Kitty kitty kitty, come down."

In the climbing rose on the wall a cat picks its silent way through the vines. The cat creeps, flattens down, freezes straight-tailed. Its head shudders side to side in a kind of feline petit mal. But what looks like a goofy palsy is really deadly triangulation.

"I see him now, I see him," Marcy says. "Watch out, bird. Go, bird!"

Out of her left eye Alice sees someone below, a black boy crouching on the sidewalk. He ducks out of sight whenever a car drives by, then returns to his spot. Maybe he is watching the house. Marcella says they watch your house for a few days before they break in. The boy darts behind a parked car. She doesn't see him again. The hammock swings into cool shadow now.

The cat makes its move, springing through the tangled rose to land where the old woody vines have interlaced to make a solid-looking spot, but the sticks snap and the cat falls through, thuds on the ground like something in a bag. For two seconds it looks dead. It lies motionless and awkward, uncatlike, then suddenly, without a warning tremble or even a lifted head, it is streaking away, under the house. The girls sing out, delighted at the cat's bad fortune. Then their voices fade back to the corner of the yard where the swing set is. The rusty chains squeak as they swing, two sets of squeaking. Alice lights a cigarette. She smokes most in these sinking late hours, when she feels her sharpest pangs of homesickness and hunger. Smoking helps to deaden the gnaw before it swells out of control.

As a child she always had an afternoon nap, in the old Chalmers Street house. Estelle would drive her out of the kitchen because Elizabeth insisted that Alice take a nap every day to prevent polio, and though Estelle didn't believe it made a piece of difference (Alice could tell by the way Estelle said, "Your *mama* say take a nap"—Estelle always blamed precisely), still she made sure Alice didn't sneak away from the house at naptime or hide somewhere. So Alice slept, on top of the white chenille spread, with the afternoon sun coming in the windows of the sleeping porch. Her mother was out. Estelle was downstairs, but would Estelle protect her if something happened? Her cheek was pocked by the tufts of the spread, her hair damp. It was a fitful, uneasy sleep.

Now, maybe what thickens her afternoons is leftover anxiety, the residue of childhood fret visiting the grown-up woman.

She tosses the cigarette butt into the street. It hits the asphalt and rolls from the crown down to the gutter, still lit, and a green Cadillac pulls up, running over it. Marcella. Alice watches her mother-in-law get out of the car. First, all the windows roll up simultaneously and automatically; the door opens, Marcella's long legs come out, then the rest of her, in flowered silk, peach and cerulean blue fluttering around her knees and in short flounces at the shoulder. The door closes with a heavy *chunk*.

"Yoo-hoo," she calls through the gate. Alice hides.

Marcella is living proof that unexpected things can happen, fast. Only two years ago Marcella was old. She was in the same house she'd been in all her adult life, her husband long dead, her pastimes the little amusements offered to widows in Charleston: unlimited christenings; a tea during the debutante season for somebody's granddaughter; one or two chamber music concerts during the Spoleto Festival, but none of the strange things, the Negro modern dance company or the nude Japanese theater group. In the summers she might go to Brevard or Flat Rock for a week. All of this in the company of other widows. She lived the life of an old lady even though she was only forty when Edmund died. But she had lived all her married life as if she were twenty years older than she really was, moving in the social circles of her husband's peers, her friends the wives of his friends. And when he died, her friends were the widows of his friends; it was like a club. One morning fifteen years after Edmund's death, widowhood lost its hold on her. She cut an ad from the paper, and within a month she was selling houses. It turned out she had a gift for selling houses. The first year she sold four of them, for a total of $570,000. The next year she sold "a million-four," including one to the man from Ohio who wanted to live in a house with columns.

She sold Duncan Nesmith a monster overlooking the harbor and the Battery, built in 1953 on landfill—on garbage, in other words—but it had columns. Then she married him. She left her dark, eighteenth-century house on Legare Street and left her blue-haired friends, who told one another the man was really rather unattractive but very wealthy and the family was said to be upset. (Meaning Will, the upset family. Marcella's one uncle and a cousin are farmers upstate, never heard from. Will is her only family.)

Sometimes Alice likes Marcella. The woman is flighty, yes, and maybe vain, but there's an independent air to her that Alice admires, a dumb toughness. Her feeling for Marcella is certainly not the affection of a daughter, but it is like the affection of a girlfriend. Girlfriends put up with a lot and don't make demands. They don't even demand loyalty, knowing their bond is tentative; it is always understood that something else can take precedence over their friendship at any moment, with no explanations necessary. Alice can imagine a friendship like that with Marcella and with Claire: a sisterly link.

Under her hammock, Iris lets Marcella in the gate. The wedge of porch sunlight is moving and narrowing, so that now only Alice's arm and shoulder sweep into the warm spot on the upswing. She knows she will not stay once the light is gone; she waits out the dwindling minutes while Marcella and Iris talk in low tones. Really, if all these women would simply step forward and acknowledge their roles in her life, she could step out of it herself. Marcella could tend to the house, its upkeep and furnishings; Iris could care for the children, feed and love them; and Claire could look after Will. They have all been just dimly enough involved to be less than adequate.

When the whole length of her swing is in chilly shade she goes down.

"Does she have tea?" Iris is saying in the kitchen.

"Somewhere. But if you've looked around the house, you've found out there isn't much organization here. No telling where the tea is kept. Alice probably doesn't know where it is herself."

"It's behind the salt, over the stove," Alice says and hopes it is there.

"Marvelous," says Marcella. Iris has found the Singapore Bird cups and put three of them on the table with saucers and spoons, and sugar in the sugarbowl, where there has been no sugar for months; Alice usually spoons it out of the bag. They are so efficient, other women, so in control of tea and cups and sugar, so beautiful. Marcella is tall and fine, silken; Iris is strong, rich in the way certain foods are rich —the two are almost opposites but they meet in beauty. Maybe that is why they seem to like each other, fussing over the teakettle and tea bags as if the tea were not real, the cups a tea set—those tiny gold-rimmed cups that require little girls to pinch the handles between their fingertips and take prissy lip-pursing sips of fake tea, and talk to each other the way they imagine women talk; so that when they are grown they can imitate those imitations. Iris is good with Marcella. She listens when Marcella talks, and when she speaks it is on Marcella's subject, not her own. Alice is surprised. Iris is more at ease than Alice would have thought.

"I hope you are fattening these children up," Marcella says to Iris. "They're little starvelings."

Alice says, "I was just like them, Marcella. You can't fatten up somebody who has thin genes."

Iris says, "They're healthy, that's what counts; they could use a little fat on their bones, but that will come. What's important is health—you can see it in their eyes and hair: health shines through." Iris has on Alice's kitchen apron. With her left hand in the apron pocket, her right pouring hot water over the tea bags with the flat, papery sound that just-boiled water makes, she stands at the end of the kitchen table. A mother's helper, that's what she should be called, instead of a baby-sitter; or she's a substitute mother.

It would be nice to have children without being a mother. People think mothers are maniacs. No one trusts them. Teachers hate them; men don't even listen to what they say. Alice saw it in the face of Beth's teacher, the fake smile for mothers shivering on her face. No, a mother's only hope for sympathy is from other mothers. Watch how they crowd up together at playgrounds, like prisoners in a camp. Yet in spite of that sympathy, maternal despair remains an unshared secret. It is a singular, focused despair that will not generalize or diffuse. It bores in and feeds on detail: a baby's curled fingers, a man's smooth still back.

Twice Alice postponed her interview with Beth's teacher. Finally, a week before school started, the teacher called. "The parent interview is mandatory, Mrs. Reese," she said, half-apologetic, half-imperious. The teacher turned out to be red-haired and shockingly young, with the kind of skin that comes close to being blue, the skin of a stomach or a thigh, and a face that gave the impression of being embarrassingly naked: short eyelashes, uncolored lips. She smiled, then her smile trembled and fell apart, the hand slipped out of Alice's handshake. *I want to like her,* Alice thought. *I really want to be like her.*

But it was a meeting of natural enemies. A teacher knows her power. It isn't over children, who will always talk behind her back and laugh and move to the next grade, anyway. It is over mothers. Always the mothers fear, What if the children fall under her spell?

She made Alice sit in a first-grader's chair. Alice saw what Beth would see: the teacher's face from underneath, chin lengthened, forehead receding, nostrils open. Around the top of the room the capitals and lower-case letters marched in military uniform, carrying a Confederate flag. The room jumped nervously with stuff on all walls, the numbers 1 to 40 riding in an open train, the days of the week and months of the year and a giant corrugated cardboard clock with movable hands made from yellow yardsticks. Beth wouldn't go for it, Alice decided. There was nothing interesting anywhere in sight. The teacher explained the dress code. Halter tops and certain kinds of shorts were not allowed for girls, although another kind of shorts was okay. She showed Alice some of the learning materials, the reading-lab boxes, self-paced arithmetic modules, individualized color-coded spelling kits. Everything worked on its own. There was a television set. As she demonstrated the video equipment, strands of the red hair loosened and fell out of the hairpins, and the teacher bit her fingernails. *They make eight thousand dollars a year,* Alice thought. *They're too young to have any interest in children.* By the time Alice left, she felt sorry for the teacher and confident that Beth would hate school.

Now, Iris . . . Iris is a cipher. She is not ignorant. Watch how she handles Marcella, looking straight into Marcella's eyes, listening as if she were really interested in what Marcella has to say. She listens to the children the same way. If Iris were a teacher, she'd be dangerous.

Marcella waves a spoon at Alice. "You are skinnier now than you've ever been," she says. "You're wasting away. How much do you weigh?"

"I don't know."

"Don't you weigh every morning?"

"No."

"But you should. It's a good way to start the day—sure of your own weight. I'm not joking. Iris, look at the circles under her eyes. Are you getting enough sleep, Alice?"

"Enough."

"Beth told me you don't watch television anymore."

"She's right."

"Marcy told me you threw their dolls into the garbage."

"She's right, too," Alice says. Marcella stirs her tea past what is necessary to mix the sugar in. Alice sips. Marcella sips, looking out over the cup at Alice. This is a showdown, Alice thinks. It is what little girls practice for, down to the angle of the glances and the tones of voices.

"I certainly don't want to meddle," Marcella begins, but Iris, aproned and standing to the side, touching the pot on the counter, interrupts.

"If you ask me," Iris says, "it's a good thing she threw them away. They're dangerous. I fell on one when I was little and cut my lip open. Look." She leans down to show Marcella the scar on her mouth. Marcella reaches up toward it with a pointed finger. Alice watches dumbly. The tip of Marcella's finger touches Iris's lip.

Marcella's forehead wrinkles between her eyebrows. "My goodness," she says. "I didn't even think of that. That the dolls might be *sharp.*"

"After that, I made my own out of a sock. My friend drew on the face. Children don't need anything fancy."

"You're a hundred percent right about that. They don't need half of what they're given. Why, Will never had all these toys when he was a boy, the cows that give milk when you pinch their little udders, the mobiles with live fish in them. People go overboard on that sort of thing these days. Iris, I believe you're going to do these children a world of good."

Alice could never have touched that scar. Yet Marcella did it so easily and fast, it might not have happened at all. Her hand is back on the table. Iris is back at the sink. What do they have in common that she does not have? Everywhere people are coming together in love notes and touches and kisses, but the best she can manage is a wreck with a black man who flees from her, an obscene message cut into a chicken skin, an artificial scream.

Marcella's cheekbones have a sort of Appalachian lift and her eyes are set high in her face. It's a face you catch sight of driving through a mill town, a country girl's face staring into your car from the edge of the road, stopping your heart, the culmination of generations. Whole clans can rise and spread plain and blank till by some fluke, a slight shift in pattern, the family bones resettle themselves in one child's face with a sudden beauty.

Today she looks older. Today her skin is just that, *a skin* pulled like a loose cover over the bone. Alice sees the cheekbones, the skull's curve, and the deepening hollows of the eyes and nostrils and mouth. Marcella is fifty-five. Alice is thirty-three. Iris is seventeen. Iris's face is still puffed with youth, springy to the touch perhaps, with a resilience that makes Alice think of the skin of old dolls with hollow legs of thick rubber; plump; dimpled. Iris likes the kitchen. She moves away from the table to clear the counter, dampens a rag, squeezes it, wipes the Formica. She doesn't mind slipping into the background; she seems to feel at home. That's it, what Alice likes about her: the way Iris eases into a room, comfortable at once.

It is centuries since Alice was seventeen, and longer since she felt at home.

Marcella is saying, "But you have your own life to live. I've meddled enough."

"What?"

"I've never had his confidence. Or his affection, for that matter. He was a distant child. But now I think we might all sort of pull together again." Marcella doesn't seem to mind Iris's presence, as she leans across the table toward Alice, for intimacy. "Now that I've remarried," Marcella says.

"Will doesn't really like Duncan very much, Marcella."

"I know that. He doesn't have to. There's more to it than that. Plenty of families get along without liking or admiring each other. Can you prevail on him at least to come have dinner? And be polite? That's all."

"I'm not sure I can prevail on him for anything."

"Of course you can." She draws herself up, pulls in her chin. "There's something you mustn't forget, Alice."

"What?"

"How much he was in love with you."

"That was a long time ago. Ten years."

"Ten years. Ten years is nothing." Marcella looks out the window, then back, as if ten years were just that close to nothing. "Love doesn't just fade away. Edmund's been dead for fifteen years, and a wonderful man has come into my life, but I still dream about Edmund. He was like Will, he never would have admired Duncan. But he'd have been polite."

"Will is still . . . not sure of things, I guess."

"Still?"

Alice looks toward Iris, whose back is turned as she rinses the cups and saucers at the sink. "Well," Alice says. "There is something new . . . It was . . . I saw . . ." She can't say it. Marcella would know what it means, that it is not good news.

"What?" Marcella says.

"Nothing. There's nothing new."

Marcella collects her possessions from the table, her brass-clipped leather pocketbook, a pair of gray suede gloves. Her Cadillac keys. "Good-bye," she says in a louder voice. "Good-bye, Iris. Good-bye, Alice," waving the floppy fingers of the gloves.

Another dream Alice has is this: Something catastrophic has happened—sometimes an earthquake, sometimes a huge explosion. Her children are not with her. The devastation is complete, worldwide; it is certain that everyone will die, but she can't decide what to do: Should she strike out through the crumbled walls and burning houses of the city, among the looters and the wounded, in search of the children? Or stay where she is? And does it make much difference? Shall we die separately and alone, or shall we make the immense, pointless effort to die together?

"Oh, magic!" Marcy's voice, shrieking with delight, comes from the front steps.

"What is it? Who did it?" Beth says, and Iris is laughing. The three of them are standing together looking onto the ground when Alice comes up behind them. Peering over Beth's head she can see nothing.

"What?" she says.

They part to make way for her, pointing down at the sidewalk two steps away from her feet, where a garden has been chalked from one side of the house to the other, day lilies in all their colors, yellow, orange, pink, delicate and freckle-throated, in clumps of long green leaves.

"It's Emory again," Iris says. "It's Queen's Emory, gone crazy. That boy. Someday he'll get arrested."

"What for?" Beth says.

"Messing up somebody's sidewalk like that." Iris stands with her hands on her hips, talking in the same fussing sort of way she used with Jacky, but she is smiling just the same, and when she leaves she is careful not to step on any of the flowers.

Tears run down Alice's cheeks. *I'm losing the world: not just Will, not just the children, but the cat in the vines, the gray gloves, the artist who covers the sidewalk with lilies. I don't want to lose Claire. Let me keep it all!* But new holes are opening up, discontinuities and singularities where she was not prepared to find them.

She had made a deal for the real world! That's what the marriage was for. To get to the man and the children, to get to the cat and the gloves, people on porches, dogs, trees, and the satin falling away on either side of the fast, merciless scissors.

Twelve

On Queen's doorstep Iris and Emory sit as the theme songs of different television shows blend in the night air, with an occasional human voice from the kitchens that open onto small stoops. Then one by one the doors close against the chill and the dark, and the sounds diminish; and Iris begins to ache with the loneliness that you get under a night sky. The stars are so bright it looks as if the ozone has already been destroyed, leaving no protective haze between earth and stars.

After a while she says, "I've got to get Fay out," talking more to herself than Emory. When she was staying with Fay nothing seemed bad about living in the black project. Things had changed around them, and it wasn't their fault. But now that Iris is out, her view is different. Other people, who couldn't understand it was only time that had put Fay there and left her stranded, might think of other causes. A white woman who would live like that would have to be a whore or feebleminded, somebody abandoned by her own people. Even the black people would think this. Emory doesn't argue with Iris when she says she has to get Fay out, but she goes on to explain, anyway.

"So the end of her life will be an improvement. It's bad if a person's life doesn't pick up at the end like they always expected it to. I've got to get her out before she gets old."

"Well, it's no big rush. She isn't all that old."

"She's turning old. I want it done before she *gets* old, which happens quick."

"I thought you were letting her go. You said she was going to have to take care of herself," Emory says.

"I said she'd have to feed herself. She'll never be able to take care of herself past what she's doing now. She could never move to another place—not unless I do it for her."

"I guess Mama's old," he says after a few seconds.

"No, she isn't."

"Sixty-seven."

Iris is shocked. "Queen? I thought she was fifty."

"Sixty-seven."

"But you're sixteen. She didn't have you in her fifties."

"Well, no."

"Then she can't be that old."

Emory breaks off a piece of poinsettia growing next to the step and watches a drop of white milk globe up on the torn stalk. He shakes it off onto the concrete step, and another one comes up but not as quick and not as big.

"She is, though. She never did have me; she isn't my mother."

Iris looks at his face to see why he is telling this story; she can tell more from Emory's face than from what he says, but she can see right away it is no story. She has a feeling of having bumped into something mysterious in the dark; she is curious about its shape but afraid to feel around to find out more.

After a minute she says, "Who is, then?"

"Oh, some girl. You know the one in Woolworth's last year, when we looked at those goldfish?"

"That was her?"

"Yeah."

"Is Queen that girl's mother?"

"Naw. Queen took me from her." Emory laughs, tilting his face up toward the stars. "Queen stole me!"

"How?"

"This girl had the baby. They were in Bayside and Queen was, too, then. The girl wasn't real bright. Queen just took the baby."

"The mother didn't call the police?"

"The mother didn't want nothing to *do* with the police. The mother had hit the baby."

Iris never has known the names of stars. She knows they do have names, and they fit together to form the constellations, but she has never been able to make out any shapes. When she looks at the sky she sees the stars scattered across it like the dots in a connect-the-numbers puzzle, and she knows there are hidden images, a lion and a hunter, bears, a princess's throne; she might be looking right at one but can't make it *take shape.*

"How old was it?" she says quietly.

"Two weeks. It got a broken rib."

The third drop on the stalk is tiny, so tiny that it can't be shaken loose. Emory touches it with his finger and it disappears.

"That stuff is poisonous," Iris says.

"Not through your skin," he says, tossing the stalk and its star cluster of leaves onto the ground.

"I've got to go. They don't know where I am and it's past suppertime," she says.

"It doesn't make any sense for you to be taking care of those drifters," he says. "You don't have enough people to worry about, you need to keep adding on to your list?"

"It's not my need, it's theirs."

"You sure?" he says.

"What do you mean by that?"

"Looks like you can't get enough people lined up waiting for you to feed them. You got Fay, those men, the white children . . ."

"They're not white children to *me.* They're children."

"Excuse me. I done forgot, Miss Iris. 'Scuse me, *ma'am.* Yes, *ma'am.*"

"Emory, don't."

"Look, you're gone from here. I didn't expect you'd stay, I didn't expect to see you around much—but I didn't expect you'd be knocking yourself out for no good reason. I mean, I'm not asking anything for me personally, but I want you to keep on being yourself, keep on being *Iris.* You understand me?"

"No. You don't want me to get out of here."

"Oh, I do. I'm getting out myself, don't worry. I do want you to get out, Iris, and make a good life, and I know you can, *if* you don't go and waste yourself first. You need to finish school. That's the first thing."

"I am. I'm *in* school."

"Two courses a semester. You know how long that'll take to get a degree? Ten years if you pass everything," he says.

"Listen, I'm not asking you. I'm doing the best I can. It's going to work, too."

"What is?"

"I'm going to be on my own. Have my own family," she says.

"You want that, after what you've lived with here?"

"Mine won't be like that one. My children will be happy, I'll teach them to be happy."

"I don't think you can teach someone how to be happy."

Iris turns to him. "Oh, yes, you can. You do it by showing them things like the stars, you teach them the names of the stars and the constellations, the names of flowers. You tell them stories. Like Queen told us, about Dave-Nero Jones. You cook food for them."

"All the things Fay never did."

"Yes, but it wasn't her fault. Fay made one big mistake in her life, and it ruined everything for her, she didn't have a prayer left after that."

"What was that?" Emory says.

"Owen."

"But if she hadn't made that mistake, you wouldn't have been here."

"Like I said. It ruined everything for her."

"So you aim to have a family without a mistake like that."

"I sure do."

Emory breaks off another stalk of poinsettia and drains it.

"Next year I'm going to art school. Away somewhere," he says.

"I know." He always had planned to go away.

"You want to, you can come with me," he says without looking her way.

"No."

"It would be different in another town."

She knows what he means, not just that she might be happier in another town, but that maybe they could be together.

"I don't think so," she says. "But thank you." From the doorstep she can see the window of Fay's kitchen, and Fay walking by one way, then back the other. "I better go see her for a minute. Then can you walk with me?"

"Sure."

"Wait here a minute," she says.

She means only to say hello to Fay, then leave. It was Queen she came to talk to and tell about the job, but once here she can't leave without a visit to Fay. Fay is not expecting her. Iris goes into the kitchen and then the living room, where Fay is watching TV, with a glass in her hand and a bottle of liquor right on the table. She doesn't have time to hide it, so she tries to joke her way out.

"Have a drink with me, Iris," she says. Iris picks up the bottle and takes the glass out of her hand, and goes to empty them in the kitchen sink. Fay doesn't bother to object. She covers her eyes, scared of Iris now.

"Don't joke with me about liquor," Iris says.

"I won't. I won't again."

"If you start drinking liquor now, it's all over."

"I won't, Iris. You can look at the bottle, it's only just opened. It's full."

"It's empty now."

"All right."

"I mean it, Fay. After all I've done to keep you in good health. If you turn to liquor now, I'll be out of your life forever, for good. I'll leave you."

"All right."

"I'll leave you all alone. You'll be a hag. Stuck here with niggers, Fay, no better than the niggers."

"Iris, don't. Iris . . ."

"I don't know why you don't believe me. You don't believe I'll do it, you don't believe what I tell you. You never did."

She leans down till she is close to Fay's face, so close that the face seems to fall apart, close enough to see one eye, and another eye, and the nose and mouth, but not the pattern of the face.

"You'll starve to death," Iris says. "Understand me?"

"Yes." Fay is pulling back, her face begins to reintegrate, shrinking toward the back of the sofa.

"And don't think someone else will come. No one else cares about you enough to show up and help you. Not Randall or Patrice, not your sweetheart either. He's not ever coming back here, not unless he thinks you might give him money again."

Fay is whimpering, twisting her legs to get out from under Iris's stare, when Emory steps into the kitchen and calls out.

"If we're going, let's go," he says.

Fay's sobs quicken. Iris hisses, "I *mean* it." She leaves Fay collapsed on the sofa, crying without covering her face, crying out into the open air of the room and watching Iris go.

"You're wrong," Fay cries. "He's coming back, he is going to show up!"

Emory ushers Iris into the yard. Frowning, he says, "What was that?"

"That was Fay and me."

Walking back to the rooming house she doesn't speak to him, angry at him for being black and for being her best friend, two things he ought never to have been. Most of all, she is angry at him for not being Queen's son. She remembers the goldfish girl at Woolworth's, a dull-eyed girl ladling the fish out into plastic bags. Iris wanted one, the way it looked in its transparent bag, a watery world magically floating on through the airy world, its fish all unaware. But Emory held her back, wouldn't even let her walk over to the tank. She saw him glance at the girl, whose face was sour-looking but not ugly, and Iris teased him. "Oh, Emory, I didn't know you had a girlfriend." She would never have said it if she'd thought it was true; but when she saw his face harden she changed her mind and decided it was true, so she shut up. They walked away from the fish. The girl was hanging the bags over the tank's edge, so all the fish were back in the tank again but separated now, each in its own bag. Iris could see the girl was older than she'd thought—thirty maybe, new in the job and not likely to hold it long, by the way her eyelids drooped and her mouth went down.

That girl, less than ordinary, and not Queen, is his mother, and no trace of Dave-Nero Jones sparks his veins.

Still, he's Emory. He doesn't have to walk her home, especially considering how snitty she was to him. He didn't have to come in and stop her cruelty to Fay, or watch over her as he has evidently been continuing to do, drawing those pictures on the Reeses' sidewalk. She knew the pictures were for her and her children. She and Emory did not always spell things out, but she knew, when he drew pictures, what they meant.

In the night air the smell from the paper mill up the river is sharp and sickening. It must blow with the wind down across the peninsula, but not in a cloud, for the sky is still clear all the way to heaven's bright coded patterns.

At the rooming house Emory says, "Look. Are these people okay, the ones you work for? Are they good to you?"

"Good to me? I guess so."

"Just don't make more out of it than's there."

"Meaning what?"

"Don't plan on them taking you as part of their family."

"I'm not!"

"Okay."

"You're saying I should know my place," she says.

"I'm saying don't look for love where it's no chance of getting it."

"The children will love me."

He gives her a long look. "You're something," he says. "Boy. You hang on to nothing."

"You can understand that."

"Yeah. I guess what I don't understand is what you think I'm going to do. I'm about the only one you aren't feeding now."

"You're going away," she says.

"For what?"

"Painting or school or whatever it is you've had your heart on. You're going to move. Aren't you?"

157

"I guess I am."

"Okay, then. What are you acting so jumpy about?"

"You always had the prettiest hair," he says.

"Oh, funny."

"No, I mean it. Even when it was short it was nice. Showed your head shape."

"Thank you."

"Good night, then," he says.

"Good night."

Why are things hidden and buried from her, so she always has to dig, dig, dig, or she has to *think* so hard. She thought she had worked it all out and gotten everything set up right. She did it all: got the place to live, some financial aid, a better job, just as she had planned for the new life. Now it isn't going the way she had thought it would. Fay is going to drink herself into ruin, Emory is saying it's all wrong, he's hinting she's taking the wrong steps. Without a car she is stuck in Charleston, and has no place to take Marcy and Beth. Iris is tired.

She has been wondering, at the back of her mind: What kind of children has Owen got in St. Cloud, Florida? If they are small children, the mother might welcome a helping hand around the house. Knowing Owen, he probably didn't pick out a homebody for a wife.

Thirteen

Will always did like night driving, used to drive Charleston to Chapel Hill in under five hours by doing it at night when there were no cars on the road. You had to let go of caution. You had to follow your own headlights, forgetting that the source of the light was you, not something guiding you. There is adventure in traveling by night, because it is pure motion, not sightseeing; it is like the night migration of birds. Once, when he was in a duck blind before dawn, the air above him filled with bird voices and wingbeats. In the dark he couldn't tell what kinds of birds they were, but there had to be thousands of them, small birds, maybe warblers. They sounded frantic; he imagined them driven into the night by a force stronger than hunger or love, flying blind, scared stiff but having no choice in the matter. Is it something akin to that, an urge without a name, that drives husbands into the night? The streetlights, the lights from signs and other cars decorate the night, each light distinct but crucial to the whole string. He is driving to Cardozo's apartment across the river.

When people get divorced they move across the river, as if in the knowledge of their broken pact with society they relinquish their place in it. Danny lives in the Old South Apartments, a place with a pool and plenty of hibachis, a West Coast style of place that took ten years to get to South Carolina. At first lots of secretaries and nurses lived in the

159

Old South, but security was nonexistent and they moved to the places with guards. Now the residents here are a tougher bunch. There was a murder in the Old South last year; the police found little stamps with pictures of Goofy and Mickey Mouse and Pluto. A cop licked one and went bonkers.

Danny isn't home. It's eight-fifteen. Will can wait, even if it takes all night. He pulls an aluminum chair to the edge of the pool, into one of the yellow circles of light from four lamps on poles around the pool. The pool paint is too blue; it looks like something from outer space, a turquoise puddle of radioactive liquid. The surface is flecked with pin-oak leaves and the bodies of dragonflies. Now and then a mosquito sizzles in the violet tubes of a bug-fryer hung up over the pump house.

There is not much action at the Old South tonight. A few cars pull in and out of the parking lot, but the hibachis are empty, the green-carpeted patios deserted. Will's thoughts run to speculation on the length of time required for vegetation to retake an area the size of the Old South—building, pool, parking lot. If you jackhammered the concrete and asphalt just enough to bust it up, let seedlings through . . . With the help of kudzu the place could be green, even dense again, in two, three years. It would look like the jungled-over pyramids of Mexico, green humps on the flat land.

" 'Vegetable love,' " he says out loud. " 'Vaster than empires.' " Is it Andrew Marvell? Ah, he should never have read those poems, wouldn't have if he'd known they'd shadow him the rest of his life.

When he is old and deep-eyed, with love and woe all past, will they still come around? Sure. It's what they're after. Now they come teasing, only flirting; but they'll make the old man weep.

At ten Danny drives into the lot. He is alone. He doesn't bother to lock the car or roll up the windows. He tosses his keys into the air once before putting them in his pants pocket, and the gesture confirms Will's suspicions. A man who is suffering doesn't give his keys that jingle, or stroll so carelessly across the grass. Before he gets to his patio Will calls out to him. Danny peers toward the pool.

"Thought I might see you here," Danny says. "But I wasn't sure you really knew where I lived."

"I helped you move in, remember?"

"Actually, no. I wasn't in the most lucid state of mind."

"No, you weren't. Carol had thrown you out and you spent one night in the street drunk and howling. Claire found this place for you and I went to Carol to beg for your clothes. It was supposed to be temporary," Will says.

"Yes, well, I liked it so much I had to stay. It's much classier than it looks. And I get along real good with the manageress."

"That will have to stop, won't it?"

"I hope not. It takes the pain out of the rent check," Danny says.

"But a married man doesn't fuck around."

"I never knew it to slow you down, son." Danny pulls up a chair but doesn't sit.

Will says, "You aren't planning on bringing Claire here to live in this shit hole, are you?"

"Can't say for sure. Don't know yet." He drops his head down in a low crouch with his fists up under his chin, making circles in the air. "Want to fight about it?" he growls, dancing under the yellow light.

"No."

"Let's drink, then. I have a bottle out here somewhere." Reaching into the middle of a clump of pampas grass behind them, he pulls out a half-full fifth of Rebel Yell. "You'll require a glass and ice, I guess. Get it inside. Door's not locked."

The apartment has not changed since the day Will moved Danny in. The only things he brought with him were clothes. In the living room are one of the orange-and-white webbed chairs from the pool, a *Playboy* on the floor, and two beer cans in the window. Claire had looked for a furnished apartment, but with one day's notice all she could get was a "semifurnished," meaning it had a stove and a refrigerator. Luckily, the last tenant left behind a bedframe and mattress. Through the bedroom door Will sees the bed, unmade. Only two kinds of people live like this: assassins and divorced doctors. He tries to imagine Claire's plants in this carpeted cardboard box, her oak chairs in this kitchen. They won't go.

The ice is in a plastic bowl in the freezer, but it's been melted down once and refrozen; the cubes are all stuck together in a hemisphere. He looks for an ice pick, a hammer, a knife—anything. There are a fork and a dirty spoon in one drawer; the other drawers are empty. "Holy shit," he mutters. Was he sent in here just to see this? He smashes the hemisphere in the sink and puts the pieces back in the bowl. He despairs of finding glasses. But he spots one on the floor and another empty in the refrigerator, next to an open bag of Doritos. He rinses the glasses and eats a dead Dorito.

Outside, he asks Danny, "Do you ever eat?"

"I dine out. Or at the hospital or not at all. Food doesn't appeal to me the way it used to. I'd just as soon do without it as much as I can. I've spent the last two years in Hardee's. For a while I quit Hardee's and went to Captain Jack's for the fish-boat special, a hunk of fried fish in a toy boat. You get to keep the boat. Then I was going to Arby's awhile, Wendy's, Popeye's. They're all good, all fine places, but in the end I went back to Hardee's. I feel at home there. They always take me in, give me a good hot meal, get me back on my feet. I appreciate that. You know?"

"I know."

"The fuck you do. You know nothing about it. You've had your head up your ass so long, son, it's a wonder you know where you are."

"What are you talking about?" Will says.

"You want it? You don't want it."

"Want what?"

"I'm talking about all of it. Claire. What you've done to her. Alice. Me. Yourself. I've been cursing you a long time."

"Well, go ahead. Get it off your chest. Don't hold back out of politeness."

"You want to know why I held back? It was because

162

Claire was in love with you. I never saw a woman so stupid-in-love before. Jesus. I always knew you were a thick-hided bastard but I hoped it was all for show. But ever since you dumped your little 'problem,' as you called it, on me last year and had me scrape your carelessness down the drain, I've known better."

"You were sympathetic at the time," Will says.

Danny leans forward in his chair. "Sympathetic? Sympathetic? There is no sympathy in those things, son. You've done it, you know what it is. You try not to think about what you're doing, and you get the lid on the god-damned dish just as fast as you can, and you pass it over to a nurse to get rid of. But yours I didn't pass on. I dumped it myself."

"Ease up, Cardozo."

"And I thought, God, this is the last chance, for all of us. For you to pull things together, and me, too, and never get this close to the edge again. But it didn't happen. I should have known. I should have known, because you did the same thing before, when your father died. Instead of seeing into it you looked past it and hardened your shell even more. Know what you said to me at the funeral? You don't remember, I'm sure."

"I remember, but it was because you were being maudlin."

"Maudlin? As I recall, what I said—and this was under the funeral tent, your mother standing there, everybody waiting around for the shovel detail to finish up—what *I* said was I loved your father. It took me two days to get the guts to say it, but it had to come out. Your mother was bawling; your father, who in my and everybody's opinion was a great man, was going into the ground. I was standing with you and her, and I said, 'I really did love that man.' And then you said, 'Go fuck yourself.' "

"Okay. I'm a son of a bitch. You've proved your point." Will puts his glass on the ground.

"Not a crack. Not a chink in the old armor, is there? Oh, well," Danny says. "Let's get drunk. Your way is better than mine, anyway. Look at me. I'm a wreck." He stands up, pours his drink into the pool. The ice cubes bob up and down; the brown stain of bourbon sinks a little, spreads, and then is lost in the turquoise glow.

"Got to get up at five tomorrow. Marshfield hunt. Tell you what. It'll be my last one. I'll get a buck tomorrow and I'll never hunt again after that," Danny says.

"Makes sense," Will says. "Since you'll be having full-time pussy again. Hard to leave a cunt for a hunt."

Cardozo is heavier than Will, but drunker and standing in the wrong place. He lands one hard punch in Will's belly but loses his balance; Will's fist in his ribs sends him lurching backward into the pool. He goes in fanny-first, his arms and legs reaching forward together. Will sees him sink to the bottom in a sitting position. Will sees his face, the eyes open, the mouth clamped shut, hair floating out. Parallel streams of bubbles rise to the surface from air in the folds of the clothes.

"Come up, asshole," he says. He can tell from the mouth that Danny is holding his breath. Will sits in the chair out of view of the pool bottom and counts the seconds on his watch. You can't drown yourself that simply. All good suicides involve speed and irreversibility, because the body will always move to protect itself against the sicko mind trying to do it in. The mind has to trick the body. Fill its pockets with stones. Tie a concrete block to its foot.

Thirty seconds.

He used to watch his father swim underwater in the creeks. Edmund would try to stay under a long time, playing, swimming underwater in a circle to come up behind Will or pinch his toe, or come up in the marsh without making a sound until Will cried, "Dad . . . *Dad!*" Sometimes, when his father went under, Will held his breath in order to get an idea of when his father's lungs would start to hurt and force him up.

Sixty seconds. Seventy. Cardozo's lungs aren't that good. Will moves to the edge of the pool. At its bottom the long arms still float out perpendicular to the body. The hair lifts out slowly. Will jumps in, surprised at how hard it is to get to the bottom. He grabs a handful of waving hair and kicks off against the concrete. They come up together, spitting water, thrashing and making noises like two bull alligators. Water sloshes up over the sides of the pool.

"I was starting to think I'd made a mistake in judgment," Cardozo's voice wheezes as he grasps the gutter. "I was starting to really believe what I said about you being a thick-hided bastard."

"Fuck you, Danny. Fuck you."

"That's all right, boy. Go ahead. I know I made you wet up your doctor shoes and your doctor watch and all. But it was worth it. Whooee, it was worth it."

"You're crazy, you know that? Carol was right. You are certifiable. Goddamn you." He unbuckles his watch and taps it on the concrete.

"Water-resistant doesn't mean waterproof," Cardozo says. "You gotta be careful, notice exactly what it says when you buy one. Everything this side of a sponge is water-resistant. Carol," he says, still in the water at the edge of the pool, laying his head down on his arms, "didn't save me. If she thought I was crazy she'd have tried to save me."

"I didn't save you either. Get out of the water. I'm going home." Will pulls himself out, walks to the car with water sloshing in his shoes, sucking at his feet. "Get out," he yells. Danny waves.

"Meet me at the Texaco station on Highway Seventeen. Five-thirty," Danny hollers. "I promise it'll be the last hunt."

Will unlocks his car.

"Well? What do you say?" Danny pulls himself out of the pool, black and bearish with the lights behind him, and dripping water.

"I don't think so."

"Come on, you fucking faggot! You saved my life; I know you want to go. Old times."

Will's elbow is out the window like a teenager's. The bourbon, the fight, the pool, his right hand on the key, the imminent grumble of the powerful engine make him feel like a young boy.

He says, "I don't want any more of your shit."

"There won't be any." Danny comes to the car.

"All right. Five-thirty."

"Yeah, five-thirty. If you have any bourbon—"

"I'll bring it."

"Good. I'm out. Look, it'll be all right, Reese. It'll work out. Watch."

"I want to ask you one thing." Will has some trouble getting the words out.

"What?"

"All this time, all these years, you've been following me. To Chapel Hill, med school. You've followed me, and what's more you've done dirty work for me all along. If I fucked up, you always made it right."

"Hell. I fucked up much more than you did."

"How could you help it? You were putting everything into my life instead of yours. I want to know why."

Danny runs his hand up over his forehead and through his hair in an uncharacteristic gesture, without irony; straight, worried. "Your life was always realer. I was a ghost to myself, a fake Jew, a poor imitation of a Southern gentleman, a masquerade as a student. I couldn't ever see anything there, no skin on my bones. Carol found out, I think. She said the same thing, said I had gotten myself confused with you."

"Claire is your way out."

"Out of your life? Maybe. But I love her. I've gotten more out of your life than you have, Bud." Danny hits the car door as you'd slap a horse on the flank, in encouragement and affection. "I've learned some things. I appreciate the use of your life. But when I really think about it, I'm not so sure it was always a case of me following you. Think it over. Sometimes maybe it was the other way around. What the shit difference does it make, right?"

"Right."

"One other thing," Danny says. "I don't know if she mentioned it to you: she's going back into nursing. Not OR, but something. Maybe ICU."

"Christ! ICU will kill her. What are you thinking of?"

"No, it won't. She can do it. She's born for it. She wants to go back."

"I don't believe you. Mind if I ask her?" Will says.

"Well, that's what I'm trying to get to. She's going back to nursing. She's not working for you anymore."

"Starting when?"

"Now."

"Okay. Now? Okay. Well, then, I guess you know what she wants. I always thought—"

Danny doesn't ask for the rest of the sentence. It would have been "that I'd rescued her and now you're shoving her back into it." But Danny is backing away, bending to untie his shoes at the same time, saying, "It'll be fantastic. Bring two bottles. I swear, Will."

His drive back into town is easy, for he is moving now with the current of time and events. That he is soaked through to the skin hardly occurs to him.

So Danny remembers that day, the funeral; Will, too, has a clear memory of the three of them under the canopy, the metal folding chairs, the plastic grass that gave an uncertain springiness to the earth they stood on, and the anger building in him like steam. All of the funeral requirements and paraphernalia started him off angry. It's all right when the dead person has been a long time dying, and death was expected: all right to have the tent and the hearse, the gray steel coffin and the fake grass and fake flowers. (Later he found out they were real: gladiolus and chrysanthemum wreaths with dark, shining greenery. How were they made to look so fake?) But when the death is a surprise, these trappings are wasteful, and almost an insult. People aren't ready for ceremony, still puzzling over the event itself. For Will it was unseemly that a funeral could be got up so quickly, as if these wreaths and drapes had been waiting in a convenient storage room just for his father. It was whipped together too fast. That morning he had fought with his mother when she came downstairs in a black dress with long sleeves and a small white collar.

"Where'd you get that?" he said. "I've never seen it."

"Belk's. Did you have breakfast?"

"Yeah." A plate with a cold fried egg was in front of him. Couldn't she see?

"When?" he asked, watching her pour a glass of tomato juice.

"When what?"

"When did you get the dress?"

"Yesterday." She drank the whole glass of juice, slowly and carefully, holding her upper lip out of the liquid, just resting the glass on her lower lip and pouring the stuff down her throat.

"You went out yesterday? You went *shopping* yesterday?" He yelled and jumped up from the table, which must have surprised her; she spilled a dribble of juice out of the corner of her mouth.

"I had to. I didn't have a good black dress. Why are you screaming?"

"Wait." He sat down. "Let me understand. You went to Belk's. Looked through the dress racks, picked out a dress. Or a couple of dresses. Then you went into the dressing room and tried them on, and looked in the mirror to see which one was best."

"Of course."

"What else did you buy?"

"Stockings. A slip."

He hated that puzzled look on her face.

He left the house and walked to the cemetery north of the city. Up East Bay Street, past the docks and tugs, two freighters, a banana boat white as the gulls circling it, and the sun on the water in chips of light; under the Cooper River Bridge, past the old jail to parts he'd never walked in before, a stretch of auto dealers and then the scrap-metal yard where rusting cars were piled six high on each side of the narrowed road. Beyond the junkyard the old cemetery was hidden, a secret garden the developers had not been able to touch. Graveyards may end as the last undeveloped land left to us.

A system of low walls and iron fences delineated the sections of the cemetery: Old Magnolia, where Confederates and statesmen and a poet or two were buried with their descendants; a Jewish section, with Hebrew letters on the stones and Joseph Cardozo under a slab of granite; a Lutheran section; a Catholic section, with the terrible rows of nun's graves sterner and lonelier than the nuns alive ever were; and an ancient tiny square dotted with the eighteenth-century graves of men who had only first names: Pompey, Nathaniel, Elijah. There were almost no vacancies now. The Reese family plot in Old Magnolia had room to squeeze in two more, Edmund and Marcella; Will would have to go out to one of the new cemeteries with flat bronze markers sunk deep enough into the earth so that a lawn mower could go right over them, the whole spread looking like a golf course. Here in Magnolia the stone markers were mossed and tilted; vines and briars obscured whole families. Well. Children might tend the plots of their parents, weed them and keep the stones clean, but sooner or later the living forget the dead, and the dead's stones, too. In a golf-course cemetery you pay the company for perpetual care. They mow you for eternity.

He was two hours early.

After a brief search among graves he half remembered from the funerals of aunts and grandparents, he found the place he was looking for, near the Reese plot along the riverbank, an old live oak thirty feet around at the base, its heavy limbs dropped to the ground, but still alive, still sucking out so much water that nothing else could grow beneath it, not even grass or weeds. In the white, soft dirt, the tree's roots surfaced and twisted and dove under again in their search for what they needed. Feathery resurrection fern covered the limbs like an unexpected growth of hair on an old man's back. He climbed onto one of the low limbs and followed its rise to the trunk, pulling himself with hands and knees up the last hump of it, then into the fork, a spacious hollow behind the ferns and massive limbs, ten feet above ground.

Past a barkless dead pine, yellow and raw, that partially obscured his view, he watched two old black men come down the road balancing shovels on their shoulders. They peeled the tarpaulin off the hole and looked in.

One said, "We got to pump it again. Put a box in this hole, it'll float up before the widow be home." The funeral director, a white man, came through the underbrush from his van with a contraption that he set at the hole's edge, letting a hose down into the hole. He braced his foot on the motor and gave the belt a couple of yanks. The pump sputtered and got going and then with a hungry *gurgle-suck* it pumped up a brown liquid and spewed it out a back hose down the hill.

"Run it till they come," the director said, wiping his hands on a towel. "Then get it out of sight. After the box is in, fill the hole fast." He looked down into the hole.

"Y'all done dug a goddamn well."

Then he busied around, fidgeted with the hoses, smoothed out a wrinkle in the grass, and brought wreaths out of his van to set between the tent and the hole. Over the noise of the equipment he didn't notice the cars till they were there, slowly pulling up off the road. He leaped to the grave, ripped the hose from the pump, and with the black men dragged the equipment into the azaleas. Then he unrolled another length of artificial grass over the edge of the grave and slunk back into the bushes. The black men came all the way to Will's tree. Car doors were slamming. People began to converge on the tent. Will saw Danny Cardozo take Marcella's arm and guide her through the old graves, so numerous and close together there was no pathway through them, to the new grave, while his father's friends shook hands with each other, moving in a quiet clump together. What Will could see from the tree was not unpleasing: the white-robed minister at the front of the plot, the people gathering in the noon stillness. He was just far enough away to get the view he wanted, and his strange downward perspective humbled the mourners: they appeared to shrink back as if toward those others under their feet. Yes, this spot would suit him fine.

But then the black men saw him. One looked up, and the other; then they both looked down. He hoped they wouldn't care. It was none of their business. But one called up to him, "Where you belong now, honey? They going to start up now," and the other one laughed. They shamed him out. He jumped down on the river side of the tree and circled around to avoid their laughs; he made it to the cars and waited until everyone was under the tent, and then he stepped out into their midst.

She had on perfume. Standing next to her, all he could see was her hands fiddling with the prayer book, turned to the wrong page. While the minister read the service Will watched her hands and thought of the brown water seeping back into the hole, and his anger began to build against her for the way she was seeping into his mind. He wanted to feel love for his father, he was waiting to feel it, but what was brimming in his heart was this disgust with her. He tried not to look at the hands, the skirt and feet in the corner of his vision; he tried to concentrate on the coffin, the steel-gray metal box, the man inside. He tried to send his love out to penetrate the box and be buried with the man, but then her hands moved, the wind moved the black hem of her dress; and her hand felt for his and grasped it. He jumped, he almost yelped. He thought he might possibly endure the hand for a minute or two, no longer, and he prayed for the minister to read fast and finish up. Finally it was over. The minister stepped forward to embrace Marcella, and she dropped Will's hand. Seconds more and he would have had to make a break for it, leaping over chairs and wreaths and coffin in his rage and fear.

Cardozo stepped up. Wearing a new suit. His eyes were red-rimmed. Marcella took both of Danny's hands, as if they were about to dance; then they hugged. Marcella sobbed on Danny's shoulder. Past the embrace, past the shade of the tent and their new black finery and the tears, Will could see the two old men lift their shovels in tandem, dirt flying in a spray through the sunlit air. Danny turned, his face teary. "I loved him," Danny said; whereupon Will uttered the obscenity that became Danny's sharpest memory of the funeral.

Will knew it was he who should have spoken of love. Not Danny Cardozo. Will stood in the sun under the old trees, twenty years old, hating his only remaining friend.

Driving home, he is happy. Oh, yes, things are going to turn out all right. Good, that Danny and Claire have paired off, solves a lot of problems when you really think about it. His big car moves powerfully and smoothly over the bridge, past the marina and the lighted boats. Like a boat himself now, he is floating on a tide, going along without a fight or a struggle. Let them have each other if that's what they want.

He won't be meeting Danny in the morning, that's sure. "So long, so long," he says out loud.

Marriage is a wordless dance, he thinks, swinging into his driveway, swinging again away from the world and into what is meant to be his heart's home. Like a dance around a pole, weaving the dancers together in a loose, unbreakable net. James Taylor is on the radio singing "Country Road." James Taylor and Carly Simon broke up. That split had to be a rough one. It's hard enough for ordinary people to part; but James, try forgetting Carly! Carly's mouth, eyes, those songs she sang. A mind like James's, a true North Carolina mind, doesn't divorce easy.

"James, son," he says, "why is that?"

In his ear some water breaks loose and runs out down his neck. Water has dripped all over the car seat and the floor of the car. He takes his clothes off on the back porch and hangs them across the railing, and has the feeling he is living one of his dreams, the nude-in-public dream, in which he marches down the street naked, not quite understanding why people are watching him. But no one watches him now. Naked and cold he has to reach back into his trousers for the kitchen-door key, as a shiver of memory raises the hair on his neck: a memory not from dreams or poems but from real nakedness as a boy, when they played in the yard under the spray of the hose into the nightfall, until his mother came and sent Danny home and picked Will up. She held him tight, carrying him inside; he tried to wrench himself away but found he could not move at all, not even his arms, because hers wrapped him hard, and he had to give up. She must have hated him even then. He was five. On the other hand, later on there was some evidence that she had loved him. When Beth was born, Marcella gave him a small heart-shaped box. He opened it suspiciously, and found it full of little white kernels, some hollow and brown inside, rattling around like unstrung beads.

"What are these things?" he said.

"Your baby teeth."

He was so embarrassed that he didn't ask any questions. It was as if they were the remains of a child who had died. Had she kept them for him? For herself? What but love could want to save a box of teeth?

He sneaks naked into the kitchen. All the lights are off. It must be past twelve, Alice will be asleep. Still, he closes the door as quietly as possible, pours a glass of bourbon in the dark, and opens the side-by-side freezer for ice. Its light falls on his body with an unwelcome glare, like a searchlight surprising a thief. His skin looks purplish; the hair on his belly is like the sparse hair on a sick dog, not enough to make fur to cover the skin but just *hairs,* separate and useless. Boxes of frozen food are piled in the freezer, with pictures of serving suggestions on the labels. Incredible. Who thought of it first: freezing food? He marvels at the shelves of it, still and silent and not rotting, in *his* freezer in *his* house. The animals are killed and washed and "flash frozen," whatever that means—it sounds like the work of a nuclear ice-bomb—and then the meat sits unchanging in the freezer while outside *he* grows slowly old. In the icy air coming at him like smoke his penis has shrunk back into itself. Cowardly son of a bitch. He closes the door and stands there to drink, hoping the bourbon will warm him from the inside. He can't risk a hot shower; the sound of it might wake Alice. He carries his drink with him upstairs, going slowly to keep the ice from clinking.

She sleeps light.

"You awake?" he whispers. She doesn't answer. He bends his knees to get down close to her face, but it's too dark to tell whether she is really asleep or not. He finishes off the drink and crawls into bed with regret for his lost shower. He tries to keep the mattress from moving and betraying his presence; he tries to slow down his breathing.

"Lost your pants at the hospital?" she says. Awake, then —watching him come into the room, watching him crouch naked to scrutinize her face.

"I fell in the pool at Danny's."

"Oh. I thought you were at the hospital."

"I was. Then I was there."

173

"Wild party, huh?"

"Nope. No party at all. Me and Danny." He could have had his shower after all, goddamnit. She was awake. Pretending. She rolls over and faces him. Her warm fingers touch his shoulder and spread out, and slide down his arm.

"You're frozen," she says. "You have goose bumps." It is unusual for her to touch him: the touch is what gives him the goose bumps. His body grows rigid. Her hand gets to his, her fingers snuggle up inside his the way her body would snuggle against his if he invited it. But only their hands touch. It is the most, right now, that he can do.

He has to keep reminding himself that he is alive. He has to try to remember that this woman is his wife.

It isn't that nothing is left. It is that what remains is such an old sad ghost of the thing that used to be, and he can't bear lying down with the vestiges. Hasn't he been looking for the thing that used to be, looking for it in Claire, looking for it in every woman giving birth on that stainless-steel table, looking for it desperately and pathetically even in the unfinished faces of his own daughters? And now he knows it is not to be found whole again; it is scattered and dispersed, past reassembling; blown ashes.

He wakes long before dawn, smiles, buries himself farther down into the covers, savoring the thought of Cardozo waiting in the gas station, at this moment still expecting Will to show, the fool—still not yet realizing there never was a chance of it. He'll wait a good half hour, maybe longer, and then when the sky is lightening in the east over the city skyline, it will come to him: he was duped. He'll know Will's warm in bed.

It isn't much in the way of consolation. But it's something. What did Danny think, that they'd all be pals?

He adds one more gratifying detail to the picture of Cardozo pacing up and down at the pumps, checking his watch. *No bourbon.* Then he goes back to sleep.

Fourteen

How fat Duncan is! He was fat when he first came to town, but now he is fatter. People fatten up near the sea, Alice has noticed. Air off the ocean is clean and makes you eat and sleep. Duncan has the habit now of walking along the Battery wall every evening, filling his lungs with clean air, and then going back to his big house on the boulevard to eat his supper.

What does a fat man look like naked? Fatter? Not as fat? She has never seen one. Duncan's belly hangs out over his belt, a cartoon of a fat man. His Madras jacket is too big in the shoulders. He shoves his hands down in the pockets and flaps them like an angry bird. Naked, she decides, Duncan would look nobler. In his funny jacket and his wrinkled linen trousers he looks like a man in another man's clothes.

He's nervous. He says, "Thank y'all for coming. Marcella will be down directly, I guess." He glances up at the winding stairway at the end of the hall. "You know how she is, getting dressed."

Alice doesn't know, but she can imagine Marcella sitting before her marble-topped dressing table, the mirror lit by bulbs all around, the surface littered with jars and pots, creams and perfumes. Marcella would take her time. She would pick out certain underclothes, silk and lace things, instead of grabbing whatever's clean. Alice has never had expensive underwear. Her mother used to make underwear for brides, stitching on lace that the bride had ordered from

Europe, but Alice always had cotton bras and pants from Sears. Marcella's bed is as fine and expensive as her lingerie; Alice has seen it, the beige-and-white silky spread, scalloped and trimmed along the edges; ruffled shams embroidered white-on-white with Marcella's initials (her new ones); and an assortment of organdy-over-pastel pillows, round, oval, shell-shaped. The bed is huge. And under the pillows and spread the bedclothes are made up in a special way, with the corners of the heavy percale sheets folded down tight, and a soft white blanket as light as air, then a thin blanket cover and the satiny spread.

All—the mirror and creams and camisoles and carefully laid bed—all for fat Duncan Nesmith. Proof of love, proof of irony. When Marcella does come down the stairs her eyes are on her husband. Love makes fools of its spies, those watchers who think they know, the ladies who thought she married for money, the scornful son. Duncan takes Marcella's hand at the foot of the stairs. Her dress is beige, her only jewelry a miniature basket of woven gold, holding flowers with diamond heads. She is beautiful. She loves a fat man.

Will is sullen and clumsy. He pours a bourbon drink and stirs it by swinging the bottom of the glass in circles. Some drops of the drink splash out onto his shirt. Marcella steps in front of him to blot the damp spot with a handkerchief. Alice, standing to one side, sees a muscle tighten in his neck as Marcella dabs at his shirt. Duncan, too, stands aside, holding a drink in each hand. When Marcella moves back, Duncan passes a glass to her.

"When did you start drinking?" Will says to Marcella.

"Start? But I've always had a cocktail when I wanted one."

"I thought only sherry and wine."

"Oh, no," she says. "Whatever gave you that idea? All these years you thought I was a teetotaler? I suppose it just shows how we make mistakes about each other."

Alice notices a smell in the house, like the smell of incense, but Marcella would not have incense. The candles on the dining table must be scented. She can see them through the open door. Alice knows how important this dinner is to Marcella, who is doing a good job of appearing to be careless and indifferent. Maybe that is what she always does.

"Y'all come on in the dining room," Duncan says; he leads the way. His jacket is too short in the back. The seat of his pants is tucked up between his buttocks, and his feet, in tasseled loafers, splay outward. In the dining room one wall is a mirror, reflecting the chandelier and the table, the crystal and candles, the four people clotted together at one end of the room like the first guests at a party, carrying on a makeshift conversation until the others arrive and they can get lost in the crowd. But here there will be no others.

"I'm going to need another drink," Will says to his reflection in the mirror. "Alice? Marcella?"

"You haven't even finished that one," Marcella says.

"I will, by the time I get to the bar." He gulps down the last two inches of bourbon.

"How is he?" Marcella says when Will is out of the room.

"I don't know," Alice says.

"Has he been sick?" Duncan says. "He looks fine." Will comes back, and that brief intimacy among the other three, whispering about Will, is gone.

"Will, I want to tell you about our latest venture," Duncan says. "I know you don't like the Tahitian, but—"

"The what?"

"The Tahitian. The hotel. We named it the Tahitian."

"Good name."

"Thanks. It gets across the idea of relaxation, with a slight exotic touch."

"Sure. Thatched cabanas?"

"Yes! You know, I thought you'd come around to the idea after a while. Not to put anyone down, but you Southerners sometimes balk at the idea of something new; then, when it comes to the real thing, you'll go for it."

"I believe that's true," Will says, taking another long drink. "The flesh is weak."

"Anyhow, what's on the boards now is even more exciting. We think you and Alice will be real enthusiastic about it. We sure are." He looks at Marcella; she smiles.

"What is it?" Will says, and swallows more bourbon.

"A theme park."

"Theme park?"

"Yes, you know, like Six Flags or Carowinds."

"Disney World."

"No, no, we want to avoid any comparison with Disney World. This will be much more low-key, more in tune with the environment and related to the historical traditions of the area. I don't need to explain to you that it's all strictly confidential right now, I mean because we've got to sew up some federal money. You don't put something like this together with private dollars. Not anymore."

"I thought grant money had dried up."

"Not yet, not yet. That's the thing, why we've got to hurry. We can get it. I've talked to the fellows who know. We can get it if we don't run into any trouble—objections and so forth."

"But who could object?" Will says.

"Well, no one really, this thing is going to be a shot in the arm for the local economy. Three hundred jobs the first year, what with waiters and maids and maintenance and up to a quarter-million visitors. But we do have to fill in a limited amount of marshland."

"What's the theme?"

"Pirates. To tie in with the riverfront. We'll have a couple of pirate ships that actually go out, take people on the river, out to Drum Island, where we'll give them maps to dig for buried treasure. Everything will have the pirate theme. Our hotel, the restaurant, the villas. It's a natural because there really were pirates here. One of them was hanged on the Battery. We plan to reenact it."

"What do you think, Mother?" Will says.

"I think it's marvelous. Don't you?"

"I'm a little worried about the timing. The idea is out of this world. But hasn't its time come and gone? Aren't we running out of gas, isn't the day coming when no one will be able to travel?"

"I don't think so," Duncan says. "Not at all. Gas is down again. Americans will always travel. And the South is where they'll travel to. Don't you know this is the boom region, this is the Sun Belt?"

"Yeah. I know that. But I've got a feeling the boom is about over. The New South is about to age overnight like those children in the tabloids. I see empty hotels and abandoned villas and unthatched cabanas all over the Sun Belt. Rats scurrying through the deserted theme parks."

"Oh, Will, do stop," Marcella says. She smiles, with a glance toward Duncan.

"I'm serious. We're on the verge of collapse," Will says.

"That's ridiculous," Marcella says. "The city is thriving. A house on the peninsula now runs two hundred and fifty thousand dollars, average. There's no collapse coming."

Alice asks for another drink. Duncan makes one for everybody and serves them on a tray.

"What's more, we're in for a doozy of a racial war," Will says in a lower voice, eyebrows slightly raised.

"Why don't we just take our drinks with us to the table," Marcella says. "I think Queen probably has everything ready."

"You really think some kind of serious trouble is in store?" Duncan asks as they all take seats. "I thought all that was over and settled. Everything's integrated, right?"

Marcella sits up suddenly straighter in her chair to indicate that Queen has come into the room, but Will does not stop.

"Look at it this way," he says to Duncan. "If you were trapped with no way out, wouldn't you try to bust out—no matter where you were—slit the throat of whatever's in your way?" Queen passes the oysters in a silver casserole. When everyone has been served she leaves the dish on the table in front of Marcella and returns to the kitchen.

"I heard of a hotel in Eleuthera burned down by the waiters and maids," Will adds.

"Oh, for God's sake." Marcella rises out of her chair.

"No kidding. The Bahamas have big problems in that respect. Jamaica, Bermuda. Tourists don't like racial war."

"He's right," Duncan says to Marcella. "He's got a point."

"What is this?" Will says.

"Oysters."

Duncan drops one into his mouth. "I never thought I'd

learn to eat the damn things," he says. "Your mother's a heck of a cook. I'll eat anything she puts before me."

"I thought this was Queen's work," Will says, looking up.

She smiles at him. "My recipe," she says. Queen brings in more food: rice and salad and bread.

Between mouthfuls of lettuce, Will says, "The only other thing that really concerns me, Duncan, because of your location at the Tahitian, is your water supply. How is that holding up?"

"Water supply? Just fine. I wasn't aware of any trouble with water over there. I mean it tastes funny, but all beach water—"

"Tastes funny?"

"Well, you know . . . yeah, it tastes funny. Why?"

"At least you still have some. Here's what's happening. This was in *Newsweek*. Groundwater is being pumped out of the aquifers faster than it can be replaced. And when that happens . . . sinkholes. The ground drops out from under whatever is on it. Swallows up cars, trailers, buildings. Then salt water backs up into the wells. The process is irreversible. There's no way to get fresh water back in there. Salty tap water is already showing up in Beaufort." He pushes his plate toward the center of the table. "I am proud to say I never ate an oyster in my life. When I was a child I swore I'd never do it, and I haven't yet."

"When you were a child you were a sissy and a scaredy-cat," Marcella says. "You still are. You are taking your own sense of doom and casting it over the rest of the world. When the rest of the world is just fine."

"I get your drift," he says. "And you may be right. I can't say I haven't thought of that possibility."

"Always afraid. He *was,* Duncan. That's why he's a pessimist now. Edmund was pessimistic but at least he kept it to himself."

"But what was Will afraid of?" Duncan whispers.

"Nothing real," Marcella says, and folds her long, thin fingers over Duncan's stubby, square-nailed ones. Alice looks away, embarrassed by the hands: the intimacy of the fingers touching each other.

"Alice. What do you think? Of Duncan's project?" Marcella looks hopefully down the table.

"Oh, Duncan, can't you do something else? Why not build another mall? It's about time for another one, people are tired of Northgate Square. A new mall in North Charleston?"

"Well, yes. But somebody else would do the park, anyway. No question about it. The land is available. It's zoned recreational-residential."

"Then build houses and playgrounds on it."

"The acreage is too expensive. All that waterfront, right on the highway. I barely got the jump on an Atlanta outfit for the options, and there's a bunch of Kuwaitis making *me* offers already."

"Oh God," Will says. "Let him have the goddamned thing. No, Duncan, you're right. We'd rather have you than those fuckers. Atlantans and Arabs! They're the same, except the Arabs are cleaner. Atlantans will mess with anything."

"Confidentially, son, it isn't just the Nesmith Company in on this deal. I represent a group of investors who prefer to remain in the background, so to speak."

"Who are they?"

"Well, as I said, at this point they want to keep a low profile."

"So! The Cincinnati connection."

"Oh, no. This is local money. Local people. In fact the initial idea came from them. Quite a few names you'd recognize. But with the environmental groups the way they are now, these people want to wait till the idea kind of sinks in, in the community. They think since I'm sort of an outsider I'm the best one to get it off the ground. Later, everybody'll be behind it."

"Local money? Wait a minute. Local money is going into a pirate park?" Will laughs. "Don't kid me. There is no Charleston man who'd put money into something like that."

"It's a sound investment, son."

"That isn't what I mean. I mean *no true son of this city*

would back a goddamned pirate park right there on the river! Don't try to tell me it's local money. Names I'd recognize! I know where the money comes from, Duncan. I've seen how it works."

"What do you mean?" Marcella says.

"It's money without history. It's cut loose, and roams, raids us. Buys what of us it wants. It's cur-dog money. It is without training, without honor."

"You're worse than I thought you were," Marcella says. "You're unforgivable."

"I never asked for forgiveness, Mother."

"Then what is it? Tell me. What is it you want?"

Will stands, knocking his chair to the floor behind him. "I want . . . a bracelet of bright hair about the bone. A fine and private place. I want to keep house unknown." He picks up the chair and nods to Duncan with a little bow, then sits. Marcella stares at him. Duncan clears his throat.

"How about coffee, Marcella? Don't we need a little coffee?"

With Marcella gone for coffee, no one speaks. Alice sinks gratefully into the silence. Will is past her reach now, into the gloom of poetry and bourbon. She wishes she still smoked dope. When she used to do it, it wouldn't matter to her how far away he got. He could go to the moon, float out past her fingers, skimming into blackness: she didn't have to care. Sometimes just by remembering what it was like she can get to feeling a little high. She can snap the lines that hold her and drop into carelessness. Who cares if poor Duncan fiddles with his fork, drawing the heavy tines over the tablecloth? Who cares that Will is already out past Earth's pull, as he leans in his chair and stares into his cold food?

She is dreaming: I will get the children grown, at least. Then there will be nothing.

Oh, Claire should have thanked her lucky stars and held on to him. Didn't she know what she had? His tall lankiness, the way he moved like an adolescent boy not yet comfortable with his filled-out shoulders, long arms and legs, and the way like a boy he made love with astonishment, with surprise! He used to like to sleep with his head on her belly.

182

Sometimes he dressed her in the mornings. She was sure for a long time that she was the only one he'd ever want.

How can Claire give him up?

Maybe love doesn't fade; it just moves on. But so easily? The man and woman she saw in the red car were smiling. They weren't bruised or wounded. As for Will, if he knows, there's been no visible damage to him either.

Marcella comes back with coffee, composed now as if she had shed her anger in the kitchen. Nothing is wrong, her face says. Her long arm reaching out to the cups pours coffee for everyone. Alice relaxes.

But when Marcella speaks, her voice is tight. Alice has underestimated her. That voice is full of rage. Her first words are shaky.

"Your father forbade me to take a drink in front of you," she says. "I thought he was wrong. But he had a certain light he wanted you to see me in, to see the world in. I went along with it, but I wish I had not. You got a warped view of things, the way he protected you. And from what? He protected you from false dangers. Then he died, and you were lost. He taught you that the world was calm and dull. When you found out different, you got even more scared."

"Spare me this analysis of my childhood, please," Will says.

"Oh, of course. You just go on ignoring us, leaning back in your chair, pretending to be so happy. You discourage other people's plans because you're unhappy yourself."

Will laughs. "But I'm not unhappy. Your whole argument fails because you're wrong on that. I'm not unhappy."

"No?"

"No."

Marcella's voice now has lost its trace of shakiness. It is iron. Will does not seem to notice that the voice is set toward him and not about to let him go.

"Well, good," she says. "I guess you do have cause for happiness. Considering the events of the day."

"What events? I haven't had any events. I spent the day at the office. What are you talking about?"

"I'm talking about Danny Cardozo and Claire Thibault getting married."

"Oh." Will looks at Alice. "Yes. They're going to get married," he says.

"No. They got married. Danny called me just before you came. They got married this morning," Marcella says.

Will's chair slowly comes up straight. "When?"

"This morning."

"Ah. Pretty sneaky. I guess I'm out a receptionist. Well, I knew they were planning it, but I didn't know . . . Danny called you?"

"Yes. He's been very thoughtful toward me. Duncan, you remember the note he sent when we got back from our honeymoon. It was dear. I'm very happy for him. He says she's a dream girl."

"She is," Will says. Marcella drops a cube of sugar into her coffee.

"Nice for Danny to get a new start," she says.

"Yes," says poor Duncan. "I guess we know what a new start can do for you, eh, Marcella? Everybody should have one."

"They're hard to come by," says Marcella.

On the way out, Will lifts a fifth of bourbon from Duncan's bar. No one stops him. He walks in front of Alice to the street. Marcella and Duncan stand together in the doorway until Alice and Will are in the car. Marcella's face is drawn. In the car Alice says, "I know all about it."

"Claire and Danny?"

"Claire and you."

He is dumbfounded. *At least he doesn't try to hide it,* Alice thinks. He stares at her, then takes a breath.

"Alice, if you could do me the greatest favor in the world, we would not talk about this right now. Just let's wait awhile. I— How did you find out about it?"

"Marcella. Someone told her. She told me."

"I'm sorry."

"What will you do?" she asks.

"There's nothing to do." He starts the car.

In the Battery gardens the oaks are lit from below; their slant, thick trunks and branches throw shadows up on the roof of leaves. From parked cars on the other side of the trees comes the music of young romance, the smooth songs accompanying what must be awkward embraces. She has never made love in a car. Or anywhere except her own bed. Near the park benches the red tips of cigarettes move and burn, where homosexuals wait in the dark on the slim chance that love will show up tonight, in spite of its repeated failures to do so in the past.

You're not supposed to count the failures, though, when you hope. It's like tossing coins. For a given toss, the chance is even, unlinked to history.

"Pirates," she says.

"Yeah. God. Maybe we should move."

"To where?" she asks. The idea sounds so good she can hardly believe he said it. A new place. A normal house, with walk-in closets and a den, bunk beds for the children. Controlled access, a guardhouse, a sentinel at the gate.

"I don't know. There isn't anywhere," he says. He's right. There isn't anywhere like that for him. She could do it. She could leave home in an instant, as most women could, and make a new one somewhere else. It is men to whom home means a certain place, a territory marked and held. He could not leave now.

"It's all right," she says. "The trouble's all over; you'll see."

"Trouble's not over, Alice. Trouble is not ever over."

"But you're drunk now. Things look worse than they really are. You— She should have told you she was getting married. She must have known it would— Or, I don't know, maybe she thought this way would be less of a shock—"

"Don't talk about it."

"All right," she says.

"I'll tell you, Danny should have called me. He should have told me."

"Yes."

"Instead, he calls my mother. What a prick."

"Maybe he couldn't get you."

"He can always get me. I can always get him."

She watches him drive. He's thinking so hard that his face wrinkles in a frown. She would rather see plain sorrow than that drunken, labored thought on his face. Can't he simply grieve, let something in him go? There is nothing to be won now. It is time for him to turn back to her. *Look,* she wants to say to him, *here I am. Have you forgotten all about me? I am still here, a backward magic trick. I didn't vanish; I stayed.*

When he stops in front of their house, she gets out, then leans down to say, "I'll send Iris down."

He says nothing, stares ahead with a burnt-out look, tapping fingers on the steering wheel.

"Will?"

He frowns. His bourboned mind is not on her.

Alice says, "It will only be a minute." She closes the door and hurries inside. Upstairs, she finds Iris sleeping on the children's bed, just at their feet; but before she can reach out to wake Iris, she hears the sound of Will's car pulling away from the curb. From the window she sees him drive slowly to the corner and stop, then take off fast. After he's gone, the street is empty. She can hear no other cars. It is entirely possible that he won't be back.

The night is rich and promising, like good soil. It is warm again. The air through the window feels like breath from a living warm-blooded animal. She knows that he is without a place to go; he'll have to wander, drive the night streets. She has a clear notion of what assails him, too; what thoughts have made him take to the darkness. Women have failed him, he's thinking. He always thought he was doing such a service to them all, in work and love both; pictured himself as the man who helped women; and now he is the man women have let down. Marcella left him, early in life and again when she married Duncan. Claire has failed him now, and he's thinking how comical she has made him look, how dispensable. At last it is all too much for him.

Warm, moist night comes into the house. When Alice walks downstairs, her hand on the stair railing gathers dampness. She looks in the rooms, the hall and kitchen. The house already seems empty, the furniture waiting to be packed up. She goes upstairs again and takes a shower. It is past one o'clock, but she is not sleepy.

In the shower she washes her hair and lets the water rain into her mouth. She dresses slowly and carefully, then gets her suitcase out of the third-floor closet and packs it.

"Wake up, Iris," she says. "Carry Marcy for me. Come on, you must. We're in a hurry. We've got to get them out of here fast."

Fifteen

He loves his car for the loyalty with which it moves him over the surface of the earth. It's a big, silent pal like Silver or Trigger who'll stick with you when the going gets rough, who'll help you make a getaway or round up bastards or mosey on home. There will never be cars like this again, with the world in a general shrivel. The future is so small! A round, tiny place at the wrong end of a telescope. Living quarters will be mean, like Danny's. Jesus. Surely Claire won't go there. They'll have to live at her place. He imagines Claire crouched in a corner of a bare room with old magazines and carpet remnants about her. He is as helpless as a bride's father, slammed out, wanting to follow where he can't go. Private, keep out. And you can't know whether a marriage is good unless you are in it. You can't draw conclusions from a couple's behavior. He never thought his parents' marriage worth a dime: they talked to each other like business partners. But he must have been wrong.

Could have been wrong, too, about Marcella and Duncan. He is surprised that Marcella knew about his affair, yet never mentioned it to him. He never thought she had the patience to let events unwind at their own speed, to refrain from interfering. So she did tell Alice. But she didn't come to him, she didn't go to Claire. She didn't meddle. He is surprised. And he is surprised by the way she behaved with Duncan around. He had expected flirtatiousness, the coquettish eye-batting that identifies a woman who's sold her love. He had not expected those hands on the table together. Or the way she stood on her porch a half step behind Duncan, her arm loose about his waist, when Will and Alice were leaving. In Duncan's company she was not the woman who had irritated Will so many years. She was solid and measured, and, God, even subtle, even dangerous. She went for his throat instead of allowing him to drag on with his usual despicable games. And she'd made the right lunge. It was a shock to him, though they'd warned him. He had not believed the marriage would happen.

When you are proved wrong about one thing, as he was about Danny's intentions, you forfeit faith in your powers of judgment. When men found out the earth revolved around the sun, they knew they were in trouble. If they'd been wrong there, what about the circulation of blood? And the four humors? What about music of the spheres? They had to go back over everything and rethink the world. Shift, slide. Everything must move when the error is discovered. Everything is called into doubt.

He'll never know. He'll see Claire on the street, dressed in wife's clothing, smiling, and he won't know whether she is all right or not.

He circles the city. Drives past Marcella's house again, where the lights are all off. Then north up one riverbank, across town, and south on the other river. This place could never be evacuated in an emergency. Traffic would snarl on the bridges and on the one main road out to the north. Best way out would be by boat if you had one, and maybe he ought to get one, just a dinghy kept hidden in the marsh.

After completing the circle he cuts into the peninsula to the middle neighborhoods, and Claire's house. He parks and turns off the headlights. The block used to excite him at night, the lights on in apartments, the occasional shadow of a figure in a window. Sometimes he would sit in the car awhile just for the solitude, considering her street his own. Now it is not. He reaches for the bottle of bourbon under the seat. He has a long suck on it and carries it with him down the driveway.

Back in the small courtyard her lights are still on, in the

upstairs room. He settles down under a tall hedge by the far wall with a hand on the neck of his bottle. Through black twigs and leaves he stares at the lit windows. When he closes his eyes, the yellow squares are still on his retina; they sink to dark red and brown. He dozes for a few minutes, recognizing sleep by the chill it brings to his bones. At two-fifteen there is activity in the streets. Car doors, revved engines, people calling to one another in darkness. The bars have closed. People have to come home now, whether they want to or not. By and by they settle down, finding places for their cars, getting into their apartments and shutting themselves and their troubles inside. Oh, he'll go home, too. He's no wanderer, capable of taking off to who knows where just because home hasn't held him. He thinks he's like most men. Most men will take off when they can, but after a while they get tired of it, drink too much, miss their children, need what's back home. He'll go home.

One long last night is all he asks. Bourbon. Cold air. The ache in his legs, the hard ground he sits on. It's a hunt, after all. One last hunt, to see what he can see.

Her light goes out. Two-twenty. The schedule's a little different from the old one. When he was here they never had the lights on past one o'clock. Even when they stayed up late, the lights were off, she liked them off, and then they could fall asleep without the bother of reaching for the switch. . . .

He scratches in the leaves and rubble. He makes a bald spot on the ground. The surface of the hard dirt is broken by pieces of ancient junk that haven't gotten fully covered yet. Two nails, half a hinge, a piece of blue-and-white china. Dead men's trash lies everywhere under this city.

At three-twenty he crawls out of the bushes, runs in a low crouch across the empty courtyard into the shadow of the carriage house. He waits there until his breaths come slow and even, which is quite some time. The moon hangs fat and low. The key is ready in his hand, the small, Clairelike key, pretty key. He unlocks and opens the door without a noise. His heart drums again and his lungs speed up. The room is different. Everything is in its usual position, but the room is different, it's against him now. The sofa and wooden chairs, the plants seem all turned to face him, hostile. The smell of the room is not at all the old smell. It is partly cigarette smoke, Danny's, and partly something foreign. Will tries to remember which boards creak as he crosses the room and starts up the stairs, but he is not overly careful. If they are already asleep, as he has calculated, they won't hear. If they are awake, well, what's he got to lose.

The sight is not the shock he thought it would be, the low mound they make together in bed. At first that is all he can make out, a whitish hump. Then legs become clear, and the rest. They are facing him, dead asleep. Danny lies behind Claire, holding on to her, his arm beneath her and his hand coming out under her thigh, his top arm resting on her side, hand up to her shoulder. They are like two naked children, trusting. They both knew he had a key, goddamnit! Why didn't they take it away from him?

They are breathing at different rates. Claire's breasts and stomach move, Danny's shoulders rise and fall, their rhythms together for a while and then not together, then together again. Lovers' flawed synchrony. This fascinates him for a while. Then he scans the room for other details. Danny's clothes on a chair, shirt and jacket draped on the back, pants on the seat, shoes toed in underneath. What does that mean? She has not made space for his things yet in her closet or in her dresser. But she will. She will have to double up her sweaters and other folded clothes so that he can have two of the drawers. Yes. This is a permanent arrangement, this bed and marriage. The way they are lying close, the way the man enfolds and protects the woman, even in sleep. It's real. Claire's upturned face is without expression. He did not actually hope to read happiness in her sleeping face. But her closed eyes and mouth have a peaceful look at least.

What they have done is eliminate the middleman. They needed him, but when he failed them both, they skipped over him to get to each other.

It is hard for him to take his eyes from their two bodies. Claire's nakedness, directed toward Will, hypnotizes him. Her nipples and hair look darker, as if already she has undergone change, turned foreign. In Danny's sleeping body is an unguarded peaceful look Will has not seen since the earliest days, the boyhood days. Now that it is done, now that they are gone from him for sure, the pure wonder of their being a couple strikes him as lucky and marvelous. He is almost proud of the match, as if he had thought it up and arranged it himself. They are perfect for each other! Why did he miss it before? Look how they fit, his knees behind hers like that.

There is one more thing he needs to know. The extent of his losses. How deep must his mourning go? But miraculously now, after seeing them, he finds no mourning at all in his heart. Some things will be hard, he knows. He looks at Claire's feet, which are nestling against each other, ball into arch, trying to get warm. He has seen them do that before. She needs a cover. But covering her is something he leaves to Danny, along with every other intimacy. It will be hard. But his big feeling is regret, not grief. He will miss her. He won't die. In fact, the other loss is almost more grievous. Danny is gone more finally and certainly than Claire is.

They move. The woman is turning over, still under the man's arm, turning within the embrace to lie facing him. Will sees the man's face now, and the woman's white back, haunch, leg.

So long, then. There was something that could have been important but never made it. Will lost it by pretending not to see. Three years Danny lived in that squalor and Will never went there, not even to give him a ride to the hospital, pretending he didn't know, pretending he didn't care. *I did care, though, Dan. Jesus.*

He lets his sadness settle, waits for his throat to relax and his eyes to dry. Leaning against the wall, he lets his breathing approximate theirs. Their breaths are deeper. He has to take in more air to stay with them. After a while he is ready.

So long, then. He begins backing down the staircase, more quietly than when he came up, with more to lose. He is free of them now, and no sense risking that freedom. On the narrow landing he turns and takes the remaining steps with care, lets himself out the door noiselessly, and relocks it. In the moonlit courtyard he fairly leaps away from the carriage house across the yard. The night is open. Thin clouds move fast across the moon. Roofs and chimneys make a crenellated silhouette between him and the lower sky. On the way out he tosses Claire's key under the Japanese plums.

At home the gates are open. Alice does these favors for him and he never acknowledges them. This time he'll thank her, for more than opening the gates; he'll thank her for a lot of goddamned things. He'll tell her everything at once, all about Claire, and he'll admit to having made mistakes. Admit that Marcella deserves happiness, and that Duncan is good-hearted, and that outsiders are not the only pillagers afoot in the land. Should he tell about Claire's abortion? That might be going too far. Maybe, depending on how she takes the rest . . .

He had thought her car was in the driveway. But there is no car, and no one in the house.

Then he remembers. He had driven off without taking the baby-sitter home; the idea of going to Claire's blocked out more responsible thoughts. So maybe Alice has taken Iris home. In the children's room he tries to piece together what happened. Their bed is empty but rumpled, the feather pillows still keeping the shape where their heads had lain. Once in his hunting days a rabbit started up out of the marsh at his feet, and leaning down he noticed the rounded-out hollow where it had slept; but even as he watched, the bent grasses began to straighten, began to refill the rabbit's space. He lifts a pillow, and its feathers plump out, leaving no trace of a child.

Fear comes back, the fear that first seized him last year when a dentist showed him the X ray of Beth's skull. A skull itself is unidentifiable, symbol of a general, not a particular, doom. But in this film, barely visible around the death's-head, was the soft envelope of a profile, flesh of Beth's cheeks, Beth's nose, Beth's chin, unmistakable. He had crumpled the film and threatened the astounded dentist with his fists.

Where are they? Where can they all have gone?

He thinks. Alice doesn't like to leave the children alone at night, so she might have taken them along when she drove Iris home. But it's too late. They've had plenty of time to get to Iris's and back.

He calls the emergency room. A nurse he doesn't know says there have been no admissions since a stabbing at eight o'clock. In desperation he dials Claire's number. Danny was sleeping on the phone side, he remembers.

"It's me," he says when Danny answers.

"What do you want?" Danny says, anger already in his half-waked voice. "No. Let me warn you first. This could be the last straw. I mean it, watch your step. All the funny stuff is over."

"I can't find Alice. She's gone, and the girls are gone."

"What do you mean, gone?"

"I came home and they were gone. I'm afraid something has happened to them."

Danny doesn't speak for a moment. Then he says, "Will, is her car there?"

"No."

"Okay. Now just wait. She'll call you, probably. Wait for her to call you."

"How the hell can she call me, Cardozo, if something's happened to them? I think someone broke into the house."

"Was the door forced?"

"No."

"Or a window?"

"No."

"So just wait, Will. It's all you can do."

"What do you mean?"

"She's left you," Danny says.

"No, she wouldn't do that."

"She would."

"I think I should call the police."

"How drunk are you?"

"What does that have to do with it? You think I don't know what I'm talking about? She isn't here. I looked everywhere, Danny, and now I'm really beginning to worry, I really am, what if they—"

"All right, Will. All right. How about if I come over there and we'll decide what to do. How about that?"

"Yeah. I think so, Danny. And I think we should do something, because if someone took them, he's just getting a head start. I think I'm going to call the cops."

"Wait till I get there. Wait," Danny says.

After he hangs up, Will stands in the hall.

"Alice!" he calls, as if she might be hiding in a dark spot that he missed. "Alice!" He moves through the empty house, bottom to top, in one room after another turning on lights, ending on the third floor, where in a corner of the guest room he sees two suitcases on the floor, pulled out of the closet. Alice's small canvas bag is not there in its usual place. The house is blazing with light.

Sixteen

Iris had not known right away what was happening. Sleep still fuzzed her thinking, and the house was dark. Mrs. Reese was pushing her down the stairs, out of the house, saying, "Hurry," and her hand in the small of Iris's back gave a shove when Iris hesitated at the door. Marcy's arms around Iris's neck weren't hanging on tight; Iris had to tilt herself to keep the child's loose head from lobbing backward. Was it fire, burglars? She locked her arms around Marcy and held her so close the weight seemed like her own.

Mrs. Reese was whispering orders. "Put her in the back seat. Here! Hurry!" She took Iris's elbow. "You get up front," Mrs. Reese said. Iris had never heard her talk like that. Mrs. Reese backed the car out of the driveway, nervously looking up and down the street. She drove off without closing the gates.

"Where are we going?" Iris said.

"I don't know yet." The voice was sharp, so Iris didn't ask anything else.

Then she went numb with wonder. It was a turn of events: she and the children kidnapped by the children's own mother! She should have foreseen it. She had read an article. Most kidnappings now are done by a parent. If she had only thought of Randall, she might have had an idea this could happen.

"First I have to see something," Mrs. Reese said.

She drove across town and down a side street, slowing the car to a creep, stretching her neck to look at the cars parked on the left side of the street.

When she stopped, Iris recognized Dr. Reese's car, the Oldsmobile. There was no one in it.

Mrs. Reese sat still, looking at the empty car. "I'll be back," she said. "Wait here, Iris."

In Claire's dark driveway Alice walked close to the trees. Her half-formed thought was to get him and take him home, like a wounded animal that has to be caught for its own good. She thought he'd be sitting in the courtyard, the way he sat on his own porch at night when he was at loose ends. But the little bench near Claire's door was empty. Claire's house was dark. Unaccustomed to being outside in full darkness, Alice shrank back under the spindly trees. He was here somewhere. It took all her courage to come looking for him, to come stalking her husband in another woman's yard. But it was a last chance. If she could get him now and stop his pain, he could recover. She understood his obsession better now; understood that it was not exactly with the person of Claire. He'd always had a nameless, unanchored longing; and when, at critical points in his life, a period of intense longing coincided with the appearance of a suitable object, he fell for it head over heels, and believed he had discovered a great passion. Poetry, friendship, work, women—each at one time he'd held to be the center of his life.

But since the origin of his passion was internal, the chosen objects couldn't hold him long; and he had to feed his yearning with yet more loss. The deepening spiral could not end well for him; she had to get him out of it.

Across the yard she saw the hedge tremble. Then a man broke through the foliage. She didn't call to him. He was running the way soldiers cross a field of fire, head down and knees bent. She didn't call because he looked strange crouching like that, not like a normal man. But at Claire's door he stood upright, and looked around. Then he put both hands on the door, unlocked it carefully, slipped in and shut the door behind him without a sound.

Alice moved out from under the trees. The cobblestoned

yard under moonlight looked glossy as wet rocks in a stream, colorless but gleamy. She stood watching the house. He had gotten away from her. How much could she do, after all, if he had lost his senses? Would another woman wait for him now? Oh, if he had given a sign! The slightest sign would have been enough, considering her auguring instincts. She didn't require verbal or even physical assurance; he could have only looked her way, leaned in her direction, and she would have taken it as a sign. But he'd lost his senses. Not wits, senses; he was mad in his heart. At last she left the courtyard, walking fast to her car double-parked in the street.

The marriage could have survived the worst of what they did to it, as long as there was a certain shared sanity. But he had gone through that door, crazed as a beaten fighter who stumbles back onto the winner's neck, stupid with defeat.

Even Claire would not help him now. Why do you think she and Danny got married, Will? To cut themselves off! They didn't want you around anymore.

Once she was back in the car she knew she was going to go. Take off, take Iris, too, go into night. Adrenaline caused a delicious energy and queer, urgent joy. But what caused the sudden alertness of her skin and the warmth at the root of her tongue? In her ears were the sounds of her body, hum of blood and throb of heart. She sucked her tongue to the roof of her mouth, tip high back in the ridged dome. She drove south. The thrill of leaving home was a bodily pleasure.

"I don't think I can drive the Interstate," she said. "We'll have to go where this road goes. That's one way to decide." They had crossed the west bridge onto a two-lane highway.

"Where does it go?" Iris said.

"Beaufort, Savannah, Jacksonville."

Iris sat back. Wasn't this what she'd always wanted? She was on a road that led to Florida; the children she wanted were asleep in the back seat. It was as if her plans had been taken over by someone else and carried out to the letter, without her having to do any of the dirty work. But now she was the victim, and that suited her fine. It was a relief from always trying to shape the sluggish world into *events*. She imagined the delight in Randall's heart when he left for St. Cloud. Snatched up, spirited away, the responsibility finally in someone else's hands.

But she hadn't considered Mrs. Reese a person who could bring anything about. Iris began to have doubts. Had Randall, some miles down the road, begun to have the same sneaking suspicion, that his abductor could not be trusted to get things right? Worse, Iris realized it was possible that Mrs. Reese didn't even know she was one.

"Hey," Iris said, half-laughing. "Are you abducting me?" *Say yes,* she prayed. *Let it be so.*

"Oh, no, I—I didn't stop to ask, I was in a hurry," Mrs. Reese said. "I guess I should have planned all this better."

Iris rolled up her window. The air smelled bad, more nighttime pollution. *Oh Lord,* she thought. *The woman has no idea. She hasn't thought it out at all, probably doesn't have enough money to get through one week. Some kidnapping. Some runaway wife.* Iris released her hopes. People are bumblers. She'd arranged her life with care, and now all of a sudden she was saddled with this woman; and she knew what it was going to mean. She'd seen it before, people thinking they can up and leave whenever something doesn't suit them. But they bumble it. To make a real break takes preparation and fortitude. Otherwise you have a half-break. Think of Owen, sneaking back for household goods, or Patrice, coming home when she needs to sleep something off. Iris knew she had two choices now: help this lady make her break clean and for good; or get her home fast, before real damage was done.

She didn't think Alice Reese had what it takes to be a runaway wife. A real one isn't just a spur-of-the-moment deserter. A real one plots it to the last detail, maybe waiting years for the right moment. When she vanishes there's not a clue as to her and the children's whereabouts, and the dodo husband doesn't even remember what he did wrong. Months later he might get a postcard from some wild place like Missouri where neither he nor the wife had been before.

It's tempting. An assumed name, a new life; one of those Florida towns where the houses are midget castles; a job serving food to retired people in a sunny restaurant . . . But she couldn't imagine Mrs. Reese as a waitress or any other kind of paid worker. Some women are useless in that respect, not through any fault of their own. There is no market for them. This lady loses the sugarbowl and her own sheets. She needs help to do the normal things of life.

Like everyone else Iris's path has ever crossed, except Emory. Always in the back of her mind Emory is the one who does not pull at her for something. She keeps him there in one corner of her head, where he'll smile, or give a piece of his mind unasked; that's probably the way it will always be, that small version of Emory tucked away up there. Never more than that. *She* is not going to be the one to ruin that boy's future. She's seen those couples—black husband, white wife—at the Laundromat or the bus stop at odd morning hours when married people aren't ordinarily seen together. They have done it to themselves, eyes open. They are desolate by choice.

But sometimes there's a child. A few steps ahead, free of them. One that Iris saw had a golden Afro and brown skin that seemed lit from inside.

Mrs. Reese must have been driving faster than the speed limit, as they had already passed beyond the lights of houses and were moving into countryside. But Iris sneaked a look at the speedometer and saw the needle right on fifty-five. They crossed a second river and were in darkness. Then the car did not seem to be moving so fast. Overhead, oaks closed together. A white owl flew with them under the tunnel of moss and leaves, then fell away into black. There were trees growing right to the edge of the road. They thinned and spread; the canopy disappeared and suddenly the sky was over them, the stars. Iris loved how pure it was, the countryside opening for her like that. It seemed very clean. She was a city girl, but this was like a place she had been to long ago and loved; and all the love came back in a flash. No wonder do-gooders in New York load children onto buses and drive them into the country: just so they'll know it's there. You can bear the city, once you know there is non-city outside. You can see that at least the original intent of the world was something different from what worked out.

They drove farther and farther into the low marshland, down the angled coast of the state. There were more rivers (salt, tidal; the ocean licking inland) and fewer towns than Iris had expected. In fact they had passed only two small settlements, clusters of houses that shouldn't even be called towns. Iris was glad to see there was so much land left. She had thought it was all gone, but now she saw there was still a remnant, in spite of the spread of cities. Charleston did not yet touch Savannah, as she had feared.

"Things are not as bad as you get to thinking they are," she said.

Mrs. Reese misunderstood. "You don't know," she said. "You just think, there's a man who loves his children, what more could anyone want, right?"

"Nothing more."

"Maybe. But the problem, Iris, is when you can't predict a person anymore. When you don't know what he is going to do from one minute to the next. If he's coming home at night. You can't really . . . *go on,* if you don't know a basic thing like that."

"Everybody else does. Excuse me, but who ever knows if the other person is going to show up?"

"The odds are better, it seems to me, in other families."

"Oh, no," Iris said. "The setup is always flimsy. Think of all the possibilities. A husband has a heart attack, a kid runs away, a mother decides she's fed up. In the long run the chances are one hundred percent that somebody's not going to come home. Eventually. You live with the possibilities."

"What if you thought somebody would be better off without you? You realized it would be better for that person if you didn't come home?"

"That's dangerous. Sometimes you think you're bad for someone you're good for," Iris said without hesitation. But she thought of Emory.

* * *

Alice's mouth was dry. The farther she drove, the weaker grew the hum in her ears, until it was gone. Her thrill, she realized, had come from a single instant, the act of leaving home. It was a discontinuous function. There might have been a thrill in that moment, but it was not repeated in the declining slope of what followed. The night was still seductive, but the future could not be all unending lovely night. Down this road was daylight, towns, traffic, waked-up children who would demand food. Breakfast at a pecan shop; alligator farms, believe-it-or-not museums, the magic kingdom. But there was little she could do. The price of leaving home must be staying away afterward.

She drove automatically, feeling progressively duller. They passed through Gardens Corner and Pocotaligo. Iris sat straight-backed next to her, eyes on the road.

"Have you been to Savannah?" Alice said.

"No."

"It's all in squares. The houses are set around the sides of little parks."

"That's a good idea. Everyone gets a view. Plain streets are depressing. You get the feeling you're just one more row. All you see is the house across from you. What I like is the way they make the streets curve in some subdivisions. For no reason. Have you seen that?"

"Yes."

"I like that. It's . . . thoughtful. Not a whole bunch of thought goes into building houses and yards and all. Last year Queen planted a flower garden by her stoop. The housing authority came and paved it, like a road running right along under all the windows. They wanted a hard place to make people put their garbage cans on."

"Beaufort's also a good town. White houses smack on the water. But it's off the highway. Anyway, we couldn't see much of it at night. Now, Jacksonville has a beautiful river. South of Jacksonville, I think, there's a summer village on the river."

"You've seen a lot of towns," Iris said.

"Not really. It's been a long time since I traveled. I used

to. I drove back and forth to Virginia and then North Carolina. Drove to New York, and to Orlando, to see roommates."

"You drove by yourself? You weren't afraid?"

"Not then. Today I'd be. New York! I'd be paralyzed. But I remember riding the subway by myself, eating alone in a Chinese restaurant."

"Yeah, New York's gotten to be dangerous, I guess."

"Well, I mean I have forgotten how to go anywhere alone. There are things you have to do. Like throw money into a toll basket on a highway. I'd pull up to it now and panic. Or what if I had to hail a cab? It's hard to believe, but I used to be able do things when I was twenty that are impossible to do now."

"But you haven't tried. You could do it. Just throw the money. Just raise your hand into the air when the cab comes by."

"It's more than the physical task. It's . . . a vision of yourself. If you don't see yourself as being able to do it, then you can't, no matter how easy it is."

Again Iris thought of Emory, and how it had been impossible for her to think of going with him when he asked.

They came to another wide river, and saw the moon behind dead limbless trees that stuck out of the marsh like black fingerbones. The concrete bridge was white and high, a bleached rainbow. It was a slow river and they crossed it slowly. Iris closed her eyes and tried to think up Owen's face, but the only ones that came were those of Jacky, Nelson, Mr. Rambo, and Emory.

"Oh," Iris said out loud.

"What is it?" Alice said.

"Nothing." Iris closed her eyes again, but she couldn't stop the faces. Mr. Rambo often waited up until he heard her come in at night. Tomorrow the men would have to get their own meals. Fay would miss her lunch. Emory would think Iris had run off the way Patrice had. She doubted anyone would mount a search for her.

Finally she said, "I have to go back."

In a flat voice Alice said, "I don't see how we can. Now that we've left."

"It's easy. Turn around," Iris said. "Just because we've started out doesn't mean we can't turn back. You and I know we've gone a long way, but back there they've all been sleeping. They'll wake up and see just another day. It's a different point of view."

"I don't know."

"They might not even know that we've been gone," Iris said.

Alice looked at her, then began to shiver and, Iris thought, to cry, although the sounds were not loud. The car slowed to a stop, slipping off the side of the pavement; Iris felt the tires meet soft ground. Alice laid her forehead against the steering wheel. Iris touched her arm and waited. With the headlights off, their only light was the moon. They were in a place where the marsh went on so far into the distance that it looked like a prairie. Iris was in love with the moonlight, the dark hammocks where scrub palmettos rose out of the marsh, the sounds of the night like sighs; she tried not to look, tried not to listen. She kept her hand on Alice's arm.

"You need to go back," Iris said.

"I can't."

Alice was afraid that if she moved or spoke again, Iris might withdraw her hand, the four fingers laid steady across Alice's forearm, the thumb barely touching underneath. She tried to think if she had ever felt a hand like Iris's on her skin before. Over the years she'd seen that she was one of that unexplained minority, women who are seldom touched. People sensed that a touch would not be welcome, so when a group met and hugged, Alice always stood slightly beyond the circle and was not hugged by anyone. It was her fault, she knew; there must be a message in the way she stood or folded her arms. She wanted to be one of those women who embrace others freely, hoot with joy on seeing an old friend, kiss near-strangers after a party. Yet it was impossible. She couldn't even imagine it.

Maybe that was the trouble. You didn't need to imagine it; you needed to *do* it. Iris simply reached out when it was time, just did it. Alice wanted that strength, Iris's unthreatening strength, unyielding gentleness. Yes, maybe Alice had abducted her. She had wanted Iris along for the strength. She had trusted that Iris would make things turn out right.

They sat there. Ten minutes passed without either of them saying a word.

"Why don't you sleep, then?" Iris said, finally. "Take a nap and let me drive some." Iris knew what was wrong. Hadn't she seen Fay enough to know what a broken heart did to a woman's muscle tone? Fay couldn't get out of bed those times. Mrs. Reese seemed unable to hold her head up.

"I can't sleep," she said.

"Let me drive, anyway. You rest." Iris got out of the car and walked to the driver's side. She almost could not make herself open the door and get in, because the night was so strange. It was not like the nights of her life. It was black and silver, and its sounds were not man-made. In the distance the dark fringe of trees where the woods took up again looked thickly sweet, and the high moon had grown small and dense as a marble over her head. There were wonders on the road. It was shameful that she should give them up and go back to the city, to the old troubles. But she opened the door. Mrs. Reese had slid over. The keys were in the ignition.

"Now I'll tell you the truth," Iris said. "My father let me drive his car a couple of times. He took me out to a baseball field in the evening and let me drive while he sat in the bleachers. I'd drive around and around the diamond until it was too dark to see him, except when the headlights aimed on him, coming around third base. He said I was ready for the road. But I don't know. I've never driven on a road."

"Was his car a standard shift or automatic transmission?"

"Standard."

"This is easier. There's no clutch. Just shift to D." Alice pointed to the letters and the red indicator that stood at P. Iris started the motor and pulled the gearshift down, found the lights. The car rolled forward. She guided it back onto the pavement.

She drove slowly, hoping she would not meet an oncoming car. The road did not seem wide enough to let one pass, though she kept as far to the right as she could. She was sure that the left side of the car was over the line. It took a while to get used to the feeling in her hands; it was frightening how quickly the car did what she wanted it to do.

Alice said, "I did think you might want to go. You wanted to see your father, you said. . . . But it was too sudden."

"That's all right."

"If you'd had some advance notice . . ."

"It's okay. How far do we drive tonight?" Iris said.

"We could spend the night in Savannah."

"It's already three-thirty. We won't have any night left to spend." But then Iris stopped talking. She counted on the sound of the car and the darkness of the night to work on Mrs. Reese's fatigue. Now and then she looked at the woman's face. Soon the eyes closed and the head dropped an inch to the left.

Iris pressed the accelerator. She knew how the car looked from the sky, zooming low on the narrow road, pushing before it one illuminated patch of graveled asphalt, while behind it everything fell back into darkness. Sometimes the road sparkled. Humps of roadside brush shot past. Iris was delighted with herself. Driving. Actually driving a car on the road. It was different from the baseball field, when she had been constantly aware of Owen low in the bleachers, fading out of sight as night gathered, watching. It was the only thing he had ever watched her do. She was relieved when he climbed down and stood at home plate to be picked up.

But this driving was her own; she was unwatched. She had a sense of being just off the ground, moving along on a cushion of air, except that the soft wonderful roll of the tires over hard road was proof of contact with the earth's surface. Most extraordinary of all was the discovery that driving did not require all her concentration. At sixty miles an hour, in near-total darkness, she was able to think about other things.

Destiny, for example. Maybe she was fated to drive this road, and to turn back would be a crime against fate.

But Iris didn't want to believe in something as drifty and vagrant as fate. Belief in it has made fools of Fay and Queen, and no doubt plenty of other people who let days and nights carry them along. Fate is what people blame when they give up.

Sooner or later she knew she was going to have to turn around. But she hated the thought, and she kept thinking, *A little farther. Let me go a little farther,* and then a new view would appear, an enticing curve ahead in the road, and she would have to get at least to that point. Emory would have said, "You've got no business here, Iris." He would have made her turn around immediately; but she'd have argued first saying, "We aren't ever going to have another chance like this one. So what if we know she ought to go back home? We aren't responsible for her. She's rich, Emory; we're poor. Let her take care of herself." She'd have told him things that lay ahead. He could go to an art school. She would enroll in a community college. And at night they'd work two jobs and save their money. It would be the life he wanted, and the kind of scenery artists like to paint, sun and water, orange trees . . . She said aloud, "What you've always wanted," before she realized how dumb that was. He wasn't even with her. She wasn't even going to that place.

Ahead in a deep curve of the highway was an abandoned gas station, an old one with a wooden roof over the rusty, round-headed pumps. Around the edge of the station someone had once planted Florida-type palms, taller than the normal South Carolina trees. Though the station decayed, those trees kept growing, till now they had reached twenty feet. Iris pulled in under the trees, circled the pumps, and turned the car back toward Charleston. Before she started off again, she stopped the car and listened to the *whush* of the moving fronds, like long, blowing grasses. Those palms were the closest thing to Florida she would ever see. Then she drove and drove and drove, back to home and all its trouble. She was picking it, the way those mixed couples picked it. Eyes open. You have to do the worthwhile thing. Happiness doesn't figure into it.

"Some kidnapping," she said out loud. "What a flop."

She liked the way her voice sounded in the car, as if it were coming over the radio.

Iris had not believed in family love. She'd thought love had to be an event, a rapture, to mean something; otherwise wasn't it only nearness that explained the love of mothers, brothers, husbands? She had pictured real love as fast and violent, a sudden grabbing robbery of your heart. But maybe it can come as something slow, quiet, that's been around or nearby all along, hardly felt until suddenly you turn on it and see an old face new: a child aglow with it, a man saddened, a woman gone tender.

Alice was never totally asleep. She ached toward sleep, but she remained aware of sounds and movement. She felt the car turn, heard Iris speak. She thought Iris said, "What a flop," and she supposed it was one, she was one. On the other hand, weren't they heading home, where they both wanted to go?

It was true that Will might not even know she had been gone, as Iris said. He might have slept at the office or come home and thought she was in the girls' room. But it didn't much matter. Something had gone. One time he'd told her they were part of history, their marriage part of the real history of the world. It might still be true; but the original *pact* with him was lost now.

Whatever happened next would be on new ground.

By five-thirty they are on the outskirts of town. First the scattered wooden houses and then the more closely bunched brick veneers, the convenience stores, the mall eerie as a prison under its floodlights, and then the whole strip of lit-up highway business. As they pass through it, dawn starts. Natural light calms things, tames the frantic bulbs of portable signs, the crime-preventing blaze in parking lots.

"I ought to call home," Alice says.

"I didn't know you were awake," Iris says. "This isn't Savannah. I'm sorry—I turned us around."

Alice looks out the window. "It would be hard to tell, wouldn't it. If you didn't know." Even these old cities have lost their identifying marks, out on the edges. "Can you turn off here?" she says.

Iris pulls up to a row of battle-scarred telephones. "What do people say to each other that causes such damage to the telephones?" Iris says. Ripped directories hang from a couple of chains. One receiver is missing.

"I wonder if you would call my house and say we're almost there," Alice says, handing Iris a dime. She can't bear to call from one of those boothless phones; he might not answer, and then she would be left standing there with the sound of the highway in her ears, reading the savage words scratched into the backboard.

"All right," Iris says.

The car is close enough to the phones so that Alice can hear what is said.

"Dr. Reese, this is Iris Moon."

So he is there. Not roaming the city, not taken off for North Carolina.

"Yes, they're here . . . she's fine. . . . I don't know exactly —a pay phone somewhere. . . . Pardon me?" Iris shifts the receiver. "You've got to be kidding," she says. "It was the other way around. Ask her. We'll be there in twenty minutes."

Iris gets back into the car. "He must have thought I'd kidnapped you," she says.

"Oh, no."

"He asked how much money I wanted to bring you back. He said he'd pay."

"Pay?"

"Yes. You have to take that as a compliment. It must prove something."

"I guess so," Alice says.

Iris has her hands on the wheel, eyeing the road, where traffic has increased with daylight. "I drove fine at night," she says. "But now I'm not so sure I can do it, with more than me and the road to take into account."

"I'll drive." Changing places with Iris again, Alice laughs. "We remind me of old ladies on a trip," she says, getting in on the driver's side. "Have you seen them? Driving like this?" She lifts her nose in the air, grasps the steering wheel near the top. "They keep changing drivers. You always see them on trips, some from out west, even. They drive all over the place."

"Probably widows," Iris says. "But I wouldn't mind that, driving a long way, like through all the states."

As they cross the bridge into town, the first segment of the sun appears over the horizon, but when they come down off the bridge, it sinks again. The city is bright, colored the gold of sand. Along the riverbank, egrets preen; one still has traces of love-feathers, tufts lighter than air, like white cobwebs. The river is pale blue with no wind on it. It's the city's best hour.

In front of Iris's house Alice says, "Who is that?"

"Where?"

"Somebody on your porch."

Iris leans out the window. "Emory, I guess. Oh, I didn't mean to make him stay up all night." She jumps out, looking toward the porch.

"Get some sleep," Alice calls. "Don't worry about coming to work."

"I'll be there. I'm not even tired. I'll be there by noon."

"The girls can entertain themselves. You really don't have to come."

"I want to." Iris starts toward the porch, then turns. "I liked the trip," she says, and looks as if she means it.

Children can sleep through anything; it is their gift. When Alice parks, they are both still asleep in the back seat, heads together. She sits in the car looking at her house. The shutters need paint. There are weeds growing up in the crack between the house and the sidewalk. One clump is flowering, small lavender starlets; and there is dew on the cloverlike leaves. A man comes down the steps, holding out his arms toward her. He must have watched from the window and seen her arrive. It is Danny Cardozo.

"Welcome home, girl," he says. "What can I carry in?"

"Me, if you've a heart to. I'm dead."

"I know. But I'd better take these two, don't you think? Help me scoop them up. You've got a wild man inside to see to."

"What's wrong?"

"He couldn't get it out of his head that something dire had happened to you. Even though I proved it to him: your car was gone, your suitcase. I kept saying, 'Face it, Reese, she's blown town. Finally saw the light and left you.' He wouldn't believe it."

"Turns out he was right, I guess. I couldn't do it."

"Good."

Will stands inside the door, backed up against the wall. His eyes are sunken and frightened.

Danny says, "I'm dumping these guys into the first bed I see," and he carries the girls upstairs to their room.

She turns to Will, who doesn't seem to know what to say to her. He needs help, doesn't he, standing there with his arms straight, neck stiff. Incapacitated. He is afraid, just as Marcella said. Alice had never noticed it before, but he is afraid, clear as day. His hair hangs down into his eyes in that particularly boyish way, and she can't help reaching up to brush it back.

"How about putting me to bed?" she says.

"Come on." He guides her up the stairs, not taking his eyes from her. On the way they pass Danny in the bend of the stairs. Alice touches Danny's sleeve, holding him. The three of them are awkwardly close, stopped there on the landing.

"Thanks for helping," she says.

"Yes," Will says.

"Sure." Danny doesn't look at them. They watch him leave by the front door.

"He came to stay with you?"

"Yes," Will says.

"That was kind."

"I know."

"You didn't deserve it."

"I know that, too."

"I've never been so tired in my life," she says.

At last in bed, every part of her body is grateful for no longer having to support itself. He lies next to her, face down.

"I'm glad you came back," he says in a muffled voice.

"Me, too," she says. She is dropping into sleep. "Let's talk tomorrow."

"Jesus Christ, am I glad you came back." He turns over on his back, his gloom lifting now, waking him. "What a great feeling. Alice—don't go again."

"I won't." All she wants is sleep. The pillowcase against her cheek is the coolest, softest thing she has ever felt.

When she is nearly asleep, he says her name once more. She will always wake to that sound, her name from him.

"Alice," he says, propping himself up on an elbow to look at her. "Something is driving me crazy. I can't get it out of my head."

"What?" she says quickly.

"It's that puzzle about the truth-tellers. Do you know it? About coming to the crossroads and asking the way?"

"Vaguely."

"What's the solution? Don't say algebra. It's something simple."

"Yes. You set it up so it doesn't matter whether he tells the truth or not. He can lie but you'll still get the truth if you ask it right."

"How?"

"You say, 'If I were to ask you if this is the right road, would you say yes?' "

"If I were to ask—Aha. The conditional."

"Turns lies to truth. Keeps true true."

"What a good thing." He lies down again, on his back, arms up under his head. "I should have asked you sooner."

After a while he says, "Well, what do you think? Is this the right road?"

"Yes. If you were to ask me, I'd say it was the right road. Please, let's sleep."

He pulls himself back to her, head down close against her neck. It is Will. They fall asleep together.

Seventeen

Iris is at the Reeses' house by ten. She knew she would never be able to sleep after a night like that. When she comes in the girls aren't dressed. Marcy is in the kitchen spreading preserves on a torn slice of bread, her nightgown sticky with purple seeds and pulp. Beth is sitting on the sideboard in the dining room, facing the mirror, with lipstick and mascara equipment spread before her.

"Where's your mother?" But Iris has a pretty good idea. This is a scene that is not new to her. When her father was in town Fay stayed in bed with him all morning behind a closed door. Sometimes they didn't come out till evening.

"Still in bed," Beth calls. She pops the cap off an eyebrow pencil and touches the color to her eyebrow in light, frightened strokes.

"They said we should wait down here for you."

"Hmph," Iris says. "Did you eat anything?"

"I got a sandwich," Marcy says. Iris sponges the jelly out of Marcy's hair. Then she makes sausage patties and fries two eggs. If these children were hers they'd never go without breakfast just so she could stay in bed with a man. She goes to the laundry room for children's clothes and glances up the back stair. After the girls are dressed she takes the rest of the clean clothes up to their room and adds them to the neat stacks she is keeping in their bureau. She was right. The parents' bedroom door is closed. She doesn't hear any noise from inside the room.

Iris used to hope that *Seventeen* would call her. Somebody would have seen her on the street and they'd want her for the makeover, where the before pictures show a girl sallow and murky, with flat hair and face bumps, and the after pictures show the same face carefully mended and enlivened, as if a charge had been sent through it. It was possible to do the same with a life. She had known it was possible ever since that doctor spoke of it so nonchalantly, not even knowing how important his words were to her. In a face what was important was the bones. *Seventeen* could change the skin, the hair, the shading, but you had to have good bones to start with, something to build up on. She has good bones for a life makeover, she is sure of it. But now she sees that it will not happen here, her makeover, not with those two upstairs, the knot of family tight enough to keep her out and keep them all in. Emory was right. They will never let her in here. She doesn't blame them. If she were one of them, she would not let her in.

Emory had been waiting for her when she got back this morning. When she saw him she was glad she had come home. Her brain was full of his image, as if she'd dreamed him and just waked from the thick comfort of his dreamed presence. She said, "You were here all night," and she knew she was the reason for his tired eyes, his cold hands. She tried to warm them between her palms, told him about the night, the car, getting home again; he only nodded. "It was like you came to me in a vision," she said. "You said come home."

He nodded again, stuck his hands under his vest. "Listen, I'm going," he said quickly, looking away as if toward the place he had in mind.

"What do you mean?"

"I'm *going*. Right away. I'm going to Atlanta."

"You can't. You have another year of school."

"No. There's nothing here for me."

"I'm here. You can't leave me here."

"Good. Come with me," he said.

"No. You stay here."

"No."

They couldn't get beyond that. She lost her temper and yelled. "What's in Atlanta? It's a dangerous city. What did Queen say? Did you tell her?"

"No, I didn't and you can't either. She'd lock me up. I'm going tomorrow. I got somebody getting me a job."

"A job? What about art school?" Iris said.

"I'll do that later."

"Oh, yeah. Right. What job? Who's getting it for you? You don't know anybody in Atlanta, Emory. You don't know anybody anywhere but me."

"Yes, I do."

"Who?" she demanded.

"Nobody you know."

"Who is it? Where are you going, what job is it?" She was near screaming. She heard the window open above her on the second floor and knew Mr. Rambo was listening, so she tried to lower her voice.

"The girl," Emory said. "I've been helping her pack her stuff up in a trailer because she's moving to Atlanta."

"What girl?"

"The one."

Her brain was scrambling for meaning, lost. Then she knew.

"The goldfish girl?"

"Yeah," he said.

"She couldn't get a *job* for anyone. You're crazy. What kind of a job is *she* going to get you? How does she know you, anyway? She doesn't know you. She nearly killed you!"

"I know. But she wasn't an adult then. She wasn't responsible."

"Emory, stay. Stay with Queen, finish school. Queen's is the best place for you."

"I've outgrown Queen. I need to go, Iris. You know what I mean. You said you had to get you a place. I got to go for the same reason."

"So Atlanta's going to be a new start? You think *Atlanta's* a place to get away to?"

"It's the only place. If I can't make it in Atlanta, there's nowhere."

"It will kill Queen." But she knew it would not. Queen has been readying herself for it for years, building up her strength to take the blow when it comes. And besides, Emory is not Queen's. She had almost forgotten that.

"Don't go with that girl," Iris said in a low, mean voice that surprised her.

"She isn't bad," he said.

"She's worse than bad."

"No, Iris. She isn't bad. She has had troubles, is all, and could use help. She asked did I want to come with her to Atlanta."

"You said yes right off?"

"No. I said I would invite you to come."

"I can't do that," Iris said.

He stood up.

"Emory, I *can't* do that. Don't ask me to. Emory, I can't. How can I?"

"All right."

"What exactly is the job she's getting you?"

"Sweeping hair in a beauty shop."

Iris's eyes filled with tears. "Oh, Emory. You don't have to go with her," she said. "Just because she's your mother. Does that mean you have to go with her?"

"No. It's just working out that way."

"It isn't fair!" she cried as he was turning.

"No, it isn't." He walked away. "Go in now," he called back. She couldn't. She sat there stunned, terrified, watching him walk away past the bus station and then around the corner. Mr. Rambo came down then and carried her inside, up to the door of her room. She let herself in and fell onto the bed, but sleep was miles away.

"Put on these jackets. Hurry now," she says to the girls. Iris, used to an empty closet all her life, is awed by the clothes these children have. Pants and jumpers and puff-sleeved smocked dresses. And yet even after they're dressed, in corduroy overalls and quilted parkas, they look like waifs. Urchins decked out. Iris is glad the clothes don't seem to fit. May they never fit! If she were their mother she'd teach them these things are nothing, the clothes and

216

toys and furniture. These things fool people into thinking they must stay where the things are. Leave it all, she'd teach them, even your hopes, and all the dreams of safe, calm places. Go with what is most terrifying, the dizzying empty night and the lonely stars until night slows and you see the whole design. Always choose love over safety if you can tell the difference, she'd teach them.

"Let's get going now!" she calls from the door. "Zip your jackets."

"Get you a jacket, Iris."

"I won't need one. I'm fat, I stay warm."

"You're not fat!" they cry out together, laughing. Beth adds, "You're beautiful."

One thing is beautiful: this town. They walk down East Bay Street on the slate-paved sidewalk, blue, smooth, like slabs of the sky. It is a good feeling to take children out-of-doors and watch as their little steps, their reluctance to inhale cold air, grow into bold skips and deep breaths. They climb the steps of the seawall and look out. A black man leans far over the railing with a cast net folded across his wrist, the weighted edge held in his teeth. He turns, twists, and flings the net in a spinning circle over the water, drops of water flying out like many small pebbles in a sun-burst pattern. The net sinks, leaving its shape printed on the surface, and then the shape sinks, too. The man's children crowd around to pounce on the fish when he pulls them in, long silver mullet tangled in the meshed folds. Farther out in the harbor sailboats miss each other, follow-ing invisible paths. Who has time to fish and sail like this? The city seems full of a strange freedom. Then Iris remem-bers it is Sunday. Cars cruise the boulevard, most of them jam-packed so that when they pull up and the doors open, people spill out onto the sidewalk—children, parents, grandparents. They leave the car doors open and lean against the railing or sit on it. They have come to see the water.

Iris shows Marcy and Beth how to fool the seagulls by tossing imaginary crumbs into the air. The greedy birds swoop in, and even when they see there is no real food they stay awhile, crowded up and screeching at the girls' feet. If these children were hers she would take them somewhere like this every day, where they could see birds and fish and plants, and she'd teach them about nature. She would learn along with them. No one had ever taught her. She doubted if Fay or Owen knew one bird's true name. The gulls desert them now for a boy on the railing who is throwing French fries into the air.

Beth and Marcy want to climb the black cannons in the park. The round mouths stuffed with concrete aim out across the entrance to the harbor and the fort. Behind the cannons are the big houses, one of them the house where Queen works. Such hugeness, such richness! But the show of money has never made Iris envious or sad. On the contrary, it is a good sign for her, for if the world is rich enough to allow such houses as these, then maybe somewhere in it is a small one for her. The world's wealth gives her a hope, even if now she has nothing of it, not a scrap, not an invisible crumb.

Beth is calling from the top of a cannon.

"Can we go see our grandmother?" She points to Marcella's house. Its wide front porch is like an empty lap, comfortable and inviting.

"I suppose," she answers. But she can't go with them. Queen works Sundays and Iris can't risk seeing Queen today. Iris would be tempted to warn her about Emory's leaving. "Stop him," she'd like to say.

"Go on," she calls to Marcy and Beth. "I'll come get you when it's time to go home."

She watches them climb the wide steps, watches their grandmother let them in. Marcella beckons to Iris across the park's green grass. Iris waves a signal to say she will wait on the Battery wall.

She is aware of her own presence now, a girl leaning toward the ocean, a girl with long hair. Some of the people driving by look at her, not crudely but with curiosity, as if she were someone of interest. She pulls out of her pocketbook the red wallet with the thin mirror. In it she can see only her eyes or, moving the mirror down, her nose and cheeks, her chin line. None of it is bad. Put together, it might be a face of interest, the face of a person headed somewhere.

One of the cars in the slow dreamy parade curving around the boulevard is a purple Dodge, hood ornament broken, engine letting out the rumble boys like cars to make. This car pulls over to the curb, and Iris turns her back on it; she does not like to watch those boys who'll bring their girl down to the Battery in broad daylight and keep at her for hours right under the tourists' noses. They want to be seen; but they won't be seen by her. She looks across the water instead, to the horizon that is actually open sea. All along the seawall others are looking out with her, leaning with her— the travelers and fishermen and joggers, the families and lovers, all thrilled by something out there. Not the sea's size or power, but its everlasting plainness. Nothing could be simpler than an ocean, sea level at every point.

The purple Dodge, motor still roaring low in a lion's purr, creeps forward in the parking lane. Opposite Iris it stops again. She can hear it idling there behind her. Well, it isn't lovers. The horn toots at her, one brief tap to make her look. Just what she needs. She glances around for a way out, a path to double back on and lose him by, and then she sees him reaching to open the passenger door. She hears the driver call her name.

She had thought if this moment ever really came she would be likely to faint or cry or have an attack of hives. Instead she is calm. Flat and sea level. *So here you are* is all she thinks. Owen is smiling up through the open door, a little older-looking but dressed the same as always, T-shirt and jeans. How did he recognize her, she wonders, since she is not at all the same as when he saw her last.

His way of inviting her into the car is to nod his head sideways. She had always thought it would be hard to decide. If he ever asked her, would she go? He'd have to argue her into the car. He'd have to make certain promises, have to be sorry for his past, have to show he really wanted her. Sometimes she even thought she'd make him take Fay, too; if he wanted Iris (and wasn't she always always sure he did!) he'd have to reconcile with Fay.

But she gets into the car without a word.

It's a different car. The one he used to have was a sort of truck—at least it was truck in back, car in front. This one has bucket seats, low down so it is hard to see over the dash. She looks out the side window. The car is moving again, and this is what she wanted, she recognizes it at once. Tears come into her eyes and her throat thickens with gratitude. She sees old things dropping away behind her, new things coming up ahead.

"Hey, Iris," Owen says. His voice shocks her with its note of shyness. He looks like a coal miner, the way his chest is sunk in. The green in his eyes, which used to be the mean element, has blued some, and he has on orange rubber flip-flops, not boots. She imagines his diet is not the best, and he smokes too much. His skin is leathered on the hands and face and neck, but under his loose short sleeve the skin is washed-out white, the way skin gets to looking under a Band-Aid.

"Hey, Daddy."

"I almost didn't recognize you, Iris. Fay said you might be down here, but I about drove on by you. Didn't think that could be you there."

"It is."

"Well. I'll just say this right off. I'm here to see if you'll want to come down to Florida with me. Nell could use some help around the house, and Randall, well, you know how much it takes out of a person just to keep up with Randall. Nell's having some trouble in that department."

"Tell her don't try to keep up with him. All you have to do for Randall is leave the door open. Give him a healthy home environment and if he wants to he can live in it; if not, let him go."

Owen looks sharply over at her, surprised, she can see, by her no-nonsense curtness. But then she has changed since he last saw her. He expected the girl she used to be, the scared laundress whose whole life hung on a crazy mother's whim.

"Well, what do you say, Iris? I don't have much time; got to get back to Fay's and load up a few things."

"Like what?"

"That outdoor barbecue she doesn't use. And the red-and-white umbrella."

"Daddy, what children do you have down there? What age? Boys or girls?"

"I don't have any, Iris."

"None?"

"No. Nell had a cyst or something that gummed up the works. Too bad, because she loves children. We took in some foster kids awhile. Two little girls, and then a boy after that, but when they had to go, well, Nell's heart broke. Now she's crazy over Randall. That, maybe, is the trouble, since she can't tell him no on anything." Iris shudders, thinking of Randall given free rein. It sounds like she is needed in Florida, to help out Nell, keep Randall in line, put some fat on Owen Moon's bones again. When she last saw him, his arms just below the shoulders were muscled and thick. Now the square sleeves flap, giving no sense of something strong inside, only those quick flashes of whiteness.

"No," she says. "I can't go."

"Why not? I already talked to your mother. She says you moved out, anyway. She's getting along fine without you. She told me she was doing good and it'd be all right with her if you went with me."

"She said that?"

"Sure. She said don't worry about her one bit. Said she already got used to not seeing you around, what difference could it make if you were two states south."

"Oh."

"What's here to keep you, Iris?"

"Nothing." They pass a horse-drawn carriage, tourists gawking at the tall houses, the young driver standing with reins in his hands; two boys on skateboards confusing traffic, knees padded, arms out, daring the cars; a lady with a splotchy dog leashed to her wrist and pulling her along faster than she wants to go. Iris likes it all, but none of it is here to keep her. "Nothing," she says. "I'll go. But let's go quick, this minute. Let's just get going now. Take the next left and then a right, and I'll show you the way out of town."

Owen snickers, swings the steering wheel with two fingers stuck through it. "If there's one thing I know, it's the way out of town," he says. "But Fay was just the same. Way back when. Bossy." Iris has no recollection of Fay bossing Owen, but maybe there were things she didn't see. Maybe he has been misjudged.

"I got to swing by Fay's a minute," he says.

"No. Let's go."

"I told you there's a couple things I want to pick up."

"Forget it. They're Fay's things, not yours."

"She doesn't use them. The barbecue never has been assembled. Last time I was in town I set the umbrella a certain way in the back of the closet. I can tell it hasn't been touched."

"What do you expect? You think she's going to grill a steak or go out in the rain by herself?" Iris says.

"So let someone have the stuff who can put it to good use."

"It isn't yours."

"Tell you what, we'll ask Fay. If she says okay, we'll take it. Let her be the judge."

Iris looks nervously out the window. All of Charleston seems to be staring into this car, or is it her imagination? She wants to get on the road. But Owen's heart is set on the barbecue and the umbrella, and he won't leave without a try at them. She sighs, guessing she can stand Fay's one last time.

"Make this quick," she tells Owen as they walk up the path. He has changed the expression on his face to a sly smile. The shadow of Fay moves behind the screen door, back toward the kitchen. "Get your junk and get out fast, hear?" Iris repeats. But he doesn't answer; he is already ahead of her and through the door, his sandals flapping against his bare heels at every step, a strange womanly sound that Iris does not like. When she gets to the kitchen her parents are facing each other, Fay looking torn between escape and attack like a huffed-up cat, Owen with his thumbs stuck in his belt.

"Well, Fay, it's up to you. We're leaving it up to you," he says.

"I said she could go, didn't I?"

"I mean the barbecue. The barbecue Patrice gave you three, four years ago."

"Barbecue?"

"The yellow cooker on a tripod, except it's not on the tripod, it's in pieces in the carton on the kitchen shelf."

"What about it?"

"Do you intend to use it? Because if you don't, we'd like it."

"What *we?*" Fay says.

"Me and Iris."

"I didn't say that," Iris says. "I have absolutely no desire for that barbecue."

"Good," Fay says. "Because I do intend to use it."

"What for?" he says.

"To cook hamburgers on."

"Who for?"

"Well, that's none of your business." Fay walks once around him, so he has to turn himself to watch her.

"Okay. Okay." He lifts his hands like a wrestler to prove he's not fighting dirty. Iris goes into Randall's room, where the old cardboard cylinder of Tinkertoys is still on a shelf, its metal top dented but intact. On the label a child has built a whole carnival out of Tinkertoys. She takes the can and Randall's pillows.

Fay's voice in the kitchen has risen in pitch and volume. "My *umbrella!*" she whoops. "Dear God, my umbrella? You pitiful excuse for a man. You little weasel!"

Iris looks from the doorway. Owen, backing away from Fay, does have a weasly look, and he *is* little, now much shorter than Fay. The heel of one flip-flop catches on a loose linoleum tile and doubles under so that he trips and stumbles backward toward the doorjamb. As he falls Fay hurls a spoon end over end like a circus knife-thrower, catching his eyebrow. One elbow gone through the screen, he sits on the floor, dazed. "Hey, keep it, then," he says. "It's yours."

"And *you,*" Fay says, turning on Iris. "What have you decided to make off with? Pillows? Well, dream on. If you want pillows, buy your own, these are mine. I saved stamps

223

for these pillows. They're special foam." She grabs one pillow by the corner and yanks it from Iris's arms. The can of toys drops to the floor, and the little wooden pieces, wheels and sticks and propeller fans, scatter across the linoleum.

"Lord. She wants to take her old toys." Fay starts to cry. "That is the end," she weeps. "When you begin taking useless things. Taking mementos."

"Exactly what are Tinkertoys a memento of?" Iris says.

"Of a time. A certain time."

"When?"

"When you and Randall would build a Ferris wheel."

"We never did. You can only do that with the deluxe set. This is the starter set. It hasn't got enough pieces for a Ferris wheel."

"I remember," Fay says.

"You're thinking of the picture on the can."

"See? You're trying to destroy my memories. I know what you built. I was the mother. You were only the kid, you can't even remember."

Fay's entire back, turned toward Iris, shivers with sobs.

"You're wrong, Mama."

"It isn't enough that he has destroyed the future. You want my past as well."

That sorry past is the last thing Iris wants. For the first time, Fay's helplessness does not fill her with rage. She is able to feel the sympathy that people discover when they are about to leave each other after a long and bitter struggle. She places her arm around Fay's shoulders. "You're wrong," she says. "I only wanted to take Randall a little something. That's all. You can keep everything you want." Suddenly she lets go of Fay and wheels around to face the door.

"Where is he?"

The screen door stands open two inches, the way it does if you don't give it a good push shut.

Fay's sobs come to an immediate stop. "Gone," she croaks.

"No!" Iris runs to the window. The parking place where his car had been is empty.

224

Fay begins to laugh. "Never turn your back on that man."
"I should have told you that. One time he left while I was
gone to the refrigerator for his dessert. Another time I slept
a little late and when—"

"You! You drove him away!"

"I what?"

"You bossed him. It's your fault he never married you.
Oh, why did you pick him in the first place, Mama? Why
him?"

"At least he didn't get what he came for," Fay says.

I despise you for letting him be my father, Iris thinks. *For
teaching me to wish him back. For raising me where the one friend
I had was always a danger to me, for giving me Patrice and Randall
for family, for letting your teeth decay to those ugly, stained, broken
nubs!*

"I'm going to hide this thing." Fay is climbing onto a
chair, reaching into the cupboard to drag down the barbecue. "Next time he comes he can search the place. He won't
find it. I'll put it under the floorboards."

Iris kicks the chair out from under Fay's stockinged feet.
First her thigh strikes the counter, then she drops to the
floor as the chair crashes against the refrigerator. Iris kicks
once at Fay's hip; it is like kicking a sack of sand that gives
some but doesn't jump away, sags back to where it was
before. Fay's eyes are open in terrible surprise, a surprise
so great it must block pain; she makes no move to protect
herself. Iris can see black women dressed all in white pass
by on the sidewalk, white dresses, hats, shoes: members of
a choir coming home, walking with a stately swing left over
from the hymn-singing, massive and bright in the sunlight,
reminding her of Queen in the white slip. Big. Trustworthy. And here her own mother has let herself be
knocked to the floor without a fuss. Looking down on the
head, Iris can see through Fay's thin hair.

"Get up."

She says it only once. At first Fay does not move. Iris sits
at the kitchen table. After a while Fay stirs, still not making
a sound. No moan or whimper. Then she pulls herself up
by the chair, turns it right side up, and sits in it, not drawn
up to the table, not facing anything, just there in the middle

of the room, not looking at Iris, not looking anywhere.

And the room like this is suddenly familiar! The emptiness, the two of them left together again, not talking. It is their life. This is the very heart of it, and it's a hole. It always was. Only now the outer coverings are gone: the false hopes and artificial memories that both of them threw up around themselves to cover their embarrassing hollow center. Her head goes down to the table top, forehead resting against the cool white enamel; her arms hang. She will never move from this table, it dawns on her. She will never be able to lift her head again, or her arms, or her feet. A thicket will grow up around her, thorned vines as big around as an arm, hiding her from any rescuers that might come looking. She will never get to another place.

One thought flashes to her clearly, with the intensity of a last hot flicker before the fire goes out. Fay could save her. Fay is still here. She tries to open her mouth, tries to roll her head to look Fay's way, but everything is jammed. ESP is all she can try, or maybe it is prayer, but she chants in her mind and directs her thoughts at Fay. *Help me.* Then *Please help, please help, please help, please help.* She thinks the words so hard they lose their regular meaning. They take new forms. They have colors in the dark behind her closed eyes, and then they turn into a peaceful slow music. Of course there is no reason for Fay to help. Fay would be better off if Iris were wheeled away to a hospital bed and hooked to life-support systems, a curled-up, withering vegetable.

Then, slowly, across the room, for she is hurt, Fay walks to Iris's side and sets her hand on her daughter's rich, shining, brown head. Iris lifts her head and Fay holds it close to her in an awkward embrace, as unsure of herself as a mother with her firstborn. But Fay never had a firstborn. The baby that was taken was the one meant to teach Fay how to love, the way all firstborns teach their mothers. Instead of learning love Fay learned, at age fifteen, that giving birth is an end, no start at all; so the children she had after that, she said good-bye to in the delivery room. Iris wraps her arms around Fay at waist level. From here they can start. She can teach Fay how to love a child, and the place she's in won't make a difference

226

—a project, a rooming house, a rich man's house, a Florida bungalow. She can do it anywhere. She starts by letting Fay stroke her hair.

"He isn't a bad man," Fay says. "You haven't always seen him in the best light."

"I know," Iris says.

She sits with Fay awhile before setting out again to pick up Marcy and Beth. Fay's hand starts on the skin of Iris's forehead and runs back over her head to her neck.

"Emory's leaving town," Iris says. "Moving to Atlanta."

Fay hugs Iris's head.

"I might go there to visit him. See Underground Atlanta and all."

"Yes," Fay says. "Atlanta's real nice. You can get a non-stop bus to it."

"You could go with me," Iris says.

"Me?"

"Sure."

"Maybe."

"Sure you can," Iris says.

"I'd like to see that hotel with the glass elevators. They're no more dangerous than closed ones, are they?"

"No. The danger is the same. The difference is that you can see it."

"I've always wanted to ride that thing, I don't know why."

"We'll do it," Iris says. She sees herself lifted skyward, cased in glass with Fay, smiling down on the entire city of Atlanta.

Eighteen

Alice and Will woke late Sunday morning, astonished to find themselves in an embrace. She felt his arms around her before she opened her eyes. Who could this be? It was like the first time she ever woke in his arms, surprised to discover arms around her, a face next to hers. When you are used to sleeping untouched, waking like that is a shock. In continuing surprise they made love, fast, like shy teenagers who still think what they are up to is bad and very unusual. He slipped out of bed and locked the door against incoming children, then came back to her and held her. He was tentative about it though, offhand, as if to say *Don't put too much stock in this.* But when he drew back and looked at her, he seemed to remember something. It was almost as if all at once he recognized her. Then he was out of bed again, while she lay naked in the chilly morning air. He was like a traveler come home, a cautious Odysseus not about to take up where he left off until he'd made sure of things.

He was prowling the room. He might be having second thoughts, getting ready to go for good this time, packing his things. She heard him pull out a bureau drawer, close it, open another one. She lay with her breath held. By turning her head to the left she could see when he crossed her line of vision; her eyes, open in a slit, caught him in the web of her eyelashes. He was in front of the closet, moving shoeboxes on the top shelf. But he had no suitcase out and open. He was looking for a specific thing, not belongings in general.

"What do you need?" she asked. "There are clean socks down in the dryer."

"No . . . My old blue bathrobe."

"But you haven't worn it in five years. You never liked it. I wore it more than you did." How could he expect her to keep track of clothes he didn't even want to wear?

"Got it," he said in triumph. He gathered a rolled-up blue terry-cloth ball from the back of the closet and spread it, capelike, over her. "I never liked it on me. I always liked it on you. You're cold."

There had been times long ago when he had covered her and warmed her . . . but none of the old omens and signs meant anything now. New ground. She had to be cautious, too. So she withdrew her eyes from his. When he helped her get the robe on, she thought he meant her to get up. "Thank you," she said. "I'll fix you a big breakfast." She felt stiffly formal. Thank you? The man was her husband of ten years.

"Now?" he said, disappointed. She lay back down. An inch of her cheek touched his shoulder. He put his hand inside the wide sleeve and grasped her elbow.

"Why have I been angry at you?" he said, almost to himself.

"I don't know," she said. She was frightened. Was he staying or going? Could she influence his direction at all?

"Maybe for expecting me to take care of you," he said.

"I didn't—"

"Wait. That's also the reason I fell in love with you. I remember one night looking at you and thinking, Jesus, this girl isn't going to make it unless someone helps her get through life, and I couldn't stand the idea of it being someone else. It had to be me."

"But why did you think that? I was doing all right then, wasn't I?" Of course she was. She'd been a 4.0 student. She'd won the Hollins Prize in calculus. She'd been happy. Alone, yes, and quiet, a little foggy maybe. But certainly not in desperate need of him for her survival. Hadn't he been the one who had insisted on the marriage? He'd said if she didn't go with him he would stay in the Hotel Roanoke the rest of his life; if she didn't marry him he would be lost, cut off from the world. Oh, well. It isn't worth an argument, these many years after the fact.

"Yes, you were doing all right," he says. "I see it now. I probably saw it then and married you so you would need me."

"Oh, well," she says. "It isn't worth an argument now."

"I'm not arguing. I'm asking for forgiveness."

"Do you love me?" she said.

"Yes."

"That's all I want."

The children knocked on the door. "Fix some toast and milk," she called. "Iris will be here soon." Bells rang, some nearby, which were not real but came out of a speaker on the roof of St. Luke's, and some more distant, from the old real bells in the steeple of St. Michael's, deeper and slower. Together they played a medley that wound together strands of half-familiar hymns, and the effect was of a pure music, uncorrupted by words or tune.

Later she heard Iris come and take the girls outside, so she stopped worrying about whether they would burn their fingers on the toaster. She was rubbing his back.

"You lead a charmed existence," he said. "Like a person walking down the street and just missing getting hit by a falling piano. I figure if I stick close to you it'll miss me, too."

"But I don't. I get hit by plenty of things."

"Nothing destroys you, though. You regenerate."

Is that what it is, then? Her tendency to wait and watch: is that regeneration? She always thought of it as torpor and failure. But there may be something to what he says. In the long run all this lassitude may prove to be peace in a kind of disguise, and all this despair turn out to be the purest shape that hope can take. Hope's last stand.

He smokes one of her cigarettes, something he has never done before. She knows it is a new signal, a gesture to tell her something. And not an empty one, no more than Adam's bite into the half-eaten apple was an empty gesture.

She has to ask, "What about Claire?"

"That's over."

"I mean, Claire herself. What will she do? Does she love Danny? Will she be all right?" Alice's Claire, whom she'd dreamed and followed and watched, was vulnerable. She hopes the real Claire is hardier.

"I expect she does love him. Love is not difficult for her. It's almost her natural state," he says.

Alice is silent. The implied contrast stops her.

He says, "For us, love is not a natural state. Love has to modify our natural state, which is solitude. But I think it will."

This is what gamblers feel like when they win back an enormous sum they'd lost earlier: no richer, but aware of ruin averted, of luck in the world. *Let me keep him now. Let me keep him.* He seems exhausted. He lies on his stomach like a man washed ashore after a night in the sea. She rubs his back harder, thinking of the way a lifeguard would rub and push.

"Alice, I have lost some things," he says.

Socks? Collar stays? She hopes it isn't something she's responsible for.

"I lost them by pretending they didn't exist. By willful neglect. I don't want to do it to you," he says.

"Shall I keep reminding you I'm here?"

"Yes. Remind me every day. Remind me every night."

"All right. I'm here. I am still here."

She calculates: How much time is left? Maybe they've lived half a life, with half to go. But they are tired out already. Where will they get the energy for the second half? Lying beside him with her hand moving slowly across his back, she searches her mind for sources of energy for the future; her arm drops onto him.

At eleven, more bells ring long peals of a permutating octave. CDGABEF, DFCAGEB, AEFBCDG . . . Alice's hand still lies in the small of Will's back, but she can only see it there, not feel it; the hand appears to be someone else's. No blood is getting to it, since the course is uphill and constricted. She gets up and shakes blood down into it the way you shake mercury down in a thermometer.

Alone in the kitchen, hearing the bells, aching from unac-

231

customed lovemaking, she cooks bacon and grits. The years she had thought would be so slow will be fast. They begin their spin now, this noon; she can feel them gathering for it, ready to send weeks and days flying. She wants to help Iris get a driver's license, maybe take her to a driver's-education school, let her drive one of those cars with the sign on top. And she wants to have a dinner some night for Marcella and Duncan, not fancy. In the spring she'll take a trip. New York or the coast of Maine, all the way to the top. She makes a little well in the grits for a pat of butter, and sets three strips of bacon on the side. It looks good, like a real breakfast.

Then everyone comes at once into the room: Iris from outside with the children, pulling off jackets, filling a glass with water to hold a bunch of lavender flowers; Will from the dining room, stooping in the doorway to receive the girls' hugs, pretending to get knocked over when they collide with him.

"Daddy!"

"We picked you some flowers, Dad."

"Aren't those weeds?" Alice whispers to Iris.

"No," Iris says. "Weeds? With a flower like that?" She holds up one of the tiny stars. In the center is a bright yellow eye.

Alice watches the children climb onto Will. They always save that raucous affection for him. He gets all their tickling and bear hugs and smack-kisses. But when they see her standing alone in front of the stove, they come to her with their quiet, soft arms held out.